SILVER LADY

Books by Mary Jo Putney

The Lost Lords series
Loving a Lost Lord
Never Less Than a Lady
Nowhere Near Respectable
No Longer a Gentleman
Sometimes a Rogue
Not Quite a Wife
Not Always a Saint

The Rogues Redeemed series
Once a Soldier
Once a Rebel
Once a Scoundrel
Once a Spy
Once Dishonored
Once a Laird
Other titles
Dearly Beloved
The Bargain
The Rake
Lady of Fortune

Anthologies
Mischief and Mistletoe
The Last Chance Christmas Ball
Seduction on a Snowy Night
A Yuletide Kiss

MARY JO PUTNEY

SILVER LADY

KENSINGTON
PUBLISHING CORP.
www.kensingtonbooks.com

KENSINGTON BOOKS are published by

Kensington Publishing Corp.
119 West 40th Street
New York, NY 10018

All Kensington titles, imprints and distributed lines are available at special quantity discounts for bulk purchases for sales promotion, premiums, fund-raising, educational or institutional use. Special book excerpts or customized printings can also be created to fit specific needs. For details, write or phone the office of the Kensington Special Sales Manager: Kensington Publishing Corp., 119 West 40th Street, New York, NY, 10018. Attn. Special Sales Department. Phone: 1-800-221-2647.

The K with book logo Reg. US Pat. & TM Off.

Library of Congress Card Catalogue Number: 2023936115

ISBN: 978-1-4967-3921-6

First Kensington Hardcover Edition: September 2023

10 9 8 7 6 5 4 3 2 1

Printed in the United States of America

For John, my ever-patient Mayhem Consultant, because he is also a writer and he *understands!*

Acknowledgments

Luckily, the history of the Royal Navy is very well documented online and it's possible to find lists of what kinds of ships were in commission during different time periods, complete with names, number of guns, and the size of the crew. Wikipedia, the online dictionary, has a lengthy and very interesting article on the shipyard under the title HMNB Devenport, complete with maps and photographs. It was always a major facility, with 2,464 employees recorded in 1730.

I was fortunate to find a Kessinger's Legacy Reprint document that reproduced an original account of the *Dreadful Explosion Of His Majesty's Frigate Amphion, Of Thirty-Two Guns, in the Hamoaze, Plymouth Dock (1800) by One of the Survivors.*

That was a very bad day in Plymouth Dock, but reading about it did provide inspiration for part of the *Silver Lady* plot. I was grateful to this Survivor for his first person account of this catastrophic event.

SILVER
LADY

Chapter 1

London, 1780

The play had been good, but an icy wind bit to the bone as Rhys and Gwyn Tremayne emerged from the Theatre Royal. "Our carriage should be down to the left," Rhys said. "And the sooner we get into it and head for home, the better! Shall we end the evening by sipping brandy in front of a roaring fire?"

"That sounds most appealing," Gwyn said as she took his arm. Then she halted, feeling a powerful intuition. "But not yet. Let's take a bit of a walk first."

"You sense something that needs to be found, Lady Tremayne?" Rhys asked mildly. Since his wife was one of the best finders in Britain, he knew better than to argue. He merely raised an arm and gestured for their coach to follow them.

"Something, or someone." Gwyn drew her cloak more closely around her as she purposefully started threading her way through the mass of waiting carriages and playgoers who were happily discussing the show they'd just seen.

Two turns took them from Covent Garden into a narrow lane. Halfway down, Gwyn paused, then turned left into a dark alley barely lit by capricious moonlight. It dead-ended at a wall, where a pile of rubble had accumulated against the dingy brick. Heedless of her expensive cloak, she knelt on the frozen ground and said softly, "You can come out now, my lad. You're safe."

There was a rustling sound, but no one appeared. "How does warm food and a fire and a bath sound?" she said in her most persuasive voice.

A child's voice snarled, "Don't want no bath!"

"Then we'll start with the food and the fire," she said peaceably. "Will you show yourself? We won't hurt you."

Rhys stood silently behind her, knowing a frightened child would fear a rather large grown man more than a soft-voiced woman. The rubble shifted and a small, filthy face became visible. A boy child, perhaps five or six years old.

Gwyn brushed back a lock of fair hair, then peeled the kidskin glove from her right hand and offered it to the little boy. He hesitantly took it. As she clasped his freezing fingers with her warm hand, his eyes widened and he sighed with relief.

"You can tell I'm safe, can't you?" Gwyn said.

The boy frowned up at Rhys. "You may be, but not sure about *him*!"

"I'm safe, too," Rhys said in his most reassuring voice. "I'm very good at protecting others."

Unconvinced, the boy narrowed his eyes warily. As Rhys stood very still, Gwyn said soothingly, "I'm Gwyn Tremayne. What's your name?"

The boy hesitated, as if his name was too precious to share. After a long moment he said, "Caden."

"Caden. That's a good Cornish or Welsh name. My husband and I come from Cornish families." Knowing there was more to find, she moved her gaze back to the rubble pile. "Your friend can come out, too."

Caden gasped and jerked away from her. For a moment she

feared he'd try to bolt, but a thin, childish voice emerged from the rubble. "It's all right, Cade. These are the people we came to find."

An even smaller boy emerged from the rubble, his ragged garments almost indistinguishable from the trash around him. His gaze on Gwyn, he said, "I'm Bran."

"For Branok?" Again Gwyn offered her hand and Bran took it without hesitation. His small fingers felt as if they were carved from ice. In the darkness it was hard to see the boys clearly. Though both were dark-haired, there was little other resemblance. Bran's eyes were light, Caden's were dark, but the color wasn't visible in the shadows. "Are you brothers?"

The boys exchanged a glance. "We are now!" Caden said fiercely, challenging anyone who might deny that.

They both had soft West Country accents, and she wondered what their story was. How had they made their way to London? Bran seemed to have the ability to read people's nature and to decide what must be done. Caden surely was gifted as well, perhaps in other ways.

Learning more about them could wait. What mattered now was getting the boys out of this vicious cold. "Come with us now and we'll take you to our home, where you'll be warm and well fed."

Bran stood shakily and almost fell over from weakness and cold. Her heart hurting at the sight, Gwyn said, "I'll start warming you now." She leaned forward and scooped Bran into her arms, then rose to her feet. The child weighed almost nothing, and his torn shirt revealed something on his right shoulder blade. If she had to guess, Gwyn would have said it looked like a tattoo of a dragon.

It was a question for another day. She pulled him inside her cloak, covering everything but his head. His thin body was cold against her. "Is that better?"

He peered out of the folds of her cloak with a smile of great sweetness. "Much better, ma'am."

"No! You won't take him away!" Caden exclaimed as he lurched to his feet.

"Don't worry, Caden, we won't separate you," Rhys said as he lifted the larger boy in his arms and tucked his own cloak around him as Gwyn had done with Bran. Caden struggled some, but the warmth seemed to soften him.

They carried the children back to the wider street, where the carriage waited. Their driver, Jones, gave them an expressive glance, but didn't speak. This was not the first time he'd seen them rescue children.

Rhys opened the carriage door. Knowing Caden wasn't comfortable with being carried, he set the boy in the vehicle. "There are carriage robes on the seats to warm you." The child scrambled inside and there was a rustle of fabric as he pulled a robe around himself.

Rhys then helped Gwyn into the carriage. She continued holding Bran as she settled on the forward-facing seat. Before climbing in and closing the door, Rhys called up to the driver, "Home now, Jones."

As the carriage rattled westward over the cobblestones, Gwyn asked, "How did you boys come to be here in London?"

The silence stretched so long that she wondered if either of them would answer. Then Caden said warily, "What's it mean to be 'gifted'? My da called me that before he threw me out of the house."

Gwyn's heart constricted at the thought of such a young boy being treated in such a beastly manner, but his question confirmed what she already knew. "Gifted people are just better at some things than most others are. Better at sensing emotions, perhaps. Better at persuasion, or maybe better at finding lost objects. Perhaps good at telling if someone is lying or telling the truth. Small gifts, but often useful."

Bran asked, his small voice hard, "Why do people hate us?"

As Gwyn wondered how to explain bigotry, Rhys said in his deep, calming voice, "Sometimes it's from fear. Sometimes from envy. Some people just need to hate anyone who is different."

It was a good explanation. Gwyn said softly as she cuddled Bran against her, "Some people hate, but there are also those who love you exactly as you are."

Chapter 2

London, Early Spring 1803

The British Home Office had broad responsibilities for protecting the public in general, but also for safeguarding the rights of the individual. It was not only concerned with all issues of law and order, but also very quietly operated a secret service to investigate potential threats to the nation and its people.

Bran Tremayne worked for the Home Office, which suited his more unusual talents, and he took his responsibilities to protect all Britons very seriously. It was vital, worthy work. The only part he didn't like was writing reports.

He was halfway through a report about a problem he'd unearthed when he investigated a dishonest magistrate in Berkshire, and what he'd done to solve the issue, when a twinge of intuition made him pause, his pen in the air. His instincts usually manifested themselves in silver sparks and threads. The brighter the silver, the more urgent the situation.

This time he sensed a faint silver line to his parents' house. He'd been planning to go there for dinner in an hour or so, but he realized he should leave now. He didn't have a sense of danger, but it was definitely time to go.

He rose from his desk, happy to quit work on the report. After donning his coat and hat, he left the rooms he shared with Caden. His brother Cade was away, also on Home Office business, so Bran was in the mood for company.

The late afternoon was mild, and the fresh air was invigorating as he walked the ten minutes to Tremayne House. He was pulling out his key to unlock the door when it swung open to reveal his mother, her lovely face welcoming, her fair hair barely touched with silver.

He smiled. "In a family where everyone is gifted, there aren't many surprise visitors, even one who is early for dinner."

"Sometime there are surprises, but you aren't one of them." Gwyn Tremayne pulled him into a warm hug. Whenever he felt her arms around him, Bran remembered that magical moment, on a bitter cold winter night, when she'd embraced him and become his mother.

He hugged her back, then closed the door quickly before one of the household cats could escape into the wilds of Mayfair. "Are you implying that you've had a real surprise visitor?"

"Yes, you just missed him."

"Should I be sorry?" he asked as she slipped her hand onto his arm and guided him toward the small sitting room. He caught a glimpse of himself in the tall mirror at the end of the corridor and felt his usual surprise at the image of a polished young gentleman. He never forgot his first view of the mirror, when he'd been a pale, scruffy child cuddled in Gwyn's arms. The house's spacious rooms and elegant furnishings had made him think he was in a palace. It wasn't long before he realized that Tremayne House was even better than a palace. It was a home.

"I suspect you'll be meeting our visitor soon."

They entered the sitting room together. Tall and authoritative, Rhys was there, and he poured drinks for them all.

"Brandy?" Bran arched his brows when his father handed him the glass. "Is the news that dire?"

"You might find it so." Gwyn accepted a sherry from her husband, and they settled next to each other on the sofa. They always liked to be within touching distance.

Bran took a chair opposite. "So tell me about this visitor."

"Mr. Davey is a solicitor from Plymouth working on behalf of Lord Penhaligon," Rhys replied. "He's seeking a Cornishman around thirty years of age who has a dragon tattoo on his right shoulder blade."

Bran's hand jerked and brandy splashed on his fingers. "The devil you say! Why?"

"The young man he's looking for is Branok Penhaligon, third and youngest son of Lord Penhaligon of Plymouth," Gwyn replied. "Mr. Davey said that the boy had shown early signs of being gifted, so he was fostered out to avoid disrupting the household."

Bran was known in Tremayne House for his calm and control, but Gwyn's words caused his temper to flare. "Damnation!"

He drew a deep breath, then said apologetically, "I'm sorry for my language. But I wasn't 'fostered.' I was sent to the worst kind of baby farm, where people dump children when they don't care if they live or die! No heat, barely any food, larger bullies beating smaller children. I would have died if Cade hadn't managed to get both of us out of there. Why would people who treated me as rubbish want me back?"

"Apparently, the two older sons have died, and you're now the last direct male heir," Rhys explained. "Lord Penhaligon's desire for an heir of his blood must have overcome his distaste for those who are gifted."

"He may rot in hell," Bran said through gritted teeth. He lifted his brandy glass and tossed the contents down in one burning swallow. "You didn't tell this lawyer about me, did you?"

"Of course not," Gwyn said. "He called on us because we're

known to have helped gifted children in need. We said we'd make inquiries."

"We understand how furious you feel," Rhys said gravely. "But perhaps you should think about this before rejecting the possibility out of hand."

"You're right, of course." Bran drew a deep breath and closed his eyes, centering himself so he could think clearly about the Penhaligons' search for their despised and discarded son. A lawyer named Davey . . .

After he'd released his anger and considered what he'd just learned, he sensed a pulsing silver line that led southwest to Cornwall. Exhaling, he opened his eyes and said, "I think I have to talk to Davey and likely go to Cornwall as well. I've been feeling that there was something in Cornwall that requires further investigation."

"Something personal, or something that relates to your work?" Rhys asked.

Bran thought a moment. "Both. I suppose that the first step is calling on this Mr. Davey."

"The first step," Gwyn said firmly, "is to have dinner!"

The next morning Bran called at Davey's hotel at the earliest time that could be considered civil. The clerk confirmed that Mr. Davey was in his room, so on the back of one of his cards, Bran scribbled, *I believe I'm the man you're looking for*, and asked that it be sent up to the lawyer.

Then he moved to a private parlor to wait. It was a plain room with only a small table and several chairs. He considered ordering tea to be served, but decided against it. This was not a social occasion.

Davey appeared in the parlor in record time, holding Bran's card in one hand. He was a lean, shrewd-eyed man about Bran's age. His gaze moved from the card to his visitor's face.

"Your card says your name is Branok Tremayne. Are you a connection of Lord and Lady Tremayne?"

"They are my parents in every way that matters." Bran stood and gestured toward a chair. "They told me of your visit, but left it to me to decide if I wished to respond."

Davey took a seat. "You have the look of the Penhaligons."

"What a depressing thought." Bran seated himself again. "I'm not ready to take my shirt off to confirm the tattoo, but assuming I am indeed the man you're seeking, can you explain why I should want to claim a Penhaligon heritage?"

"The property and fortune are substantial, and there's the title, of course," Davey replied.

"I've never craved a title and my finances are comfortable, so those aren't particularly compelling reasons," Bran said. "Why should I bother responding?"

"Curiosity?" Davey suggested, amusement in his eyes.

Bran almost laughed. He could learn to like Davey. "I'm mildly curious, but what kind of family condemns unwanted children to starvation and an early death?" He was unable to keep the bitterness from his voice.

"A foolish family," Davey said, surprisingly. "All children are a gift, but Lord Penhaligon is . . ." He hesitated, then stated, "Very old-fashioned."

"Is that the polite term for a 'pigheaded bully'?" Bran asked.

"Lawyerly decorum forbids my answering that."

He could definitely like Davey. "Tell me about the family. Do they all share Lord Penhaligon's prejudices? What is the rest of the family like? How did the older sons die?" The words struck Bran with unexpected force. He'd had two older brothers, blood kin, who were now dead and beyond knowing. It was a strange feeling.

The lawyer's brow furrowed. "The eldest son, Arthur, was rather wild. While living in London, he engaged in a duel and died of his wounds. The second son, George, loved sailing. He drowned in a storm at sea two months ago. There is a daughter, Glynis, the youngest child, but of course she can't inherit. Lady Penhaligon is very reserved, but well thought of by those who know her."

Bran suspected that Lord Penhaligon—his father, God help him!—was a bully and the females of the family were beaten down by him. He'd probably despise the man, if and when they met.

Strange. He'd always felt that his Tremayne family was all a man could want or need, yet he was curious about these blood relatives. Moreover, there was that nagging sense of some trouble in Cornwall that he should investigate. "Were you ordered to find the Penhaligon heir and drag him down to Plymouth?"

"In essence, yes. Lord Penhaligon would like me to find his missing son and immediately escort him to Penhaligon Castle," Davey replied. "He was sure that Branok would be surprised and grateful and would happily move into the castle to start learning how to run the estate. Ideally, Branok would be unmarried and willing to take a bride acceptable to his lordship."

"Is Penhaligon naïve enough to believe that will happen?" Bran asked incredulously.

"He is not naïve, but he is used to being obeyed."

"I hope he handles disappointment well," Bran said dryly. "Who would be heir if you don't succeed in your quest to find the missing Branok?"

Davey paused before answering. "Lord Penhaligon had a second cousin, whom he despised. I've heard that the cousin had a son, who would be the next closest heir, but obviously his lordship would much prefer a son of his own to inherit."

"Even one who is gifted?"

"I believe he would consider you the lesser of two evils," Davey said blandly.

Bran definitely liked this man's sense of humor. "So he's desperate."

More soberly, Davey said, "Lord Penhaligon's health is not good. He hopes to find the son he always wanted rather than the sons he actually had."

"He might have fared better if he'd treated his children better," Bran observed. "Out of curiosity alone, I am willing to visit the Penhaligons and come to my own conclusions about them. I will not stay long, and I will not reside under the parental roof. Is there a decent inn nearby?"

Davey thought for a moment. "Lord Penhaligon will not be pleased if you refuse to stay at the castle, but that is an issue for you to deal with. There are no nearby inns worthy of the name, but the castle has a dower house. It's a pleasant property, convenient without being too close. It might suit you, but Lord Penhaligon will do his best to persuade you to his will."

"I have no doubt," Bran agreed. "But he can bellow all he wishes, and I won't change my mind because he has nothing that I want."

"That will be a great advantage." The lawyer cocked his head. "If you are indeed Branok Penhaligon and have decided that you will come to Plymouth, I will need to see the dragon tattoo."

Bran had known that was inevitable. He hesitated for a long moment. If he refused to show the tattoo, he could deny being Branok Penhaligon and walk away from all the complications that would arise from his birthright.

But he realized that this was something he must do, no matter what the cost. He stood and peeled off his coat, cravat, and shirt, then turned his back to Davey. He heard the lawyer move to investigate more closely. Standing in front of a stranger half undressed was not comfortable. Luckily, the other man didn't touch him.

"The tattoo is faded and distorted because it was done when you were only an infant, but it appears to be the Penhaligon dragon," Davey said quietly. "I believe that you are indeed the Honorable Branok Penhaligon."

"I will never be the obedient son Lord Penhaligon wants." Bran pulled on his shirt and coat and restored himself to respectability. "But I suppose I must go to Cornwall and acquaint myself with the family."

"This will be interesting to observe," Davey commented. "You seem to be as stubborn as your father."

Bran loathed the idea that he had anything in common with Penhaligon. "My father is Rhys Tremayne, who is the finest gentleman in England. I wager that within a fortnight of meeting me, your bad-tempered employer will call on you to draw up papers formally disinheriting me."

"He may want to, but legally you are his heir, and you will be the next Lord Penhaligon." There was amusement in Davey's face. "Will you travel to Cornwall with me when I leave, day after tomorrow?"

Bran considered, then shook his head. He had work that needed to be finished, and besides, he did not wish to appear too eager. "I can leave a week from today. Do I need to visit the castle with you so you can prove that you successfully located me?"

"That would be best. I have an office in Plymouth. If you meet me there, we can go to the castle together." He gave Bran a card with his office address, and they agreed on a time and date.

Bran accepted the card and wondered what he was getting himself into.

The night before leaving for Cornwall, Bran finished packing and sat down to write a note to Cade. Then the door opened and his brother arrived in person, tall, broad, and utterly competent even when travel stained. Bran looked up, pleased. "Cade! I didn't expect you home till next week."

"I had a feeling that you were getting yourself into trouble, so I thought I'd better return and sort you out," his brother explained as he tossed his coat over a chair. "What's happening?"

"Not trouble, exactly." Bran rose from his desk and poured

them both glasses of claret. "It turns out that I am the third and only surviving son of one Lord Penhaligon of Plymouth. The tattoo on my right shoulder blade was the brand burned into my infant skin in case he ever needed to identify me."

Cade swore and swallowed most of his claret before settling in a chair opposite Bran. "Tell me all about it."

When Bran finished his account, Cade asked, "Why are you cooperating? All you had to do was keep the tattoo covered up."

"I considered denying the connection," Bran admitted. "But I believe that this is something I need to do. You know I've had the itchy feeling that there is something going on in the Southwest that bears investigation."

"You've mentioned that." Cade frowned. "I think there will be consequences you can't even imagine."

"Should I be alarmed or excited?"

Cade hesitated, his eyes drifting out of focus as he considered. "Both."

Bran sipped his claret and wished that Cade wasn't so very good at sensing trouble.

Chapter 3

She had been drifting in darkness for eternity. Now and then she would be pulled closer to light. Given food, forced to rise from her bed and move around before being allowed to slip back into her mindless sea of darkness. They called her Girl.

Hands pulled her up, guided her to a chair, gave her food. Bean soup.

As she sipped the soup from a mug, she heard voices around her. The harsh voice that belonged to the one she thought of as the Crow said, "Are you sure you can pull her out of this far enough to do what needs to be done when the time comes? It's not long now."

The other voice belonged to the hands that pulled her to eat and walk. A lighter voice, a woman, the Starling. "She'll be fine. Her gift is powerful and will be stronger for all the rest she's getting. Just let me know two or three days before she's needed so I can wake her up properly."

"Is she eating enough? She's very thin."

"Thin but strong," the Starling said. "I take her for walks every day to keep her healthy."

The words were just meaningless sounds. The Crow left. Girl finished her soup and waited dully for whatever came next.

"Time for your walk," the Starling said, pulling Girl to her feet. "Almost dark and a bit cool, so you'll need this shawl."

The Starling wrapped the length of scratchy wool around Girl's shoulders and led her outside, holding Girl's left arm firmly. Fresh air, a hint of the sea, gathering night.

The Starling led her along a familiar path through the woods. The night darkened quickly, and rain began spattering down. The Starling stopped and tried to turn Girl around. "Time to go back now."

Girl resisted. Something had changed. She felt . . . a spark out in the night. Something, someone, that tugged at her, lifting some of the darkness. She realized that the blankness surrounding her wasn't right, that once there had been more. She'd had a different name . . .

The Starling uttered an angry word Girl didn't recognize, then pressed a hand to Girl's forehead. Darkness flowed from the Starling's palm. "Do as I say, Girl! It's time to go back before the rain gets worse."

Blankness closed down on her again, but not quite as strongly as before. As she docilely returned to the cottage through the rain, she held to the knowledge that there was something beyond the dark.

Chapter 4

⁓

Bran presented himself at Davey's Plymouth office on the appointed morning, at exactly nine o'clock. The lawyer met him with a glint of relief in his eyes. "I wasn't sure you'd come."

"Curiosity, you know," Bran said as they shook hands. "I've brought my horse so I can escape quickly if necessary." That was a joke because he knew he must be here for a while. How long a while he couldn't even guess.

"How did Lord Penhaligon react when you said you'd located his missing heir?"

"It was about what you'd expect," Davey replied. "He was relieved that I'd found you, and annoyed that you had refused to accompany me back."

"I'm sure he'll be even more annoyed after we meet in person." Bran followed Davey out to the lawyer's waiting carriage. After he tethered his horse behind, they headed southwest along the coast. It was wild, beautiful country.

"The castle is an hour or so south of Plymouth, and the village of Penhaligon is right below and has a good harbor. Polperro is the next village of any size along the coast," Davey said.

"I've heard of Polperro. It's a center for smuggling, isn't it?" Bran gazed along the rugged coastline. "One can see why. There seem to be an endless number of coves and creeks and places to conceal ships and contraband."

"There are. It's quite a challenge for the Revenue Service, though they've had their share of successes in capturing smugglers and illicit goods," Davey replied. "The struggle between the law and the free traders has been going on for centuries."

"Are any Penhaligons involved in the trade?"

Davey gave a half smile. "It's one of those questions one doesn't ask. Most of the landowners officially disapprove of smuggling, but they serve French brandy at their tables."

"Heaven forbid that the rich and powerful be deprived of their pleasures," Bran murmured.

"Where there is demand, there will be a supply," the lawyer said cynically. "Most French contraband comes up through the island of Guernsey. Usually, it's broken down into smaller quantities that are easier to transport. Then it's shipped to various places along the coast. Sea caves are very good for hiding spirits while they mature."

They talked in a desultory fashion as the carriage rattled along the road, with Davey offering explanations about the sights and the history of Cornwall. They'd progressed some distance when the carriage crested a hill. Davey signaled the driver to stop, and they both exited the carriage to stretch their legs. They had a good view of the coast sloping below them.

They'd been driving through woodlands, but ahead of them was a bare, windswept headland, crowned by a sprawling walled castle. Bran saw a subtle silver shimmer around its weathered stones. He had no sense of familiarity, even though he'd been born there, but the shimmer said the place would be significant. He wondered what awaited him. Being gifted was all very well, but the feelings that came to him usually lacked detail. "I imagine that very Gothic structure is Castle Penhaligon?"

"Yes, it's real Gothic, built by the Normans, not the imitation Gothic ruins that romantics like to build in their back gardens." Davey pointed. "There's a road that runs through the woods until it reaches the open area around the castle. See the building surrounded by trees on the far side of the road?"

"With a slate roof?"

"Yes, that's the dower house. You can't see it from here, but there are stables behind. It's pleasant and private."

"It's a bit of distance from the castle," Bran observed.

"It was built several generations back when the Lord Penhaligon of the time had a wife and a mother who didn't get along. He thought putting some space between them was a wise idea. No one has lived here since the current Lord Penhaligon's mother died some years ago."

"I like your suggestion of staying there," Bran said as they climbed back into the carriage. "I'm going to want that distance."

Bran felt his tension increasing as they traveled the last stretch to the castle. The broad doors in the curtain wall were open and the carriage rolled through, coming to a halt in front of the steps leading up into the castle. A groom appeared almost immediately to take charge of their chaise and his tethered horse.

Bran glanced up and saw people peering out the windows. He tensed and raised his mental shields so he wouldn't feel battered by their emotions. "We're being watched."

"It's inevitable, but the novelty will wear off soon," Davey assured him.

"I certainly hope so." Bran felt like an insect on a plate as he stepped from the carriage.

The castle doors swung open as they approached, revealing a black-clad butler and two footmen. Though the castle retained its Norman exterior, the interior had been modernized and looked like other sizable country houses Bran had visited. The paneling and furnishings were less dramatic than the original castle stones, but surely more comfortable.

"Good day, Morris," Davey said to the butler. "Is the family in the upstairs drawing room?"

The butler inclined his head. "Yes, Mr. Davey." His gaze moved to Bran. "Mr. Penhaligon."

Nerves taut as strung wire, Bran started up the sweeping staircase with Davey beside him. The lawyer murmured, "Remind yourself that Penhaligon has nothing that you want."

The thought was some comfort, but Bran would much prefer to be dining with his real family at Tremayne House.

The butler opened the door to the drawing room and announced, "Mr. Davey and the Honorable Branok Penhaligon."

The drawing room was expensively furnished, and the sight gave him a sharp stab of memory. He'd been in this room, and something bad had happened here. He slammed shut the door to memory, to be explored later. Now he must concentrate on the people in front of him. His family, for better and worse. He felt the pressure of their interest. Curiosity, resentment, anger.

The high-ceilinged chamber contained several small conversational groupings, and his family was gathered in one such area directly ahead of him. A wing chair facing the door held a scowling older man with a cane. Two women were seated on a sofa to the left, one older, one younger. His mother and Glynis, his sister, presumably. An empty sofa was on the right.

After a swift evaluation, Bran inclined his head to Lord Penhaligon. "Sir." To his regret, Davey had been right that Bran had the look of the Penhaligons. His father and sister shared his own long, strong-boned face and gray eyes.

Having acknowledged his father, Bran turned to the ladies of the house and bowed. "Lady Penhaligon and my sister, I believe?"

Lady Penhaligon—his mother? really?—caught her breath as she gazed hungrily at him. "My Bran," she breathed. "You look so much like your brothers."

She pressed a hand to her lips as if trying to control herself. She was a handsome woman and must have been a beauty when young, but now she looked drained and colorless. His mother had not wanted to send him away, he realized. She'd fought to keep him, but had been overruled by her husband. She'd lost two sons, and she feared that the one who had been sent away would hate her.

"Mr. Davey mentioned the family resemblance when we first met." He smiled warmly. They must speak later, but for now it was enough not to show anger. Her expression eased and she lowered her hand from her mouth.

Bran turned to Glynis. She was dark-haired, with pretty features, but was very subdued. "I'm glad to find that I have a sister." He already had Tremayne sisters, whom he loved deeply, but this was a sister of the blood.

She raised her gaze to him, uncertain but hopeful. Shyly she returned his smile and he recognized that they could become friends. He also saw, to his surprise, that there was a silver thread running from Glynis to Davey. Affection, and it was mutual. Was it undeclared because Lord Penhaligon would not countenance a mere lawyer as a husband for his only daughter?

Bran's thoughts were interrupted by the harsh voice of Lord Penhaligon. "Look at me, boy!"

Bran did and saw that his father was torn between relief at having a living son and anger that he'd had to seek out the gifted child, whom he'd despised.

Unperturbed, Bran inclined his head and again said, "Sir. This meeting is most unexpected."

The old man's mouth twisted. "You came quick enough when you learned that you were heir to a title and fortune."

"You were the one who had Mr. Davey look for me. I almost didn't come at all," Bran said in a cool voice. "But I was curious, so I decided to take a short leave from my work."

"What sort of work do you do?" Lady Penhaligon asked.

"I have a position at the Home Office." He smiled blandly.

"They employ a number of the gifted because our skills make us very useful."

His father snorted. "Flaunting your unnatural abilities! You don't belong here. I never should have sent Davey to find you!"

"The choice was yours, not mine, but I won't stay where I'm not wanted. Goodbye, sir." He inclined his head to his mother and sister. "It's been a pleasure to meet you."

He turned and strode for the door, feeling the gazes of his family boring into his back. He'd almost reached the door when his father snarled, "Wait. Wait, damn you!"

Bran turned back and said politely, "Is there more you'd like to say, sir?"

Lord Penhaligon glared at him, visibly torn between his craving for an heir and his distaste for Bran's very nature. Davey's calm voice intervened. "A family reunion of this sort is a momentous occasion. Surely, it's best to proceed slowly and take the time to become better acquainted. You may all be pleasantly surprised by what you learn."

Bran doubted that he would find his father worthy of respect, much less affection, but he had to give Davey credit for his ability to spread oil on troubled water. Lady Penhaligon filled the awkward silence by saying, "I agree. You've only just arrived, Bran. There is so much to discuss and so much you need to learn about your heritage. I'll order tea."

The tea cart must have been prepared in advance because it was rolled into the drawing room almost as soon as the mistress of the house made a small gesture. Bran and Davey took seats on the right-hand sofa, and the ritual of tea and cakes reduced the tension in the room.

As Lady Penhaligon poured Bran's tea, she said, "One of the tower rooms has been prepared for you. I trust you'll find it comfortable. It has a wonderful view of the sea."

"You are gracious, Lady Penhaligon," Bran said. "But Mr. Davey mentioned that the dower house is currently unoccupied. I would prefer to stay there. Some distance might be useful under these circumstances."

"A good idea," his father said gruffly.

Lady Penhaligon swallowed hard. "Of course, if that is your wish. The dower house is regularly cleaned, but I'll send a couple of maids over now to make sure it's ready for occupation. I'll also assign several servants and a groom to look after you during your stay."

Bran shook his head. "No need. I like my privacy. If a groom stocks the stables with feed and bedding and a maid cleans one day a week, that will suffice. I'll care for my own horse. I assume I can take my meals here at the castle?"

"Of course," his mother replied. "You must start by dining with us tonight. My husband has invited a number of the local people you should know."

Bran sipped his tea, the calming drug of the British. "I look forward to becoming better acquainted with everyone."

The tea cart held small sandwiches, pastries, and warm, crumbly scones accompanied by preserves and a bowl of clotted cream so thick it could have been sculpted into a statuette. Bran split a scone, spread marmalade on both halves, and topped each with large dollops of the sinfully rich cream.

He sighed with pleasure after his first bite. "I've always heard that Cornish clotted cream is the best, and now I know why. This is sumptuous."

His mother smiled. "The people of Devonshire claim their clotted cream is better, but of course they're wrong."

As Bran chuckled, Glynis said, "Don't laugh, battles have been fought about which county's cream is best!"

Davey added, "There are also stormy questions about whether the preserves or the cream should be spread on the scone first."

Bran eyed his scone with raised brows. "I had no idea what dangerous waters scones float upon. I'd better eat this quickly!"

More light conversation followed. Glynis asked him about London, which she'd never visited, so he discussed shops and amusements she might enjoy. He didn't want any deep discussions with these people. Not now, maybe never. Superficial chat was better than watching Lord Penhaligon scowl at him.

Once a civil amount of time had passed, Bran rose and said, "If you'll excuse me, I'd like to settle into the dower house before dinner." Remembering that silver thread between Davey and Glynis, he added, "It's a long drive back to Plymouth, Mr. Davey. If you'd like, and Lady Penhaligon agrees, perhaps you could also spend the night at the dower house?"

"That sounds like a fine idea," his mother said. "If you stay, Mr. Davey, of course you must also join us for dinner."

"It will be my pleasure," Davey said. "I can take Mr. Penhaligon to the dower house and help him settle in." He glanced briefly at Glynis and once more Bran sensed a thrum of connection between them.

The butler escorted Bran and Davey down the stairs and sent a message to the stables to bring the carriage and Bran's horse around. Bran sighed with relief as he and the lawyer went outside to wait for their transportation.

"You survived that well," Davey said. "You were as smooth as Chinese porcelain, letting everything slide off."

That comment surprised a laugh out of Bran. "Is that how it seemed? I just thought being a perfect gentleman was the best way to survive." He'd also been shielding himself so he wouldn't be overwhelmed by everyone else's feelings.

"You were right. Lord Penhaligon may resent your very existence, but he certainly can't criticize your manners."

"Of course he can," Bran said dryly. "I think there is very little his lordship approves of."

Davey looked as if he agreed, but didn't think it appropriate to say so aloud. "Thank you for suggesting that I spend the night here. As you say, it's a long drive back to Plymouth."

"And perhaps it will give you and Glynis some time to-gether."

Davey stiffened. "What makes you say that?"

Bran shrugged. "There seems to be a connection between you."

The lawyer's eyes narrowed. "If that's the sort of thing gifted people see, no wonder you aren't universally popular."

"I don't think one needs to be gifted to see how you two look at each other," Bran said peaceably. "Nor does it take any special insight to suspect that Penhaligon would not approve of his only daughter marrying a mere country solicitor."

"You suspect rightly." Davey sighed. "If you're going to read my mind, we should probably be on a first-name basis. I'm Matthew."

"I'm not reading your mind, but I do like your sense of humor, Matthew. As you know, I'm Bran to friends and family." Bran offered his hand. They shook, sealing their alliance. He was glad to feel that someone was on his side.

Chapter 5

Their transportation arrived and Bran and Davey rode over to the dower house. It was only about a ten-minute drive, but the location among the trees made it feel very private. Inside, several maids were busy cleaning and making up beds in the two largest bedrooms. Because the house hadn't been lived in for several years, it felt stuffy, but windows had been opened and fresh air was breezing through.

Davey said, "As you're staying longer, you get first choice of the bedrooms."

Bran headed upstairs to look at them. There were four bedrooms on this floor, all similar in size and comfort, though the furnishings were somewhat worn. He almost chose the room at the front of the house that gave him a glimpse of the sea in the distance. He loved the sea. Was that an inheritance of his Penhaligon blood? Probably not—many people loved the sea.

But he sensed that he should choose the bedroom on the opposite side of the house, which looked into the woods. Important things would happen in this house, though he didn't know what. Perhaps the woods would be part of those happenings.

"This room will do nicely. I just hope I can persuade Lady Penhaligon that I really don't want servants underfoot."

"If you repeat that several times, she'll probably accept you at your word," Davey said. "She very much wants you to forgive her for sending you away."

"She wasn't the one who did that." Bran turned from the window. "It was Lord Penhaligon who insisted I must be disposed of."

"You say you don't read minds?" Davey said skeptically.

"I don't." Bran wondered how much to say. "But I'm good at sensing people's emotions. For example, I wonder if his bad-tempered lordship will be able to accept me as his heir when he hates the idea of having me in place of the sons he raised."

"He didn't like them much, either," Davey said. "I'm not sure he likes anyone very much."

Bran thought of his own loving family. "What a sad way to live."

"He has his title and wealth to warm the cockles of his heart."

"Shall we see if we can find something alcoholic downstairs, Matthew?" Bran asked. "You can tell me all about the guests I'm likely to meet at tonight's dinner."

"I'm sure the servants preparing the house have restocked the drinks in the study." Davey led the way downstairs to a comfortable room in the back of the house. A glass-fronted cabinet contained several bottles, so he removed one of claret. After pouring wine in two goblets, they settled down in the comfortable chairs.

Bran eyed the claret in his glass. "Now I'm wondering where this came from and if it was imported legally."

"Probably not. We've been at war with France, off and on, for a long time, and the current peace will surely end soon." Davey sipped his own wine. "How do you feel about smuggling?"

Bran frowned at his claret, not drinking. "To be honest, I haven't thought much about it before now. It's illegal, of course, and because I work for the Home Office, I'm generally on the side of the law. But since I haven't really considered the subject, I've surely consumed smuggled drink before." He took a small sip of the wine. "And this is blasted good. How do you regard smuggling? You're a lawyer and an officer of the court."

"Yes, but I grew up near here. Smuggling is not only a tradition, but often the only way for a man to support his family, especially when the fishing is poor."

"It's hard to condemn a man for wanting to feed his family." Bran took a larger swallow of his claret. "Will I be meeting any smugglers tonight at dinner?"

"Very likely, but I won't tell you who they are." Davey's tone turned ironic. "If you can read minds, you'll surely figure it out for yourself."

"I don't read minds," Bran said again. "Even if I did, I wouldn't leap to my feet and accuse fellow guests. I'd much rather wait and watch and learn."

"That's wise. If you speak out harshly about smuggling, when you are potentially the most powerful man in this area, it could be . . . unhealthy."

"That is not a cheering thought." Bran finished his claret and set the glass aside, knowing he needed to keep a clear head. "Who is likely to be at the dinner this evening?"

"It's apt to be a large group, since men will bring their wives and perhaps adult children. Particularly unmarried daughters."

Bran groaned. "Really?"

"Of course. You will have position, power, and a fortune." Davey was clearly enjoying himself. "You're every maiden's dream, Bran."

"Even though I'm gifted and was exiled by my family?"

Davey became more sober. "Not everyone dislikes those who are gifted."

"Not to mention that money and a title can outweigh other considerations." Bran grimaced. "Tell me about some of the people I'm likely to meet tonight."

"Certainly, the vicar of the parish church, St. Clarus. Mr. Fillmore is a good fellow and knows everyone and everything that goes on around here. His wife is a close friend of Lady Penhaligon's."

Davey thought more. "If he isn't at sea, Jacob Libby should be here. He owns several ships, both fishing and trading vessels. Likely, Devin Fellowes as well. He owns the village inn. Surely, Joseph Bidlow will be in attendance. He's the Penhaligon steward and in charge of most of the estate enterprises, now that Lord Penhaligon is no longer able to manage everything himself."

"Were the older sons involved in running the estate?" Bran couldn't bring himself to call them his brothers.

"No, Arthur was devoted to sowing wild oats in London, and George preferred the sea. Penhaligon found both of them unsatisfactory." After he thought for a moment, Davey added, "Arthur wasn't much missed by anyone, but George wasn't a bad fellow."

"I presume that Mr. Libby and Mr. Fellowes are likely involved in smuggling," Bran commented.

Davey smiled wryly. "I leave you to determine that."

Chapter 6

~

Girl's restlessness was growing. She felt a tugging to the west that was strongest when the Starling took her for evening walks. She sensed that there was more to life, more to *her*, than she could remember. But whenever Girl struggled to talk, to ask about herself, the Starling would lay a cold hand on Girl's forehead and blankness would flow through her.

Vaguely she recognized that she must not show restlessness or try to speak. She must not let the Starling touch her forehead. Perhaps then the world would become clearer . . .

Chapter 7

Bran shivered involuntarily as he and Davey entered Castle Penhaligon. "Is something wrong?" the lawyer asked.

Bran decided to answer honestly. "There are a lot of strangers inside and I can . . . feel the weight of their minds. A great deal of curiosity, of course. Along with . . . anger. Fear. Resentment. Greed. People who hope to use me to their advantage." He took a deep breath. "Time to shield myself and pretend I'm a porcelain teapot."

Davey laughed. "Surely, it won't be that bad."

"Bad enough. But you don't need to escort me all evening. Find some time with Glynis. I'll manage."

"I don't doubt that. But you probably won't enjoy it."

That was certainly true. Bran was not fond of crowds of strangers, but he was very good at managing whatever must be done.

The upstairs drawing room was now full of people sipping drinks and chatting with each other. Lord Penhaligon sat in his preferred location in front of the door, with several older men clustered around him. His lordship's face was gray and the hand clasping the head of his cane was trembling slightly.

Bran wondered just how bad his father's health was, and whom he could ask for a straight answer. Perhaps Davey would know.

In full porcelain mode he approached Penhaligon and said, "Sir," inclining his head politely.

His father scowled at him. Speaking to his cronies, he said, "This is my youngest son, Branok Penhaligon. Boy, meet my steward, Bidlow; Mr. Libby, our largest shipowner; and Fellowes, owner of the Admiral Drake Arms in the village."

Bidlow had grizzled hair and a sun-browned complexion. Eyes narrowed thoughtfully, he said, "It's good to meet you, Mr. Penhaligon. Do you know anything about farming?"

"Very little, but I can learn."

Bidlow looked cautiously approving. Before Bran could speak with the other men, his mother sailed up and gave him a light kiss on the cheek. "My dear boy! Let me introduce you to your new neighbors."

Bran was happy to go with her. She introduced him to several couples, who were pleasant and interested, but not over-powering. Mr. Fillmore welcomed him to the community with genuine warmth, befitting a vicar. His round, good-natured wife said with humor, "You must feel like a prize sheep being judged at a fair, Mr. Penhaligon."

Bran laughed. "Very true! I hope I don't end up being sold for mutton pie filling."

"We here in Cornwall don't believe in wasting a ram," Mrs. Fillmore assured him. "Good breeding stock, you know."

He winced. "I've been warned about that!"

"Are you courting a young lady in London?" his mother asked, her gaze calculating.

"No, but if harassed, I will invent a false fiancée!"

His mother and the Fillmores laughed; then he was led away, to meet more people.

His mother managed to introduce him briefly to most of the

guests. He did his best to remember names and faces. As Davey had warned him, there were half a dozen young women dressed in their prettiest gowns who studied him with predatory gazes. All were reasonably attractive, yet none interested him.

Eventually his mother excused herself to check on the progress of dinner, and Bran was free to move about more casually. Davey and Glynis were talking quietly in a corner of the large room in a location where Lord Penhaligon couldn't see them. They weren't touching and they controlled their expressions, but the connection between them was clearly visible.

Bran was glancing around, wondering whom to approach next, when Mr. Fellowes approached and handed him a glass of red wine. "I see you've been so busy being introduced that you haven't had a chance to acquire a drink. As an innkeeper, I thought it my duty to remedy that. You look like a man who could use a spot of claret."

Bran chuckled. "My thanks. I've been getting thirsty from so much talking." He took a grateful swallow of wine. It was a very good claret.

Fellowes was a solid, prosperous-looking man of middle years. He gestured around the room. "This sort of gathering is useful for getting an overview of local society, but it's not restful being on display."

"So true!" Bran sipped more of the wine and wondered when dinner would be served. He was getting hungry. "I imagine you know as well as anyone what people think of my unexpected appearance. Dare I ask what the general opinions are?"

Fellowes considered before he deemed to reply. "Your return is the most excitement Penhaligon has known in years. There is some wariness because you're a foreigner, meaning not from Cornwall, but there's also relief that there is now a clear heir to the barony. I'd be happy to give you a tour of the village and introduce you to some of the other business owners. We can talk more then."

"I'd like that. How about the day after tomorrow?" Bran suggested.

Fellowes agreed, but their discussion ended as the guests were summoned to dinner. Bran looked forward to seeing the village and wondered if Fellowes's inn had a cellar full of smuggled goods. Very likely. He was sure he'd learn interesting things in the village.

When the dinner finally ended, Bran and Davey returned to the dower house. As they stepped inside, Davey said, "Shall we see if the drinks cabinet contains some fine illegal French brandy?"

"Please," Bran replied. "I think I've earned a good strong drink."

The cabinet did not fail them. Davey splashed brandy in two glasses while Bran lit a fire against the cool night air. As Bran settled into a wing chair and sipped at the brandy, he said, "I thought that went relatively well, but I'm not sure, since most people were polite to my face."

"From what I could tell, people were wary because you're from London, but glad that you're not putting on airs." Davey chuckled. "You're considered to be handsome, gentlemanly, and very marriageable. Consider yourself warned. There's no shortage of young ladies who would like to become the next Lady Penhaligon."

Bran made a face. "One needs to want to marry in order to be marriageable, and I haven't the least inclination in that direction. I hope that you and Glynis were able to slip away for a few private minutes."

"We did, but it wasn't long enough." Davey cradled the brandy glass in both hands as he gazed at the fire. "It's so hard to leave her, when I don't know when we'll meet again. I have to return to Plymouth in the morning and there's much work to catch up on."

"Do you two have long-term plans?" Bran asked quietly. "I presume that elopement isn't being considered."

"If I was twenty, I'd be begging Glynis to run away with me, but age brings a better understanding of how catastrophic elopement would be. Most of that hardship would fall on Glynis."

"Are you waiting for Lord Penhaligon to die?"

Davey winced. "Though his death would certainly simplify things, wishing for her father to die is such an ugly, appalling idea. But it's impossible not to recognize that if he were gone, there would be nothing to stand between us."

"What if the new Lord Penhaligon should object to such a match?"

Davey's brows arched. "Would you object?"

"Of course not. I want my sister to be happy. But there is no guarantee that I'll inherit. Lord Penhaligon can barely stand to look at me. He may decide I'm not really Branok Penhaligon."

"But you have the tattoo," Davey said, startled. "And you look like a Penhaligon."

"He hasn't asked to see the tattoo. I suspect that if he doesn't see it, he can claim that I'm an imposter, not his real son at all." Bran sipped his brandy more slowly. "The Penhaligon looks are very common here, I noticed tonight. You look like a Penhaligon yourself. Earlier barons might have seduced legions of servant girls."

"I have some Penhaligons in my family tree," Davey admitted. "But you're the true heir, I'm sure of it."

"You're probably right, but his bad-tempered lordship could deny me. As I don't particularly want the inheritance, I wouldn't fight for it." Cheered by the thought, Bran continued, "Lord Penhaligon could find another man about the same age who has a Penhaligon-type face and declare him to be the true heir."

Davey swore. "I thought the succession was settled! Lady Penhaligon certainly thinks you're her son."

Bran shrugged. "She wants a son and forgiveness. She would accept any man who is reasonably plausible."

"I think you really are Branok Penhaligon," Davey said flatly. "All the pieces fit. If you hadn't shown me the tattoo, I wouldn't have been able to say that I believed you to be the missing heir, but you did show it to me. Though it was blurred, I don't doubt that it's the Penhaligon tattoo. Why did you come here if you genuinely don't want the inheritance?"

"Curiosity, remember?" Bran rose and moved to the window, which looked out into the woods behind the dower house. "I had a strong feeling that I needed to come to Cornwall, so I've accepted the possibility that I'm the missing son. At least for now."

"I've noticed that you keep looking off into the woods. Why?"

"I don't know," Bran said softly as he gazed into the mass of dark trees. "I may have mentioned that being gifted sometimes urges one in a particular direction, but it doesn't explain why. One must await the unraveling of events for clarity. That hasn't happened yet."

"I don't envy you, having to wait indefinitely."

Bran smiled as he turned away from the window. "We are what we are. How about more brandy?"

Bran rose early the next morning and prepared a simple breakfast. He was scrambling eggs with cheese, which surprised Davey when he came downstairs. "You cook?"

"Enough to feed myself and you, if you're hungry," Bran said. "My mother believed that all her children, both male and female, should be able to take care of themselves."

"By 'mother,' I assume you mean Lady Tremayne?"

"Yes." Bran split the eggs between two plates and added sliced ham and toast, then poured two cups of steaming tea. "She's my real mother in a way Lady Penhaligon will never be."

"You find yourself with a complicated family."

"Indeed." Bran sat down and buttered his toasted bread. "But I give Lady Penhaligon credit for swiftly stocking the pantry so I won't starve between the meals I take at the castle. You're returning to Plymouth this morning?"

"Yes, I've neglected my legal practice for too long." Davey ate a bite of eggs with a piece of ham. "I'll call at the castle and thank Lady Penhaligon for her hospitality before I leave."

"Will you tell her that I'm going to spend a quiet day exploring the area?" Bran asked. "After meeting far too many people yesterday, I need some time to myself, but I'll come to the castle for dinner."

"I'll let her know so she won't worry," Davey promised.

"If I hear anything you might need to know, I'll send a message," Bran said. "Assuming I don't decide I'd rather just go home to London."

"Interesting times ahead for you, Bran." Davey finished his tea and toast, then stood and offered his hand. "Good luck to you."

"Thank you, Matthew." As they shook hands, Bran added, "I appreciate all your help and guidance."

"I was just doing my job." Davey offered a quick smile. "But in this case it's been a pleasure."

After the lawyer left, Bran settled down to a second cup of tea. He was looking forward to a quiet day. Perhaps that would help him clarify just why he was here.

Chapter 8

⚊⚊

Girl had been very good, causing no trouble, obedient to the Starling. But deep inside there was a growing burn of restlessness that made it harder and harder to be a blank *thing* with no thoughts or understanding.

She was most restless during her walks outside. Fresh air stirred her, making her understand that there was more to her, to life, than this drifting, featureless existence.

On this morning the wind was brisk and carried a hint of wildness. The sea.

Thoughts of the sea stirred images. Water, waves crashing on sand and stones. She realized that she'd always loved the sea and it was somewhere past the woods where they walked. And there was something more in that direction, a spark of light that drew her.

She paused on the path that ran into the woods, feeling things she could not define, but needing to inhale more of that wind from the sea. To find that spark of light and hold it close. Tightening her shawl around her shoulders, she inhaled deeply, filling her lungs with a promise of freedom.

The Starling caught her arm and said harshly, "Stop dithering and come back to the cottage, Girl!"

Girl resisted the Starling's pull. Exasperated, the woman raised her hand and reached toward Girl's forehead to flatten thoughts and emotions once again.

Noooooo! Scalding-hot energy blazed through Girl and she jerked away from the Starling. A soundless scream echoed through her mind.

The Starling snarled bad words and grabbed Girl's arm, trying to yank her close enough to subdue. Girl shoved the Starling violently, knocking the other woman to the ground. Then she spun away and plunged into the woods toward that scent of the sea, heedless of lashing branches and rough ground. When her unbound hair snagged in a branch, she pulled it free and tied the mass in a loose knot that fell down her back.

Girl ran and ran until she could run no more, then fell gasping against a tree, the bark rough against her skin. In the distance she heard shouts. The fog that clouded her mind had thinned a little. Dimly she realized that she'd once been called something different, not Girl. She couldn't remember what, but she yearned to know that name as she yearned for the sea and the spark of light that drew her. The light was brighter now.

She would find it. She straightened and continued more slowly through the trees. When she became too tired to walk farther, she curled up under a tree and drew her shawl tightly around her. Despite the noon sun, it was cool beneath the trees. It was so good to breathe pure, fresh air.

She woke up cold and stiff to find the sun had crossed the sky. Her gown and shawl had snagged and ripped in several places during her flight and her lightweight shoes were battered. No matter. She rose and started walking again. When she found a stream, she splashed water on her face and drank deeply. Refreshed, she continued on her way.

She walked, rested, walked again. The day was beginning to

darken when she heard the baying of hounds in the distance. She shivered, instinctively realizing that she was the prey the hounds were hunting.

Her mouth set. She would not go back to the Crow and the Starling. She found a faint game trail going in the direction of the sea and began walking again. She wasn't sure what she was seeking, but eventually she would find it. If the hounds caught up with her, she would deal with them somehow.

She would never be Girl again.

Chapter 9

~⟆~

After being the focus of so much attention the day of his arrival, Bran found it a relief to spend the next day exploring the countryside on Merlin, his sure-footed chestnut horse. The weather was cool, alternating between sun and clouds, with an occasional light spatter of rain.

The cliffs and stones and crashing waves were dramatically beautiful. He headed south as close to the shoreline as he could find a safe trail. Occasionally he saw sails out on the sea, small fishing boats, he guessed. Smugglers as well? Quite possibly.

Toward the middle of the day, he felt a sharp pinch of intuition and drew Merlin to a halt. A rough path zigzagged down the low cliff and it shone silver in his mind's eye. He dismounted and tethered Merlin, then scrambled down the path, which ended in a small cove with a narrow shingle beach.

He explored and found a sea cave, whose opening was invisible from most angles. Wishing he had a lantern, he improvised a torch of dried grasses and ducked into the cave. The torch burned quickly, but lasted long enough for him to see a couple of dozen stacked small barrels that surely contained spirits.

There were also wooden boxes that could contain other illicit goods, perhaps tea or tobacco. A smuggler's cache.

It was time to take advantage of the peace and quiet to do some serious thinking. Outside, he found a convenient-sized rock and sat down to watch the waves roll in, elbows resting on his knees and his hands loosely clasped in front of him as he stilled his mind.

When Davey had appeared in London looking for the missing Penhaligon heir, Bran had felt a deep compulsion to reveal himself and go to Cornwall. He now recognized that there were multiple reasons for that compulsion. One related to his work with the Home Office, which impacted the health and security of Britain. Smuggling was involved, but not in an obvious way, he felt. Smuggling deprived the treasury of a sizable amount of revenue, but it wasn't critical. So . . . something else. Was information being smuggled south into France? Perhaps.

But the personal reasons for coming here were stronger even than his Home Office responsibilities. Was it critically important for him to meet his original family? He hadn't felt a strong connection to any of them, though he could become fond of Glynis and Lady Penhaligon.

Was it vitally important that he inherit the title and property? Perhaps, but he had trouble seeing himself in that position. He'd never lusted after wealth or status, and he didn't now.

If he did become Lord Penhaligon, he'd have to figure out how he felt about smuggling. Certainly, it was illegal, but how much of the local economy depended on the trade? He didn't like the idea of impoverishing people who had few other resources. Still another reason to hope that he wouldn't have to face that future.

So, what personal issue had brought him here? When he cleared his mind and stilled his thoughts, his imagination blazed silver. He'd come for both business and personal reasons, but most of all the personal. He opened his eyes and inhaled deeply. That silver fire faded, but still pulsed in his veins. Something critically important was about to happen.

Sighing, he stood and scrambled back up the cliff to where Merlin was placidly enjoying a patch of new grass. Bran's thinking was somewhat clarified, but he was still far from really knowing.

He glanced at the sun and realized it was time to return to the dower house so he could dress for dinner. Tonight was supposed to be a quiet family meal. Quiet was good, but he wasn't sure about the family part. Lord Penhaligon's scowls were enough to put anyone off their food.

Luckily, dinner included the vicar and his wife, along with Bran's parents and sister. They were good company and kept conversation flowing. Lady Penhaligon and Glynis were shy but friendly. Lord Penhaligon mostly scowled.

Bran was relieved when he was able to bid everyone good night and return to the dower house. There was a full moon to light the way, but he churned with restlessness.

After grooming and feeding Merlin, he went into the house and lit lamps in several ground-floor rooms. Then he poured himself a small amount of the fine smuggled brandy. He was halfway through his drink when in the distance he heard the baying of hounds.

This! He felt as if lightning had struck him. The event he'd sensed was about to come crashing down.

Brandy sloshed on his hand as he slammed the glass onto a table. He yanked on his coat and dashed out the back door into the woods. The fierce barking of the hounds rose and fell as if they were closing in on their quarry.

Bran had always had good night vision, which kept him

from breaking his neck as he raced along a path that led inland through the trees toward the sound of the hunt. The woods thinned as the ground sloped downhill to a small meadow, where the moonlight revealed a tableau that froze Bran's heart. A figure blazing silver bright emerged from the trees on the opposite side of the meadow.

The silver light was so fierce that it took time and concentration for him to see that it was a young woman. With absolute certainty, he recognized that this was why he was here. *She* was why he was here.

As the silver dimmed, he saw that she was stumbling with exhaustion, her shapeless blue gown ragged and her pale hair tumbling around her shoulders. Behind her, half a dozen foxhounds galloped from the woods, baying as they closed in on their prey.

Horrified, Bran charged down the slope, hoping to God that the dogs wouldn't drag her down and tear her apart. Before he could reach the girl, she turned and raised her hands palms up as she faced her pursuers.

The dogs halted, snuffling the ground in bafflement while she slowly backed away. Bran gave a soft whistle as he realized that the silver lady was gifted and she was creating a shield to confuse the hounds. But her ability was erratic and several dogs were starting to focus on her again. Not wanting to disrupt whatever power she was wielding, Bran slowed as he approached her.

"Well done," he said in a soothing voice as he sent thoughts of calm and kindness. "It's difficult to hold the hounds at bay. I'm a friend. My name is Bran. Please let me take you away to a place of safety."

He extended his hands toward the hounds and created his own shield to reinforce hers. After a few moments the dogs sat or lay down, panting.

The silver lady jerked and turned to look at him, her eyes wild. He wasn't sure if she understood his words, but she didn't retreat from him. She was as shockingly beautiful as she was desperate.

Shouts sounded from the woods not far away. "She must be nearby!" a hoarse voice bellowed. "Quickly now!"

"Time we left," Bran said, keeping his voice even. "You look too tired to walk farther. Let me carry you. I won't hurt you, ever."

As he said the words, he knew that was a truth from his marrow. He could never hurt her. Her gaze met his. Her fear and tension faded and she started to fold down like a rag doll.

He closed the space between them and caught her before she fell to the ground. She gave a ragged sigh and rolled into his arms as he caught her up, clinging as if she was drowning and he was her one hope of survival. She was light and slender of build, though he knew she'd feel heavy by the time he got her back to the dower house.

Talking softly, he turned and headed up the slope at the quickest speed he could manage. Carrying her meant she left no scent on the ground for the dogs if they started to pursue her again.

They had vanished into the woods by the time the harsh voices reached the meadow where the girl had been. Outraged swearing rent the air as the men debated what had happened to stop the dogs and where their quarry could have gone. The oaths and curses faded behind them.

By the time he and the girl reached the house, the night air was peaceful, except for the hooting of an owl and the distant sound of the sea. As he carried her inside, he was panting as loudly as the hounds had. Her slim body was chilled, and he guessed from her thinness that she might be hungry. He took her directly to the kitchen.

After setting her in a Windsor chair, he said, "I'll make some tea, but first something to warm you up." A woven knee rug was folded on a sofa in the drawing room. He collected that and wrapped it around the girl before he built the embers in the kitchen hearth into a fire.

She didn't resist his ministrations, just pulled the knee rug close, her head hanging. She seemed numb and confused.

Grateful once more that Lady Penhaligon had provisioned the kitchen, he put potato soup on to heat while the tea steeped. He added honey to sweeten the hot drink before cutting wedges of cheese and slicing the rather dry bread.

When he set the bowl of warm soup on the table beside her, she lifted it in both hands and drank with ferocious intensity. Silently he refilled the bowl. This time she drank more slowly and didn't empty the bowl. After setting it down, she nibbled on a piece of cheese and washed it down with tea.

Even exhausted and disheveled, she was intensely alluring, with delicate features and a gentle elegance. Her tangled blond hair had looked silvery in the moonlight, but he saw now that it was a warmer shade of blond, a soft shimmering gold. She moved him deeply, but he did his best to conceal that. He mustn't give her reason to fear him.

As he poured more tea for both of them, she raised her wary gaze to him. Her eyes were a clear light aquamarine blue and they were confused, but not mad. He guessed that she was in her early twenties, though it was hard to be sure.

"My name is Bran," he said conversationally. He tapped his chest, then gestured toward her. "What's your name?"

Her brow furrowed. Did she not speak English? Or was she simple? He studied her more deeply and sensed that someone had suppressed her essence. Someone who was gifted and was totally without conscience.

"Bran," he said again, placing a hand on his chest. Then he gestured toward the girl. "And you are . . . ?"

Her mouth opened uncertainly and she licked her lips. "G-girl?"

Her voice was thin and rusty, as if it hadn't been used lately. She looked so lost and forlorn that he impulsively laid his hand over her slim, cool fingers. "You'll be well soon," he said softly, wondering if she understood his words. "You'll know your own name and be yourself. I promise you."

Someone began pounding on the front door.

Chapter 10

His silver lady flinched violently at the sound of hammering fists. Her eyes wide and frantic, she started to rise from the table, poised for flight. The bark of dogs joined the sounds of knocking.

Sending her calming thoughts, he raised a hand, not wanting to frighten her by grabbing her arm. "It's all right. I'll protect you. No one will take you away." He made soothing motions in the air, trying to convey that she should relax and stay still. There was no need to run.

Uncertainly she settled back in the chair. As the banging resumed, Bran stood. "I'm going to send whoever that is away. Stay here and you'll be safe."

Hoping to God that she would stay, he lifted a lamp and made his way through the house. Having lights on showed that the house wasn't empty, so he couldn't ignore this rude visitor.

He peeled off his coat and tossed it over a chair, then grabbed the half-empty glass of brandy he'd abandoned earlier. That should support his appearance as a gentleman taking his ease in his home.

Another barrage of blows was falling when Bran unlatched

the door and swung it open. "Is the house on fire?" he asked coolly. "I can't imagine any other reason for you to be making such a racket."

A large, dark-haired man, who was dressed like a merchant or perhaps the owner of a fishing boat, stood at the threshold. His fist halted in midair as the door opened. Another smaller man, holding a lantern, stood behind him. At the edge of the circle of light, the foxhounds, bright eyed and restless, pawed the ground.

The stranger lowered his fist and said gruffly, "I'm Captain Crowley and I'm looking for a girl."

Using his most aristocratic London accent, Bran said, "Aren't we all? But sorry, there are no girls here. This isn't that sort of house."

The man flushed with irritation, but held on to his temper. "Not just any girl. She's my niece. My mad niece. Young and skinny and blond. Can't talk or understand what anyone says. She lives with her cousin Doris, who looks after her, but today the girl went wild and attacked Doris. Knocked her down and then ran into the woods. It's getting cold tonight and we need to find her before she freezes to death."

Bran made himself look concerned. "I'm sorry to hear that. There are more dangers in the woods than the cold." His gaze went to the foxhounds. "The dogs haven't been able to track her?"

Crowley scowled. "They lost her scent in the woods, but she was heading in this direction."

Bran realized that several of the hounds were moving restlessly as they eyed him. Since he'd carried the silver lady, her scent was on him, and the dogs were reacting. He created the same kind of shield he'd used in the woods and the dogs lost interest.

He sipped at his brandy casually. "I've seen no wandering girls, but I've only just returned from dining at Castle Penhaligon."

Crowley's expression changed. "Are you the missing son everyone is talking about?"

Bran arched his brows and looked supercilious. "I'm Branok Penhaligon, not that it's the business of anyone outside the family." It was the first time he'd used the Penhaligon name, but it seemed useful in dealing with this fellow who had apparently been the silver lady's captor.

Crowley examined him with edgy interest. "Of course everyone's interested. Sorry to have disturbed you, Mr. Penhaligon. If you see my lost girl, catch her if you can. If you can't, send word to me in the village. Everyone there knows me."

"I'll do that." Bran swallowed the last of his brandy. "Good night and good luck finding your niece." He closed the door and locked it before Crowley could say more.

He heard muttering from the men and yips from the dogs, but sensed Crowley and his companion and the foxhounds moving away from the house. He breathed a sigh of relief as he considered what his silver lady would need next. He'd provided food and safety, but no doubt she was exhausted; she needed rest. But she would need so much more.

Clothing, for example. He couldn't buy women's clothing without attracting a good deal of notice. And though he'd said he didn't need servants in the dower house, they would still come occasionally with food or to do cleaning. It would be hard to keep her presence in the house a secret for long.

He needed more people to conceal her presence. Tomorrow he'd ask Lady Penhaligon if he could invite several of his siblings to keep him company. No, ask to invite one sister, a lady's maid, and Cade. Lady Tamsyn Tremayne was also blond, and about the same size as the silver lady, so she could bring clothing for two. If the silver lady posed as Tamsyn's maid, it would be easy to keep her out of sight. Cade was good for general protection, and he could help ferret out the trouble Bran was sensing.

Decision made, he returned to the kitchen. His heart almost stopped when he realized his silver lady wasn't there. He swore softly, wondering if she'd hidden or even fled the house. "They're gone now. Are you here?"

After a long moment he heard rustling and she peered over the edge of the table, her expression wary and a long kitchen knife clutched in one hand. She was not going to let herself be recaptured.

Ignoring the knife, he repeated, "They're gone. More tea?"

Not waiting for an answer, he poured some into their cups and stirred in honey. Then he settled opposite her, hoping to set an example of relaxation.

She eased into the Windsor chair again and laid the knife on the table. After she sipped the tea, she began to look more relaxed. Tea, Britain's universal remedy.

He tapped his chest once more. "Bran. Have you remembered a name other than Girl? That's not a name, just a description."

She stared at him helplessly. "Remembering will take time," he said in a matter-of-fact way. "Do you understand what I'm saying?"

She looked baffled and worried. How frustrating it must be for her to be locked behind the barriers that Crowley and her cousin had apparently laid on her mind!

Talking to her in a normal way with explanatory gestures might help break down the barriers, and he didn't have any better ideas at the moment. He touched his chest again. "Bran."

This time she whispered, "Bran?"

"Yes!" He smiled at her. "Well done."

She smiled back, looking happy to have earned some approval.

Next step, what to call her? "Calling you Girl is disrespectful because you aren't just any girl, you're special. I need a name for you until you remember your own." He thought for a moment. "May I call you Lady? Because I think of you as my silver lady."

She cocked her head to one side, her expression confused.

He tapped his chest. "Bran." Then he touched her hand. "Lady. Do you like that?"

She touched her chest. "Lady?" she asked uncertainly.

"Yes! Well done again. Can you understand some of what I say?"

This time she gave a hesitant nod. Progress. He offered her more soup, more cheese, more tea. She shook her head at each, so that was another piece of communication she knew.

Looking at her tired face and battered clothing, he guessed that now that she'd eaten and was safe from Crowley, she was ready to collapse. He placed his hands together and tilted his head on his hands to mime sleep.

She nodded and stood when he did that, so he beckoned for her to follow and led her upstairs, carrying a lamp and a pitcher of water. He'd give her the bedroom that Davey had used, the one that looked to the sea. A maid from the castle had cleaned the room and made the bed with fresh linens to be ready for future guests, so it would do nicely.

He pointed out his bedroom and collected a comb before he led her to the front room. She looked around in wonder when he opened the door and gestured her inside. She gave a small sigh of pleasure when he opened the draperies wide enough for her to see the moonlight touching the sea beyond the castle.

He put the lamp on a table and set the pitcher of water by the basin. There was soap and a towel on the washstand. Next he showed her the chamber pot behind a screen in the corner, as that was something she'd certainly need.

She immediately poured water in the basin and began washing her face and hands. Glad she understood basic hygiene, he said, "Good night, my Lady." After he again mimed sleep, he closed the door and withdrew to his own room.

He'd write his letters to London before going to bed and mail them after he talked to Lady Penhaligon. If he was to keep his silver lady safe, he would need help.

After Bran left, she took off her battered shoes, shawl, and gown, so she wore only her thin shift. Then she washed as much of herself as possible before sliding into the bed. It was a grand bed, with a canopy and smooth sheets, so unlike the narrow cot and scratchy straw mattress she'd slept on in the Starling's cottage. She closed her eyes and let herself relax. She had aches and bruises from her flight through the woods, but for this night at least, she was safe and free.

Lady. She liked that Bran wanted to call her that rather than the harsh-sounding *Girl.* She like Bran as well. As soon as she'd seen him, she knew he represented safety. Her fears vanished when he caught her up in his arms. His strength and kindness had been an almost unbearable relief.

It was maddening that she couldn't understand everything he said, but she felt that her mind was clearing. The more he spoke, the more she understood. How long until she knew her own name and who she was? She craved that knowledge. She wanted to be a real person again.

She had no idea what the next day would bring, but for now she gave herself up to blessed sleep.

Chapter 11

Bran awoke the next morning feeling that the world had changed. It took only a moment to remember his silver lady, who now slept under his own roof. At least he hoped she did. She hadn't seemed inclined to run away the night before.

He rose and washed up, then dressed for the day. He quietly left his room and saw that the door to the opposite bedroom was open. Hoping she was downstairs, he descended to the kitchen and found her toasting a piece of bread over the embers of the fire. "Good morning, my Lady. Would you like preserves with your toast?"

Not waiting for a reply, he entered the pantry and brought out a jar of marmalade. It had been made in the castle's still room and was excellent.

Lady opened the jar and cautiously tasted the contents, then smiled with pure pleasure as she spread marmalade onto her toasted bread. Bran was already heating water for tea. There was a pleasant domesticity to making breakfast together.

He sensed that her mind was clearer this morning, though still far from normal. But her shabby blue gown remained a disgrace. She'd made some effort to brush it clean, but the garment had been plain and ill-fitting even before being battered during her escape. He made a gesture down the length of the garment. "I'll get you better clothing, but it will take several days. I'm sorry."

She gave a small nod and continued eating her breakfast. Bran frowned, wishing he didn't have to leave to visit Fellowes, but intuition insisted that he must. "I promised to meet a man in the village, so I'll be gone for most of the day. You must stay quietly in the house and let *no one* see you."

He did his best to mime his leaving and her staying, going through the motions twice. Then he asked, "Do you understand me?"

Her brow furrowed a little, but she nodded. He checked the pantry. There was still some soup, as well as cheese, bread, marmalade, and pickles. The kitchen had a water pump, so she'd be able to drink. "There isn't much food, but I'll bring something back for you. Will you be all right until then?"

She nodded again. Hoping she really did understand, he beckoned to her. "Come, my Lady. I want to show you something I think you'll like."

She obediently followed him to the study in the back of the house. There were two shelves of books that he'd investigated previously, and he pulled out the largest volume. It was a travel book with engraved plates of different destinations. He opened the book to the first plate, which was the Colosseum in Rome.

Lady caught her breath when she saw the picture and studied it intently. Bran pointed at the descriptive text on the opposite page. "Can you read this?"

She stared at the written paragraphs, then shook her head sadly. He patted her hand. "Soon you'll remember how to read." He hoped he was telling her the truth.

"I must leave now," he said. "Remember what I told you. Stay inside and let no one see you! Do you understand?"

She looked up at him, her expression earnest. "Y-yes," she said in a tentative voice.

Delighted that she spoke aloud and seemed to understand, he smiled. "Very good! I'll be back this afternoon."

He left the house and walked to the stables to saddle Merlin, praying that Lady would be safe alone all day. As Merlin whuffled happily to him, he stroked the chestnut's shiny coat. "You're probably lonesome for other horses, aren't you? But don't worry, if Lady Penhaligon doesn't object, soon you'll have more equine company. I know you and Cade's Major are particularly good friends."

He saddled his horse, wondering if his silver lady rode. After he led Merlin from the barn and mounted, he glanced at the house. He didn't see her in any of the windows, so she must be taking seriously his warning not to let herself be seen. He waved in case she was watching.

As he rode away to the castle, he again gave a silent prayer that she'd be safe on her own all day.

Lady stood behind the drawing room curtains and peered through the sliver of space at the left side. She could see out, but didn't think Bran saw her when he rode out of the stables, because there was no recognition in his face when he scanned the front of the house. She was pleased that he waved before turning down the lane that would lead him toward the castle. The gesture made her feel real.

She stared after him because he was her friend and protector, but equally because she loved looking at his horse. It was a beautiful creature, a shiny reddish brown with white mane, tail, and front feet. She gazed down the lane until both horse and rider were out of sight.

Brows furrowed, she turned and slid down the wall so that she was sitting under the window. In the hazy days when she was held prisoner in the Starling's cottage, she couldn't remember seeing any horses, though she vaguely remembered hearing hoofbeats when the Crow arrived. There was a shed where he probably left his mount during his visits.

Seeing Bran's beautiful horse made her recognize with absolute certainty that she loved horses, had always loved them. She closed her eyes and imagined herself cantering easily, gracefully, over plains of grass and rugged stones. A . . . a moor? She wasn't sure what a moor was, but the word seemed to fit.

A vision of riding sharpened in her mind. The horse was very dark, with an extravagantly flowing black tail and mane, an elegant thunder horse from the heavens, and where had that thought come from? The dark horse was a mare with a gracefully curved neck and a sweet nature. The word "Arabian" sounded in her mind, though she didn't know what it meant.

But she remembered riding that horse, grooming her, flying along on her back. Shadow had been her own beloved mount.

Shadow? Yes, she could visualize every lovely inch of her horse, including the bright curious eyes and the affectionate nudges. The enthusiasm for chunks of carrots and sugar. Her mental vision became clearer and clearer, and she could almost believe that their minds touched.

She let herself drift in these new memories, which were much more enjoyable than the memories of her imprisonment.

What had become of her beloved Shadow? Had the Crow stolen her? She fiercely hoped that Shadow lived and that they would be reunited.

But there was so much she didn't know! As her mind awakened, she was becoming more curious about the world around her. She rose and decided to search through the house to see what interesting things she might find.

When Bran reached the castle and asked to see Lady Penhaligon, he was escorted to the breakfast parlor, where her ladyship and Glynis were eating. When he greeted them, his mother looked up, pleased. "Branok! My husband prefers to breakfast in his room, so it's a pleasure to have you join us. Please help yourself." She gestured toward the well-filled sideboard.

"I accept most gratefully." He filled a plate with eggs, bacon, and fried potatoes, then refreshed the teacups of his mother and sister before he sat down. There was little talk while they ate, but when Bran finished, he said to Lady Penhaligon, "I have a favor to ask of you."

"Of course!" His mother looked ready to grant him anything.

"Would you object if I invite a Tremayne sister and brother to join me in the dower house? Since I appear to have two families, it makes sense that you start becoming acquainted with each other."

His mother looked startled and a little wary, but said, "Of course you may invite them, though you'll need more servants to run the house."

"My sister will bring her maid, and Cade might bring a groom, so we shouldn't have to impose on you too much." The more people in the house, the easier it would be to conceal his silver lady.

"What are your brother and sister's names?" Glynis asked with interest. He guessed that she'd welcome more company.

"My sister is Lady Tamsyn Tremayne. She's a bit younger than I am. My brother is Caden Tremayne, who is a bit older than I."

His mother's brow furrowed. "She's *Lady* Tamsyn?"

"Yes, she's a true-born daughter of my parents, Lord and Lady Tremayne," Bran explained. "Cade and I are among their foster children."

"It sounds very complicated," his mother said rather uncertainly. "How many children are there in your family?"

Bran laughed. "As you say, it's complicated! My parents

have three natural-born children and"—he paused to do a mental count—"about a dozen fosters, both male and female. Our parents always treated all of us exactly the same, and we all feel like true brothers and sisters." Looking back, he found it surprising that the natural-born children weren't jealous of the fosters, but they'd all been kind and welcoming, traits they must have inherited from their parents.

"Lord and Lady Tremayne have very generous hearts," Glynis said quietly.

"They do. Since you don't object to their coming, I'll send a letter to London to invite Tamsyn and Cade. Does the Royal Mail call in the village?"

"Yes, at the Admiral Drake Arms," Lady Penhaligon said. "I have some letters to send out also, so I'll have a footman take yours and mine together."

"No need. I'm engaged to visit Mr. Fellowes at his inn today for a tour of the village," Bran said. "I'll be happy to take your letters as well."

"How kind." Lady Penhaligon rose. "I'll bring them down now." With a nod, she left the breakfast room.

After her mother left the room, Glynis regarded Bran thoughtfully. He realized that her gray eyes were very like his. She said, "You're always polite and the perfect gentleman, yet I haven't the least idea of what you're really like."

"Gentlemanly behavior is an excellent shield," he said dryly. "I find it useful because this situation is so strange. I don't really know how I feel about it."

"Don't you wish to become Lord Penhaligon?" she asked curiously. "The title is old and the fortune substantial. Most men would consider it a great prize."

"It is, but I've little interest in collecting prizes," he said honestly. "I like the life and family I have in London. I don't need more."

"You don't want us?" she said, hurt in her eyes.

He gave her a warm smile. "I'm quite happy to have you as a sister. The rest of it I'm not sure of."

"Then I'm happy to be one of your many sisters." Glynis looked thoughtful. "What is it like to be gifted? What magical skills do you have?"

"Nothing at all magical," he said firmly. "It's more like having very good intuition about things. It's useful, but it's not calling up demons from the vasty deep. For example, even though I wasn't enticed by the idea of claiming a barony, I did have a very strong feeling that I should come to Cornwall. I'm still not entirely sure why, but I know it's right that I'm here." His silver lady was quite enough reason all on her own, though he knew there was more.

"Are there different kinds of gifts?" she asked, interested. "More than making good decisions."

"Yes, but they tend to be subtle." He hesitated, wondering how much to say. "For example, Tamsyn is a very healing presence. Just being around her makes sick people feel better." He was hoping that she'd be able to help restore his lady to herself. "Cade is very good at solving all kinds of problems. Send him to a place where there is trouble and he'll do a good job of sorting it out." He was also particularly good at cracking heads as needed.

"My father has never allowed any mention of what it is to be gifted," Glynis said, her eyes wide with fascination. "There's so much I don't know!"

He studied her face. "Being gifted often runs in families. Have you sometimes felt an unexpected degree of certainty? A sense that something is vitally important to you?"

"When I first met Matthew," she blurted out, then flushed and dropped her eyes. "I shouldn't have said that."

"Why not? The bond between you is very clear," Bran said gently. "It's strong and mutual."

She glanced up. "Mutual?"

"Very much so. I have the sense that your parents don't approve of him as a match for you."

"My mother likes him, but my father..." She shook her
head.

"Lord Penhaligon is not an easy man," Bran said with massive understatement. "I suspect that if you've felt instincts beyond what most people have, you've suppressed them."

She gave him a twisted smile. "Is reading minds one of your
gifts?"

"No, but I'm usually good at sensing people's feelings. It
feels as if you've been suppressing a part of yourself."

She nodded, not looking at him.

"Perhaps it's time that you explored that aspect of your nature, sister. I will be happy to talk with you whenever you
wish."

Their conversation ended when Lady Penhaligon returned
with her letters. She handed them over to Bran. "I hope you
enjoy the village. It's a very pretty place."

"From what I've seen, the entire coast of Cornwall is beautiful." Bran's words were innocuous, but as he spoke, he realized
that today he would learn something very important about
why he needed to come to Cornwall.

Chapter 12

⚘

The Starling's cottage had been small and stark, so Lady enjoyed exploring this splendid large house. Her room was the most beautiful she'd ever seen, with a blue canopy above the wonderfully soft bed. Other furnishings included a clothespress, a table and two chairs, and a washstand. The polished wooden floorboards were warmed by a thick carpet that she'd curled her bare toes into when she rose this morning.

As she turned away from the room, she gasped at a sudden vision of the Crow and Starling entering the house through the back door and searching for signs of her. She didn't think it would happen, because Bran had dismissed the Crow with cool authority the evening before, but the idea was so upsetting that she started tidying her room so it would look unoccupied.

Carefully she straightened the covers and fluffed the pillows and neatly folded the towel that hung on the washstand bar. Fortunate that she had no possessions—except the clothes she wore and her shawl, which she didn't need for now. Bran had given her a comb so she'd carefully combed out her hair and braided it into one long tail down her back.

She would return the comb to his room. What to do with the shawl? Thinking about it, she folded it and crossed to Bran's room. Since he was staying here, his room could look occupied. She placed the shawl in his clothespress under a pair of shirts. He hadn't brought a lot of clothing, but she curiously examined what he had. The fabrics were nicer than what she wore.

She was intrigued by his razor, which was set on his washstand with other items, some of them mysterious. Touching his things made him seem closer.

His room looked back into the woods, where he'd found her. A large tree grew not far from the window. Close enough that she could jump to it. She had done things like that in her past, she was sure of it.

The house had several similar bedrooms, clean and silent as they waited for future guests. As she explored, she found a narrow staircase that led up to the area under the roof. An attic? She was pleased when that word floated into her mind.

The stairs opened into a short passage with tiny empty bedrooms opening off it, to the left. The rooms were like the one she'd had in the Starling's cottage, but nicer. For people who had worked here? Servants? Another unexpected new word. Perhaps. Again, everything was clean but empty.

To the right, the attic corridor ended in a door. She opened it and found piled furniture and boxes and trunks and other interesting things, all dimly lit by a small window on the end wall. This area was dusty, as if no one ever came here except to add more boxes.

She opened one box and found heavy folded fabric. Curtains, she guessed. When she poked the material, very dusty. Another box held women's clothing of complicated styles. She lifted out an elaborate gown made of a shiny cream-colored material. There was a huge amount of fabric in the skirt and the overall size of the garment was far too large for her. It smelled of dried lavender.

As she folded the gown back into the box, she sensed that the garment held memories of the owner's youthful past. The woman had kept it to remember those long-gone days.

A pile of dust-covered books was set on a table, so she opened the one on top. It didn't have pictures, like the book Bran had given her, but she felt closer to understanding the words. She frowned at the page, but the small black squiggles remained just beyond her understanding. Maybe tomorrow would be better.

She moved toward the window and opened a smaller box. Clothing again, this time simpler women's garments. She held a gown up to her shoulders and it looks as if it might fit her. She folded it back into the box to investigate later.

The next book held garments similar to Bran's, but smaller and looking more worn. Tan trousers, undergarments, a white shirt, a blue jacket with brass buttons, a pair of shoes and another of low boots, were set on the bottom of the box. She had the sense that the carefully cleaned and folded garments had belonged to a beloved boy, now gone.

She loathed the shabby gown and shift she was wearing, which were likely castoffs of the Starling. She suspected that she should try on the female garments from the previous box, but the boy's clothing was far more interesting. She stripped off the dreadful gown and shift and donned the trousers, shirt, jacket, and boots. They were only a little large and even the low boots weren't a bad fit.

She liked wearing clean clothes and having the freedom of movement that men enjoyed. This was not the first time she'd worn male garments, she realized. Her earlier image of riding her horse returned and she realized that she'd been dressed like a boy. And someone—a woman?—had gently scolded her for doing that.

She swallowed hard at the thought. Somewhere, sometime, there had been people who had cared for her. She must find them again.

She *must*!

Chapter 13

❧

The village of Penhaligon was beautiful in a very Cornish way. It was built on the hillsides above a small river that opened into a fair-sized harbor. Steep streets were lined with rows of plain, sturdy fishermen's cottages.

The Admiral Drake Arms was easy to find as it stood on the main street and looked out over the harbor. An alley ran along one side of the inn to a small stable yard behind. Bran left his horse and entered the inn in search of Mr. Fellowes.

The innkeeper was working on his account book in the almost empty taproom. He rose and gave Bran a friendly welcome. "Hello, Penhaligon! Come for your tour of our fine town?"

"Yes, I look forward to learning my way around." The more he learned, the better his chances of figuring out what had drawn him to this part of the world. Something was going to happen, but what? "I also have letters for posting to London."

"They'll go out this afternoon." Fellowes accepted the letters and set them on a table that held several other missives. Then he donned his hat and coat and led the way outside.

Bran paused to admire the sweeping view of the village and

the harbor. Several small boats were moored near the stubby stone pier. Out in the channel beyond the harbor, he saw a scattering of fishing vessels. He shaded his eyes with one hand as he studied a dark shape well out in the channel. "Is that a Royal Navy vessel in the distance?"

Fellowes squinted at the sea. "Aye, a frigate by the look of it. Probably headed to the Royal Navy Shipyard at Plymouth Dock. Have you visited there? It's huge. They build new ships and repair the old ones. It's quite a sight."

Bran became very still as the words "Plymouth Dock" flared silver in his mind. "It's one of the largest shipyards in Britain, isn't it? I'd love to see it."

Fellowes nodded. "You should get Mr. Davey to show you around. He knows everyone in Plymouth."

They ambled down the hill toward the harbor. Whenever they passed a shop, Fellowes led Bran inside and introduced him to the proprietor. Bran met a greengrocer, a cobbler, a baker, and the owner of a store that carried everything from stationery to candles. Like most of the other people he'd met in Cornwall, the merchants were polite, curious, and a little wary.

When they reached the harbor, a ship was gliding in to moor by the pier. Fellowes asked, "Do you know much about sailing ships?"

"No, but I think I'd better learn," Bran said. "What sort of ship is this one?" He guessed that it was forty to fifty feet long, a good size for a coastal trading vessel. The name *Sea Maid* was visible near the bow.

"It's a lugger, which means that she's rigged with lug sails that hang from a spar. As you see, they're angled, which makes a ship fast and good at sailing close to the wind," Fellowes said. "The *Sea Maid* is a familiar visitor."

Fellowes waved at a powerfully built man who jumped from the ship onto the pier and called out, "Captain Dubois, I have someone for you to meet!"

Dubois approached and introductions were made. He was of

middle years with shrewd eyes and a weathered face, and to Bran's eyes, he glowed a dark, tarnished gray. He offered his hand. "Mr. Penhaligon."

As soon as Bran shook hands, he knew that Dubois was gifted, and that he was a dangerous man. Concealing his thoughts, Bran smiled. "A pleasure, Captain Dubois. Mr. Fellowes is educating me about the sea and the ships that sail these waters."

"You'll find no better tutor," Dubois said, his voice softly accented. "He captained his own ship before moving ashore to his inn."

"Is that a Guernsey accent?" Bran asked with interest.

Dubois nodded. "You may not know ships, but your ear for accents is good. Yes, I'm of Guernsey and it's glad we are that Britain and France have made peace. We Guernsey men have felt like a bone caught between two dogs."

Though the Guernsey island group was close to Normandy, it was a British domain, with a mixed British and French culture. The dialect was more French than English—and the islands were major conduits for French goods being smuggled into Britain. "Peace is always good," Bran said, "but I doubt this one will last much longer. Then the two dogs will be at each other's throats again."

"I fear you're right." Dubois sighed. "But the island has been well fortified against Napoleon's troops, so we shall pray for continued safety."

Though the captain spoke like a loyal Briton, Bran sensed that his opinions were very different. That would certainly explain his aura of danger.

Turning to Fellowes, Dubois said, "We must speak. Can you come aboard my ship now?"

Fellowes hesitated. "I was going to treat Mr. Penhaligon to lunch at the inn. Do you have time to join us?"

Dubois frowned. "No, I must unload cargo and bring on other goods in time to catch the tide."

"No need to feed me today, Mr. Fellowes," Bran said easily. "I'll stop by the bakery on my way up the hill. I'm looking forward to trying Cornish pasties."

The innkeeper looked relieved. "Thank you for understanding, Mr. Penhaligon. We live and die by the sea and the tides here. I'll serve you that lunch another day with the freshest fish you've ever tasted!"

"I look forward to that soon," Bran said. "Thank you for introducing me to the village." Besides being hungry, Bran could use this opportunity to buy food for his silver lady and perhaps learn more about the village and its inhabitants.

It was a short walk up the steep street to the bakery shop. Mrs. Rogers, the owner, was sliding small ginger cakes from a baking sheet onto a platter, but she looked up as Bran entered the shop. "Good to see you again so soon, Mr. Penhaligon. Have you come to sample my wares?"

"Indeed I have. Mr. Fellowes said that you're the best baker between Plymouth and Polperro, and I want to try your pasties."

Mrs. Rogers laughed. "He's not wrong, because I'm the *only* baker between here and there! But you won't regret coming in. Pasties all have some chopped vegetables, usually potatoes, onions, and turnips. Then I add meat or fish or cheese and different seasonings."

The counter was glass fronted with baked goods displayed on the shelves below. She pointed. "The top shelf is today's pasties. Beef is the dearest, bacon and potato the most popular, cheese and potato the best bargain. They're all fair tasty, if I do say so myself."

"I'd like one with bacon and one with cheese, and may I eat here?" Bran gestured at the small tables along one wall. "I'm too hungry to wait."

"I like a man with an appetite," she said approvingly. "Would you like some ale to wash them down?"

"You're a very perceptive woman, Mrs. Rogers." Bran settled at a table, and the food and drink appeared almost immediately. The pasties started as a circle of dough. After the filling was added, the circle was folded in half and the dough pinched all along one edge to create a D shape. They were still warm from the oven and the crusts were rich and flaky. They went well with the tangy local ale.

Bran indicated the opposite chair. "Since it's quiet now, would you be able to join me? I always make it a priority to befriend good cooks."

"You're a silver-tongued devil!" She chuckled, not realizing how accurate she was. She poured some ale for herself and sat opposite Bran. "What do you think of our village?"

"It's beautiful. Mr. Fellowes is a good guide." Bran took another bite of the bacon pasty. Delicious. "He introduced me to the captain of a ship that was just coming in, the *Sea Maid* from Guernsey. Do you know Captain Dubois?"

A furrow showed between Mrs. Rogers's brows. "We've met."

"I've read that a lot of smuggled goods come through Guernsey," Bran said, his voice relaxed. "Is Captain Dubois a smuggler?"

The baker glanced out the front window, as if checking whether anyone was there. "I have no idea. It's best not to talk about such things."

He finished the bacon pasty and started on the one with cheese. A sharp local cheese, he guessed, that went well with the potatoes and the rest of the vegetables in the filling. It was every bit as good as the bacon version.

After he swallowed his second bite, he said, "Mrs. Rogers, you seem like a plain speaker. Since smuggling is apparently important to Cornwall, I think I should try to understand it better. Would you be willing to discuss the subject? Only as much as you're comfortable with, of course."

She sipped her ale and studied his expression. "They say you work for the Home Office. That includes the Revenue Service, doesn't it?"

"Yes, but I have nothing to do with tax collection or revenue cutters chasing after smugglers." He considered how much to say. "The Home Office has many departments. Some of them have found smugglers valuable for moving information and people between Britain and France during the wars. My work is closer to that."

"They say the war will be starting up soon, so smugglers will be useful to Britain again," she said thoughtfully.

"As I said, you're a perceptive woman. I'm not a dark and dangerous spy," he said. "Merely an investigator who, in small ways, does what I can to help my country. That doesn't include giving information to the Revenue Service."

She considered for a long moment, then nodded. "Fishing is a chancy business. If the pilchard shoals don't come, or if there's a season of rough weather, so the boats can't go out often enough, many in the village will have cold, hungry winters. Smuggling is a way to earn some extra money. Spirits, tea, silks, anything that is taxed heavily is profitable for smuggling. A fair number of villagers are involved in the trade in a small way, working enough to take care of their families. There are larger operations in Looe and Polperro, but there's smuggling and caves for storage all along this coast." She shrugged. "Families have to eat."

"Agreed. Thank you for the explanation." Bran finished his cheese pasty and washed it down with the last of his ale. "I need to go home, but I'm expecting company and I'd like to take a supply of your splendid baked goods. Not just pasties, but bread and fruit tarts and some of those ginger cakes!"

Her brows rose. "I can't sell out the shop, because there will be more customers coming, but I can keep you and your guests from starving for a day or two." She stood. "I'll pack a good assortment in a canvas bag, which I expect you to return on your next trip to the village!"

He laughed as he got to his feet. "I will, so I can fill it up again!"

More customers came in as Mrs. Rogers carefully packed the bag so items wouldn't break or be squashed. Bran was paying for the food when he felt a stab of scalding intuition. He caught his breath, knowing he needed to return to the dower house *now*!

Chapter 14

⌒

Pleased with her new outfit, Lady packed her despised gown and shift and battered shoes in the box that had contained the boy's garments. She glanced around the attic, sure there were many treasures yet to be found. But now it was time to go down to the kitchen and find something to eat.

She descended the narrow stairway to the bedroom landing and was about to take the wider stairs to the ground floor when she heard people behind the house. *The Crow and the Starling!* She could barely breathe when she recognized their muffled voices.

She moved into Bran's room and peered out the edge of the window. Sure enough, the Crow was fiddling with the back door, and she knew it was only a matter of time until he got it open. It was just like the image she'd seen earlier. She opened the window a crack so she could hear the words clearly.

The Crow snarled, "Dammit, I'm sure she's here! The dogs searched the woods. She just disappeared. She must be hiding in a building. She isn't in the stables, and this is the only other building nearby."

"But the dogs lost her scent well away from here." This time it was the Starling, her voice anxious. "If them at the castle found out we're breaking in, we'll be in big trouble."

"Where else could the stupid girl have gone? That slick bastard is gifted—he might have hidden her scent somehow." There was a squeal as the back door opened. "If you hadn't let her get away, we wouldn't have to do this! Search the house."

Heart pounding, Lady wondered where to hide. In a cupboard in the pantry? She was small enough to fit, but too easy to find. The attic, among all the boxes?

She imagined herself in the tiniest, dustiest corner, under an old table—and the image immediately changed to one of the Crow triumphantly dragging her out and the Starling raising her hand to extinguish Girl again.

No!

She must escape from the house, using the tree outside Bran's window. The tree was on the same side of the house as her enemies were entering, so she must hope they were far enough inside not to see her.

Bran's window was hinged on the right and swung inward. A casement, that's what it was called. She opened it farther, wide enough for her to get out. Then she climbed onto the sill and balanced there while she judged the distance to the tree.

The branch looked farther away than it had earlier, but she must chance it. Falling to the ground wasn't likely to kill her, but she would probably be injured and unable to get away as quickly as she needed. Grimly she gathered her strength, then launched herself from the sill while grabbing for the branch.

She caught it, barely. The branch swung down with her weight and she almost fell, but she clung like a squirrel, even though the bark was hurting her hands. When the branch steadied, she scrambled along it to the tree trunk. She perched there for a moment while she drew a deep breath and listened.

She didn't hear any shouts or exclamations, so she must not have been seen. She worked her way around to the other side of the trunk. Below were enough branches and branch stubs to allow her to climb down far enough to drop to the ground without injury.

Giving thanks for her boy's clothing, she headed into the woods. When she'd escaped from the Starling earlier, she'd headed . . . west, that's what it was called. Now she must find Bran. He would protect her. Where was he? She halted and thought of him: his kindness, his pleasing looks, his warm, protective arms when he'd carried her away from the Crow and his hounds.

Yes, there he was in her mind. She headed . . . south? . . . through the woods. After she found the main road, she retreated into the woods, where she wouldn't be easily seen, and continued moving south.

She needed Bran. She quickened her pace, afraid of being pursued when the Crow and the Starling couldn't find her in the house. The open window might send them after her. She could hear the rumble of wheels from the road; that would not be Bran. Then a horse moving slowly south. Not Bran.

She was gasping for breath when she heard another horse moving at a swift pace north along the road. *Bran!* She was sure of it. Turning, she cut through the brush. As she emerged from the woods, she tripped on a low branch and was catapulted into the middle of the road.

"Damnation!" a man swore.

A horse reared over her, its hooves threatening to crush her. *Bran!*

He expertly brought his horse under control as he exclaimed with shock, "Lady!" Vaulting from the saddle, he knelt and drew her into his arms. "Are you all right? What happened?"

She clung to him, shaking with relief. His embrace was safety and warmth and more.

"You're safe now," he said soothingly. "But we need to get off the road before someone else comes along."

He stood and helped her up, keeping an arm around her

shoulders as he led his horse into the woods. After a few minutes' walk they reached a small clearing.

"Stay, Merlin," he said to his mount as he released the reins.
Then he sat down on a fallen log, drawing her down beside
him. "Can you tell me what happened, my Lady?"

She burrowed against him again, searching for words. The
only ones that came: "Merryn. My name is *Merryn*!"

"Wonderful!" He hugged her closer. "Merryn is a lovely
name. Do you know more of your names?"

She bit her lip, then shook her head.

"You'll remember soon," he said encouragingly. "Do you
have the words to tell me what sent you running through the
woods?"

She calmed her mind, then said haltingly. "Crow. Starling. In
house."

Bran gave a soft whistle. "They broke into the house?"

She nodded confirmation.

"You're a very clever lady, Merryn. You found boy's clothing, much better for escaping than your gown, got out of the
house, and found me. I wonder what you'll be able to do when
you're fully restored to yourself." He brushed a hand over her
head and down her back. "You're also very brave."

There was a small patch of grass in the clearing, and Bran's
beautiful chestnut began to graze. Noticing, Bran said, "You
must be hungry, too." He moved to his horse and pulled a
bulging bag from one saddlebag and a jug from the other.

"I raided a bakery," he explained as he opened the bag and
pulled out something golden and deliciously scented. "Have a
Cornish pasty. This one is beef and potato, I think."

Realizing that she was ravenous, she bit into the pastry with
enthusiasm, flakes of crust crumbling on her lap. It was wonderful. As she ate, Bran uncorked the jug.

"You're probably thirsty as well. There's cool tea in the jug."

She finished the pasty, took a swig from the jug, then explored the bag. She chose another pasty. This one contained cheese and potato. She sighed happily when finished.

He dug into the bag and produced a small, spicy-smelling pastry. "Have an apple tart." It was sweet and tangy and delicious. Bran ate one also. Then they both ate ginger cakes.

When they'd finished, he said, "You told me that the Crow and the Starling broke into the house. They suspected you were there?"

She nodded. "Couldn't find me anywhere else, even with dogs."

"You seem to be remembering more. Do you know why they held you captive?"

She frowned as she tried to puzzle that out. "They wanted me to do . . . something for them. Soon."

Bran looked thoughtful. "Because you are gifted?"

"Think so," she said haltingly. "Don't know what."

"As you remember more, we'll learn why they took you," he said confidently. "But now it's time to return to the dower house. You've had a difficult day."

He stood and packed away the food and the tea. "Can you ride with me on my horse? With you dressed as a boy, no one will know who you are. I'll tuck your braid down under your coat." He did that, then took off his hat and dropped it on her head.

His warmth was in the hat. She liked that feeling, but had to push the hat back so she could see. He smiled at her. "You look very charming."

She wasn't sure what he meant by that. Was it good or bad?

Unable to resist, she went to the horse's head and stroked the beautiful, sleek neck and cooed nonsense noises. The horse gave her a friendly head butt, preening under her admiration.

"Merlin likes you," Bran said. "And clearly, you are used to horses."

He allowed her to appreciate Merlin for a while longer before saying, "It's time we headed back to the house." He swung onto his mount. "Do you want to ride in front of me or behind? If you're really tired, in front of me would be easier because I can hold you."

She was tired, but she liked the idea of riding with her arms around him. She patted Merlin's haunches in answer. Bran offered his hand, and she scrambled up behind him, using his stirruped foot as a step. She settled against him with a sigh of contentment. She was well fed, on a horse, and the warmth of Bran's body was very pleasant on a cool spring afternoon.

She closed her eyes and thought of Bran and her lovely, lost Shadow, who seemed almost close enough to touch.

How long would it be until she knew who she was?

Chapter 15

⤛⤜

Bran set an easy pace back to the dower house. Luckily, there was little traffic along this road and no one who passed took particular notice of his companion. She would look like a boy to any casual glance.

He dismounted when they reached the house, then helped Merryn down, so they could walk Merlin into the stables. After removing the tack and offering water, he began to groom the horse. Merlin loved being groomed and leaned into Bran with a pleased whicker. While he checked the horse's hooves for pebbles, Merryn found the grooming tools and began brushing Merlin on the other side.

Bran guessed that she was doing it from the simple desire to pamper the horse. She was obviously experienced in equine care.

"Did you have a horse before?" he asked.

She paused in her brushing, looking wistful. "Shadow. Most beautiful horse."

"Horses are splendid, aren't they? Merlin is the best I've ever had." As she continued with the grooming, he said, "I've invited two members of my London family to visit me here in the dower house. My sister Tamsyn is about your size and is also blond. She'll bring clothing for you, and we'll say that you're her maid."

Merryn looked at him uncertainly. "Maid?"

"You'll be safer with more people around you," he explained. "My brother Cade will come with Tamsyn."

She returned to her grooming, and he guessed that she didn't really understand yet, but she would. Tamsyn was the best healer in the Tremayne family and Bran hoped that she would be able to help Merryn clear her mind. "Can you remember anything else about your life before you were taken by the Crow and the Starling?"

She bit her lip, then shook her head. With her male clothing and delicate features, she looked enchanting. He reminded himself, as he had before, that he must not think of her as a lovely, desirable young woman. Not when she was under his protection and recovering from what had been done to her. It would be good to have Cade and Tamsyn here to distract him.

Merlin was shining and happy, so Bran was about to suggest that they return to the house. Then a long, high-pitched whinny sounded outside the stable. Merryn whirled, her face lighting up with joy. "Shadow!"

She bolted out the broad open doors into the stable yard. A beautifully proportioned dark bay galloped up to her and skidded to a halt to greet Merryn with equine delight. Merryn threw her arms around the mare's neck, crooning messages of welcome.

Shadow wore a halter with a pair of broken leads dangling from it, as if she had broken her restraints to come to her mistress. Had Merryn mentally called the horse to her? Bran had heard of gifted people who could do that, though it wasn't common. Clearly, Merryn was very powerful.

The mare almost certainly had some Arabian blood. This was a horse who belonged to people with means.

Merryn used the broken lead to urge Shadow over to the mounting block. From there she scrambled up onto the horse's bare back, looking vastly pleased with them both. She looked like an ancient horse goddess who could ride her steed to the stars.

"A beautiful horse for a beautiful lady," he said warmly. "I'm so glad that you were able to call Shadow to you, but we should move her into the stables so she can be properly groomed and fed."

Merryn wrinkled her nose at the practical suggestion, but slipped to the ground and led her horse inside. Together they watered, fed, and groomed Shadow, who apparently hadn't been cared for to Merryn's high standards.

When they finished, Bran said, "I have to dine at the castle again tonight, but I'm worried that the Crow might come back while I'm gone."

Merryn closed her eyes for a moment, then opened them and shook her head firmly.

He studied her, consciously evaluating mind and spirit. "You have some ability to see the future, don't you?" he said softly. "You knew when you escaped captivity that you would find sanctuary. You knew that the Crow and the Starling would find you in the house, so you escaped again. And you knew where to find me as I returned from the village. Does this happen often for you?"

Her brow furrowed as she thought. "Only big things that hurt."

He gave a low whistle. Many gifted people had some sense of the future. For him, it was knowing he needed to go somewhere, to do something, but the strong, clear foretelling ability Merryn seemed to have was rare. "This may be why your captors wanted you. They may hope you can tell them of approaching danger if they are planning to do something bad. Does that make sense to you?"

She frowned, then nodded. She scarcely needed words to communicate.

"I hope you can use this ability to keep yourself safe," he said seriously. "While I'm at the castle, do you want to be in the house or here with Shadow?"

She gave him a swift smile. "Shadow!"

He laughed. "You have lost time to make up for." He moved to his saddlebags and retrieved the bag of baked goods and the jug of tea. "Your dinner, my lady!"

She opened the bag and pulled out a ginger cake, smiling mischievously as she popped it into her mouth and ate it.

"You'll probably have a more pleasant evening than I will," he said wryly. "You'll be all right if I leave you alone for several hours this evening?"

She caught his gaze and gave a solemn nod. It was a wordless acknowledgment that he trusted her judgment of her own safety, and that she appreciated his trust.

She was as gallant as she was beautiful. She would be formidable, once she was in full possession of her faculties.

Suppressing his desire to cup her soft cheek in one hand, he said, "Come to the house. I want to show you something."

After she glanced again at Shadow, Merryn followed him outside and through the stable yard to the house's back door.

"Can you open the door?" he asked.

She tried, but it was locked.

"Keep your hand on the doorknob," he ordered. As she obeyed, he placed his hand over hers where it held the knob and closed his eyes as he concentrated his power through their hands and the knob.

When he released her hand, she pulled it from the knob and flexed her fingers curiously. So she had felt that rush of energy. He said, "Try the knob again."

She obeyed and it turned easily in her hand, opening the door. Startled, she jerked her hand back and looked at him in surprise.

"I've taught the knob to recognize you," he explained. "You can come and go as you please, but others can't now."

She gave a delighted smile and opened and closed the door several times. "Have a pleasant evening, Merryn," he said. "I'll see you later."

He mounted Merlin and cantered off to the castle. Now that Bran knew that Merryn could sense when danger was coming, he wasn't as worried about leaving her alone. Though it was difficult not to worry some.

Lord Penhaligon joined his family for dinner. He said little until the meal was almost finished. Then he grabbed his cane and lurched to his feet. "Come with me, boy. I want to speak with you."

It was the first time his lordship has expressed any desire to talk to Bran at all, although it was obvious he was trying to be insulting. Bran rose and accompanied him to the older man's study, on the other side of the house. His father sank behind the desk, pulled a bottle of brandy from a lower drawer, then poured himself a drink, not offering any to his guest.

Bran sat down without an invitation, as it didn't seem he was going to get one. Scowling, Lord Penhaligon took a swig of the spirits, then said, "I hear you're asking questions about smuggling. Stop doing that!"

"Why?" Bran asked.

"Because it's none of your damned business," his father growled.

"I'm trying to learn about the area—and that includes smuggling, because it seems to be an important activity here."

"That still doesn't make it any of your damned business!"

"If the Penhaligons are involved in smuggling, or are protecting smugglers, surely it is my business." Intuition struck and narrowed his eyes. "Was your second son, George, a smuggler?"

The baron cursed and swung his cane at Bran. Bran caught

the end of the polished wood stick with one hand, immobilizing it. "I'll take that as a yes," he said mildly.

His father tried to jerk the cane away, but Bran effortlessly pulled it from the older man's hand and laid it across the desk.

"He was the best of my sons!" Penhaligon snarled. "Far better than you, if you even are my son! I refuse to acknowledge you, so you'll never inherit!"

"As you wish," Bran said. "Believe me, I've no more desire to be related to you than you have to be related to me. Of course, if you refuse to accept me, there is still the question of an heir. I was told that next in line is a second cousin, whom you loathe. You might do better to find a young man who has the look of the Penhaligons, obeys orders, and is willing to have a dragon tattooed on his shoulder."

"Damn you!" The baron grabbed a heavy glass paperweight and hurled it at Bran. "I should have thrown you into the sea instead of allowing you to be sent to that baby farm!"

Bran caught the paperweight as easily as he'd caught the cane. He wasn't the athlete that Cade was, but he was a pretty fair cricket player. He stood and set the paperweight on the desk. "If you have nothing else you wish to discuss, sir, I'll bid you good night."

As he turned to the door, Lord Penhaligon said in a rising voice, "You're always so damned polite! Don't you ever lose your temper like a normal man?"

Bran glanced over his shoulder. "Very seldom. I don't enjoy being angry." He smiled with a touch of mischief. "And keeping my temper drives others mad. It's quite entertaining."

Bran left the study accompanied by a spate of curses. When he returned to the dining room, Glynis and Lady Penhaligon were looking at him anxiously. "We heard shouting," his sister said.

"His lordship was upset with me," Bran said. "He said he'd refuse to acknowledge me as his son and heir, though I don't know how serious he was about that."

"That's ridiculous!" Lady Penhaligon exclaimed. "Of course you're our son!"

"The matter could be debated." Bran thought for a moment. "I think I'll go to Plymouth for two or three days. Mr. Fellowes suggested that it would be interesting to visit the Royal Navy Shipyard at Plymouth Dock. I gather it's one of the largest employers in this part of Britain."

"Will you call on Mr. Davey?" Glynis asked shyly. "I believe he knows a number of people at the naval yard."

"Of course I'll call on him. He's been very helpful, and I intend to take full advantage of his good nature. Can you suggest a good inn?" Bran asked. "I'll be gone two or three nights, but I'll be back before my brother and sister arrive."

"The Three Crowns is said to be very good," his mother said. "Glynis, can you think of others that Branok might like?"

"There are a couple I've heard recommended," his sister said. "Give me a moment and I'll write down the names and the streets they're on." She rose and went to the next room, where there was a desk and stationery.

Bran chatted with Lady Penhaligon, not surprised that it took more than a few moments for Glynis to return with her suggestions of where to stay. When she did, she handed him two folded pieces of paper, one concealed beneath the other. "Here are several places that are well spoken of. The Mariner is said to be very good and it's on the west side of Plymouth, fairly close to the naval shipyard."

He thanked her and left the breakfast room, not surprised to find that the second piece of folded paper was sealed with wax and had *Mr. Davey* written on the outside.

Peers like Lord Penhaligon could "frank" letters, which meant signing them in the upper right corner so the letter would travel for free.

Bran privately thought it absurd that the richest people had the most privileges. If he did come to sit in the House of Lords, perhaps he could address that issue. A drawback of franking in this house was that Lord Penhaligon was able to see every letter that left the house, which meant Glynis couldn't send a private letter to her sweetheart.

As he collected Merlin and started back to the dower house, he wondered whether he should take Merryn along with him as a young woman or a young boy. A boy, he decided. That would attract less comment than if he traveled with a female, and he suspected she'd like it better as well.

She did.

Chapter 16

~∽~

They rode north until they reached the river that separated Cornwall and Devon. They pulled their horses to a halt and looked across the water. To the right was the sprawl of the city of Plymouth, while directly across the estuary was the shipyard. Bran gave a soft whistle at the sight. "So that's the dockyard. It's a city in its own right."

Beside him on Shadow, Merryn also found the sight stunning. As always, she was entranced by the sight of water, and she was intrigued by the long sweep of waterfront on the opposite shore. Stone bays and basins contained massive ships that were under construction or being repaired. Behind the docks were workshops and barracks and storage buildings, and everywhere, men working.

Bran said, "This is an important site in British history. In 1588, more than two hundred years ago, the nation of Spain wanted to conquer England and force us to convert from Protestant to Catholic. They gathered a huge fleet of warships called the Spanish Armada and sent them to overpower us."

She looked at him with interest. Though she didn't understand about Spain or religion, it was clearly a powerful piece of history.

Bran indicated the water between them and the naval shipyard. "The great admiral, Sir Francis Drake, sailed on these very waters as he led a fleet of English ships out to war. With the help of a mighty storm, England destroyed the Spanish Armada. It was one of the most important events of our history. This shipyard was built not long after that, because Britain has always relied on our navy for protection."

Merryn nodded and returned her gaze to the shipyard across the water—and gasped as dark visions filled her mind. Hearing her, Bran asked sharply, "Do you see something alarming?"

She swallowed hard so she could speak. "Flames. Explosions. Death!" She closed her eyes, wanting to banish the images, but she couldn't. "A night filled with fire."

"A vision of the future?" Bran asked, looking at her rather than the shipyard. When she nodded, he inquired, "Is it soon? Far distant?"

"Not too far." She shuddered. "War."

Bran reached across the space between them and caught her hand. As always, his touch was soothing. "It's likely that Britain and France will be at war again soon. The French will attack?"

"Yes . . . ," she said slowly. "But not . . . as expected." She knew that unexpectedness mattered, but not why.

"I agree that there is danger and possible catastrophe. The yard glows like a dark silver dagger," he said softly as he looked across the water again. His face had an expression she hadn't seen before, focused on something beyond her understanding, but vitally important.

Bran glanced at her and she realized that she was clutching his hand so hard, her fingers were white. He smiled and was her Bran again. "We were drawn here to learn what might happen. We work well together, Merryn."

She gave a shaky sigh and released his hand. "I hope so."

"I know so." He gathered his reins. "And now we'll take the ferry across to Plymouth Dock and find an inn and enjoy a quiet evening and a good dinner."

A quiet evening? As she signaled Shadow forward, she had a swift mental image of sitting in front of a fire with Bran, just relaxing together. She hoped that would happen.

What experiences awaited her in this city? The more she encountered new things, the more she became herself, she thought. She'd realized that morning that she enjoyed traveling dressed as a boy. She had braided her hair into two long tails, then wrapped them around her head before donning a hat that covered her hair and shadowed her face.

She found that she liked being boyish. There was a word for that, she thought. Tomboy? Yes, that was her! She was very proud of remembering that word. Bran had approved her appearance that morning. "As long as you keep your head down so your face is hard to see, you can easily pass for a boy. If anyone asks who you are, we can say you're one of my Tremayne cousins. Do you like the name Martin Tremayne?"

She'd considered a moment, then nodded. She was getting better at understanding words, but not as good at speaking them herself. Bran seemed to understand her well without many words.

Riding Shadow in the open air was giving her a wonderful sense of freedom, though by the time they reached the outskirts of Plymouth, her backside told her she was out of practice.

That meant she just needed to ride more often!

The Mariner Inn seemed very grand to Merryn, but Bran was completely at ease. First he sent a message to his friend Mr. Davey suggesting they meet the next day if possible. Then he registered himself and Merryn as Branok and Martin Tremayne, with a pair of connected chambers so they could move back and forth freely. She wondered if she'd ever stayed in a place like this before and thought probably not.

She'd kept her hatted head down and moved idly around the entryway so no one would look at her closely. It was a relief when she and Bran could go up to their rooms. As soon as they were private, she removed her hat and released her braids, combing her hair loosely with her fingers.

Bran chuckled. "You've had enough of pretending to be a boy for today?"

After a moment while she figured out his words, she nodded emphatically.

"I ordered a hot bath to be brought up to the other room," Bran said. "You can stay in this chamber until the servants have set up the tub, the hot water, and towels. I also asked them to bring a dressing gown for you to use when you're done, so you don't have to get back into your riding clothes. Will you enjoy that?"

A hot bath and a fresh robe? *Wonderful!* She spontaneously rose onto her toes and kissed him from sheer delight.

She meant it as a friendly thank-you, but she found that she liked kissing him. She leaned into him, happier than she could ever remember feeling.

He made a choked sound and his arms circled her as his mouth welcomed hers. For a few moments it was glorious. She loved the warmth and strength of his body, the tenderness in his touch. How the kiss was stirring unknown, alarming, and delicious feelings inside her! She wanted to kiss and hold him forever.

Abruptly Bran broke away from her and said in a ragged voice, "We mustn't do this, Merryn!"

Confused, she stepped closer again and asked, "Why not?"

He caught her hands to hold her away. "Because it's wrong for me to take advantage of you when your life is so uncertain."

Her brows furrowed. "What is 'take advantage'?"

He searched for words. "Men often want women in ways that can hurt women."

"You would never hurt me," she said with complete confidence.

"I pray I don't! But you are very lovely and tempting." He gazed into her eyes, his expression serious. "I fear that I might do something I shouldn't."

She frowned helplessly. "I do not understand."

He tried again. "You know nothing of your life. Perhaps the Crow and Starling took you away from someone who loves you. Perhaps even a husband."

The idea was startling. A husband? She had only the vaguest understanding of what that meant. But she could sense that Bran was sincerely worried about what might happen between them. She gave an uncertain nod.

He was still holding her hands, so he raised them and brushed a light kiss on each finger. "When you are fully yourself, my words will make more sense. Perhaps then we can continue this discussion."

Releasing her, he continued, "I heard a knock in the room next door. Your bathwater, I think. I'll let the maids in so they can fix the bath for you. Wait here." He moved through the door that opened to the other room, closing it behind him.

As she waited, she tried to understand why what felt so good was wrong. But Bran surely had sound reasons for what he'd said.

There was a murmur of voices next door before Bran returned. "It's all ready for you. Take your time and enjoy yourself."

She rose. "You also like baths?"

"Indeed I do. I'll have one later." He made a courtly gesture for her to enter the other room, then closed the door after her.

*   *   *

She saw that the maids had started a fire to warm the room against the spring chill. The hip bath had been set up behind a screen with towels and lavender-scented soap set on a small table within reach. The promised dressing gown was folded over a wooden chair. Merryn was happy to remove her travel-worn clothing and step into the tub.

She lifted the soap and inhaled the sweet tang of lavender, then knotted her hair on top of her head to keep it out of the way. Settling into the deliciously warm water was pure delight. She couldn't remember any other baths, but knew beyond doubt that she had always loved them. This one was particularly welcome, since a day of riding had left her with sore muscles that she hadn't used in too long.

She leaned back in the hip bath, glad that she was small enough to submerge herself well. Then she relaxed, her eyes closed.

Her mind didn't still, though. She kept thinking of that kiss and Bran's initial pleasure, then retreat. She'd enjoyed touching him. Kissing him. But he'd said they shouldn't do that now. Why not?

With a snap of insight, she realized why. He was strong and she was weak, in some ways little more than a child. A good person would not use strength to control a weak person, and Bran was a very good man; she knew that.

The answer was clear: She must become a strong woman if she wished to become someone he could honorably kiss. She must work on that.

She dozed a little until the water cooled. Then she regretfully climbed from the hip bath and dried herself with the towels and donned the dressing gown. It was warm, soft wool, so long the hem dragged on the floor. The feel of it was almost as delicious as the warm water.

As she combed her hair loose around her shoulders, she realized that she was hungry. They'd stopped for a midday picnic and to rest the horses, but that had been hours ago. Time to ask Bran when their dinner would arrive.

Thinking that she must practice being strong, she opened the door to his room.

Chapter 17

Pencil and notebook in hand, Bran did his best to clear his mind and try to find a pattern in the scraps of intuition and possibilities that had brought him to Cornwall. To begin with, danger was looming, and it must be related to the inevitable resumption of hostilities between Britain and France.

Smuggling was one element. There was no doubt that French agents in Britain were sending information to France, just as British agents in France sent intelligence back to Britain. But that had been going on for centuries. This looming problem seemed much larger and more dangerous.

His first look at the Royal Navy Shipyard had felt ominous, and Merryn's vision of fire and death supported his intuition. The Royal Navy was Britain's most vital defense, and it was logical that the French might want to attack, but surely the yard would be well defended; a raid would be suicidal for the French. He made a note to learn more about the naval yard's defenses. What else?

His ruminations were interrupted by a firm knock on the door. Wondering who that might be, he rose and unlatched the door to find Davey standing in the corridor.

"Matthew!" he exclaimed. "I didn't expect to see you before tomorrow at the earliest."

"When I got your note letting me know you were here, I hoped you'd have a message from Glynis," his friend explained.

"Yes, she did send a letter for you." Bran turned and moved to the small desk as Davey followed him into the room.

The sealed letter was on the desk, so Bran retrieved it and handed it to the lawyer. "It seems rather substantial."

"Do you mind if I look at it now?" Not waiting for an answer, Davey broke the seal and opened the letter. "Sorry to be so impatient," he said wryly, "but since Lord Penhaligon sees every letter that leaves the house when he franks it, Glynis and I haven't been able to exchange private messages."

Wanting Davey to leave, Bran suggested, "Why not go down to the coffee room so you can read in private? I'll join you in a few minutes after you've had time to properly enjoy your letter."

Davey glanced up, his expression sheepish. "I'm behaving like a lovestruck swain, aren't I?"

"Yes, but there's nothing wrong with that." Bran was trying to usher Davey into the corridor, when the door to the connecting room swung open and Merryn entered. In the blue dressing gown and with her damp blond hair falling around her shoulders, she looked delectable and wickedly improper.

All three of them froze. Merryn looked horrified and ready to bolt, while Davey stared, shocked. Wincing as he shut the door to the corridor, Bran said, "This isn't what you think, Matthew."

"What am I thinking?" Davey asked blankly.

"That she's my mistress or a local lass whom I invited in for amusement. Merryn is neither." Bran did a quick check of his intuition. It was time to explain the situation to Davey. "As a lawyer and a gentleman, will you keep silent about everything I'm about to say?"

Davey drew a deep breath. "I give my word as a lawyer, a gentleman, and as your friend."

"Thank you. Have a seat—these explanations are going to take time," Bran said. "Merryn, do you want to change into your regular clothing?"

She made a face, then settled into a chair, pulling the dressing gown around her until nothing was showing but her head and her hands.

When they were all seated, Bran continued, "Matthew, remember how at the dower house, I kept looking toward the woods and couldn't explain why?"

Davey's gaze flicked to Merryn and back. "Did you find her in the woods?"

The tone was satiric, but Bran said flatly, "Yes. She was being chased by several men and a pack of foxhounds. After I took her back to the dower house, I learned that she had been held prisoner by a man called Crowley. She didn't know her own name, and could speak or understand almost nothing."

Davey gasped and stared at Merryn. "How is she now?"

"Better," she said.

"She's not one to waste words," Bran observed. "But I think she understands most conversation now?" His voice raised in question.

She considered, then said, "Yes."

"Merryn has some interesting abilities, including the fact that she was able to call her horse from wherever it had been kept. She's a very fine rider. I didn't want to leave her alone while I came to Plymouth, so she found some boy's clothing in the dower house attic and accompanied me in disguise." Bran smiled. "She's officially a young cousin of mine named Martin Tremayne."

"Do you have any idea why she was imprisoned?"

Bran caught Matthew's gaze. "She's gifted with foretelling ability. She saw several events that might happen, including her need to escape the dower house when Crowley broke in. Earlier today when we looked across the river and saw the naval shipyard, she saw fire and destruction and war. I think those dangers are why I felt compelled to come down to Cornwall."

Davey's brows furrowed. "I've been feeling uneasy myself. I thought it was a general sense that war was coming, but this is rather more specific and right here on our own doorstep."

"Though the shape of what's to come is unclear, potential disaster is looming. I can feel it," Bran said grimly. "Do you know any Crowleys?"

"There are a number of them down around Fowey, but none I know personally." Davey frowned. "You said in your note that you wanted to tour the shipyard. Is that because you're concerned about what might happen there?"

"Yes, I'd like a thorough tour so I understand the work and the danger points. How can I arrange this?"

"All you need is for a resident of the town, like me, to get permission from the commissioner who is in charge of the yard," Davey said. "That's currently Captain Robert Fanshaw. I believe he's in London at the moment, but I should be able to get permission from his secretary, particularly since you're from the Home Office. A warder will be appointed to give the tour and answer your questions."

"Perhaps tomorrow or the day after tomorrow?" Bran asked. "The sooner, the better."

"That should be possible," Davey replied.

Merryn sat up straight in her chair. "Take me."

Bran studied her. "That's not a good idea. It's apt to be noisy and overwhelming."

"I *must* go with you!" she said with unaccustomed intensity.

"Are you seeing something important?" Bran asked. When Merryn nodded, he said, "You won't be able to pass as a boy at close quarters."

"Take me as a girl."

Bran's brow furrowed. "That would work. It's fortunate that you found female garments in the attic, though the fit and style are imperfect. We'll have to find you better female clothing. Matthew, there's not enough time to have garments made for Merryn. Do you know of a good-quality used-clothing shop where she could get a basic wardrobe?"

Davey thought a moment. "Yes, but it would be best for her to go there dressed as a female in the first place. If she goes in dressed as a boy and buys only female clothing, she'll be remembered and talked about."

"You're right. Merryn, will you mind giving up your boy's clothing for a gown that doesn't fit well?"

She made a face, but nodded.

"Then you can become my young cousin Mary Tremayne."

She nodded again. "Now dinner?"

Bran laughed. "Dinner indeed. I'll order now. Matthew, will you join us?"

Davey stood. "I'd like to, but must decline. I need to send a note to the commissioner's office so we can get permission for the tour."

"Again, my thanks for your help," Bran said.

Davey tucked Glynis's letter inside his coat. "And I thank you for yours. Until tomorrow."

After the lawyer left, Bran asked Merryn, "Do you have an idea of why you need to go with me to the shipyard?"

She frowned and shook her head.

"Then we'll find out when it happens." Bran had learned early that intuition was just a general road map. Details came only when one was in the middle of things.

Chapter 18

❧

Merryn found that she didn't mind dressing like a girl, now that she had nicer garments that fit. After her trip to the secondhand shop, she had her male clothing plus a decent female wardrobe that included two gowns for daytime wear, a riding habit, shifts and other underthings, a cloak, boots, and a very nice bonnet, which allowed her to duck her head and conceal her face.

The shipyard tour would surely be interesting, but as the carriage transporting her and Bran and Mr. Davey left them off at the gatehouse, she saw that the yard was a dizzying jumble of noise and people. A heavy wagon laden with timbers and barrels rattled by next to them, and the space inside the walls was filled with people moving about purposefully. In the distance there was a deep clamor of metal, which sounded like hammers on forges. A village smithy multiplied dozens of times, she guessed, and wondered when she'd known a village smithy.

Unnerved, Merryn edged closer to Bran. He said quietly, his expression concerned, "You don't have to do this if you'd rather not, Merryn."

She scowled at him. "I *must*." She had learned that sometimes she had very clear visions of what might happen, but other times she only felt uneasy and not sure why. Today was like that. There would be some sort of danger, and it could come from many directions in this place.

She drew a deep breath and told herself that she must learn how to be strong if she would ever be worthy of Bran.

A sturdy, middle-aged man in a naval uniform came out of the porter's lodge by the main gate. Davey said, "Bran, this is Mr. Burford, the chief warder of Plymouth Dock."

The warder nodded respectfully. "Good to see you again, Mr. Davey." His shrewd gaze went to Bran. "You'd be Mr. Tremayne, from the Home Office?"

"Yes, but this isn't an official visit." Bran offered a hand to the warder. "I've been visiting family down here and I thought it would be interesting to tour Plymouth Dock. I was impressed as soon as I looked over the water from Cornwall. My thanks for your agreeing to escort us around the yard."

After releasing the warder's hand, he added, "This is my young cousin Miss Tremayne. She insisted on coming."

Merryn peered up from under the brim of her bonnet, looking about fifteen years old and very innocent. The warder frowned. "Keep a close eye on her. The yard is a busy place. Over two thousand people work here in dangerous trades, and accidents can happen." Returning his attention to Bran, he asked, "What would you particularly like to see?"

"I've heard that Mr. Dummer, the naval surveyor who designed Plymouth Dock, was devoted to improving efficiency. Surely, what he did here can be applied to other sorts of facilities," Bran said smoothly. "Also, with war on the horizon, I'm interested in the shipyard's defenses. We must be certain there are no weaknesses the French might exploit."

Looking pained by the comment, Burford said firmly, "We've held the French off for a good long time, sir, and that's not about to change!"

He motioned for them to follow him as he strode into the yard, neatly avoiding a pile of dung left by one of the cart mules. "The Devenport Lines are earthworks constructed on the land side and they circle the whole of the town, as well as the yard. Troops are garrisoned inside to man the defenses if needed. There are multiple batteries of guns on both sides of the harbor, as well as within the yard proper. Any Frenchman who tries to attack will be blown to pieces!"

"It sounds like the defenses have been well thought out," Bran agreed. "But I recall that there was a tragic ship explosion here several years years ago, the frigate *Amphion*. What happened?"

The warder's face turned rigid. "A dreadful, dreadful day. The *Amphion* had returned from patrolling the North Sea after a storm damaged the foremast. She put in here for repairs. The work was finished promptly, and she was preparing to set sail again the next day. For that reason the ship was swarming with women and children who'd come to say goodbye to their menfolk . . ."

After a long silence he continued, "I was walking toward the frigate on my usual patrol, and there was an almighty explosion. The ground shook and the sky turned red and the *Amphion* shot up into the air so high, I could see the keel before she crashed back into the water and began to sink straightaway. Flames to the sky and mangled bodies everywhere."

He stopped and looked apologetically at Merryn. "Sorry, Miss Tremayne. I shouldn't speak of such things in front of you."

"It is good that the lost be remembered," she said in a soft voice.

"None of us here will ever forget," the warder said grimly as they resumed walking.

"Indeed not," Davey said. "I was in the town, and even there the explosion was stunning. Like many others, I ran to the yard to see if I could help, but there was so little we could do."

"It was God's own mercy that there wasn't much damage to any of the nearby ships," the warder said heavily. "But only a bare handful of people on the *Amphion* survived."

From Burford's expression Bran guessed that friends of his had been among the casualties. "What caused the explosion?" he asked. "Was it sabotage by a French agent?"

The warder's face twisted. "Nay. It's not entirely sure, but some weeks later when the wreck was dragged around to another jetty to be broken up, a sack of gunpowder topped with biscuits was pulled up from between decks. The theory is that a gunner known for drunkenness was stealing gunpowder to sell and disguising the sack with biscuits when he left the ship. Being drunk, and with the ship so busy that day, he got careless and accidentally set off an explosion in the fore magazine."

Bran gave a low whistle. "So not the enemy, but criminal greed and stupidity by one of our own men caused the *Amphion* tragedy."

"No number of earthworks and artillery batteries are proof against human weaknesses," Davey said dryly.

Merryn laid a hand on Bran's arm, her grip tight. He glanced down and saw the haunted pain in her eyes. *Fire. Explosions. Death!* Had her vision the day before been of the past or a possible future?

"Do you want to leave?" he asked again.

She gave a sharp shake of her head and released his arm, her narrowed eyes scanning their surroundings. Davey noticed the interchange and looked concerned, but he didn't speak. They continued forward behind the warder, who waved a hand to the right. "This is the rope house, where rope is both spun and laid, one of those efficiencies you asked about, Mr. Tremayne. The floor above is dedicated to sail repairs. That smaller building just beyond is the rigging house."

Bran whistled. "The rope house is the longest building I've ever seen!"

"Ropes need to be long so they don't need splicing, which

means the longer the rope house, the better," the warder explained. "Setting rope manufacture, sails, and rigging close together is part of Dummer's efficiency."

As Bran glanced around at the buildings full of workshops, some of them glowed a dark, dangerous iron gray to his inner eye. They were locations of potential danger, he guessed. Likely the rope house was full of combustible materials, such as bales of sisal, so there was a danger of fire. Other shops had their own hazards.

The dry docks ahead of them were a forest of masts. Bran guessed there were at least four ships under repair or construction, perhaps more.

"The smithery is to the north of the main yard," the warder said. "A good distance from other buildings because of the risk of fire. There are forty-eight forges for making anchors and metal braces and every other metal object that a ship needs."

Even through the general racket of the yard, it was possible to hear the ominous hammering of the forges, and there was a dark silvery warning in that noise.

"Up ahead is the number one basin and dock, the first one designed by Mr. Dummer," Burford said, raising his voice because the noise increased as they neared the basin. "His design was revolutionary, and the stone stepped sides are still the best dry-dock idea ever, because the slant makes it easy for carpenters to work on the keel. As you can see, a frigate is under construction. The steam crane is lifting the masts into place today."

"The best steam crane in Britain and possibly in the world," Davey said, pitching his voice to be heard above the clamor. "I always enjoy watching it in action."

Bran studied the steam crane, a massive machine that pounded with ear-numbing noise. Steam power was changing industries all across Britain and this was no exception. But this particular engine glowed a dangerous dark silver. He frowned as he glanced up to watch as the crane swung a long mast overhead.

"*Bran!*" Merryn screamed as she hurled herself into his

chest, shoving him backward off his feet. The massive timber mast smashed down right where he'd been standing, striking with a force that made the ground shake. He hit the ground with an impact that knocked him breathless.

After a suffocating moment he managed to get air into his lungs and pushed himself to a sitting position. He froze, horrified by the sight of Merryn's unmoving body lying between him and the fallen mast. "*Merryn!*"

Her bonnet had fallen off and been flattened by the mast. She opened her eyes and tried to sit up, but couldn't.

Bran thought his heart would stop. Then Davey dropped beside him. "Her skirt is trapped under the mast. Merryn, are you hurt?"

She frowned, then said unsteadily, "N . . . no. But can't move."

Several men closed around them, exclaiming with shock. Burford barked, "Push the mast toward the basin. All together now, *push*!"

Half a dozen men lined up along the mast and obeyed. The mast rolled several feet away from Bran and Merryn. The warder asked urgently, "Mr. Tremayne, Miss Tremayne, were you hurt?"

Bran drew a deep breath and stood, glad to realize that he was intact. "Nothing to signify."

With the mast off the skirts of her gown, Merryn was able to sit up, but she looked badly shaken and her gown was mussed and dirty. Bran bent down and scooped her into his arms. She curled in on herself like a frightened kitten.

He cuddled her close so that her head rested on his right shoulder. "Brave, clever girl," he said softly. "You saved me."

She blinked up at him. There was a smudge on her cheek. "Yes."

When he'd carried her away from the foxhounds, she'd been thin and fragile. She'd put on some weight in the days since, and he was intensely aware of her femaleness in a way that rattled his wits. He didn't ever want to let her go.

He took a deep breath. "It's time we left." Holding her close, he began to retrace their steps toward the main gate. "I need to get Merryn back to the inn so she can rest."

Davey picked up her flattened bonnet. "I'll get the carriage and bring it back this way."

The warder was pale as he said, "I'm so sorry, Mr. Tremayne, but as I said, the yard can be a dangerous place."

"I understand," Bran said as he held Merryn close. "Accidents happen."

Bran carried Merryn back toward the main gate. He'd hired a closed carriage and driver earlier so he and Davey and Merryn could talk in private.

The driver brought the carriage promptly when Davey summoned it. Bran was glad to lift Merryn inside so she wouldn't be the target of curious eyes. She sat next to him and burrowed under his arm. He held her close. "It's all right now, Merryn. You're a heroine."

Davey climbed in and took the facing seat. He drew a deep breath as the carriage turned and headed back into the town. "I've been to the yard many times, but I've never seen a near-lethal accident like that."

"It wasn't an accident," Bran said flatly. "I sensed a desire to kill me an instant before the mast fell, but I don't know if I would have reacted quickly enough to avoid being crushed if Merryn hadn't pushed me away."

Davey stared. "You're sure it was deliberate?"

"Yes," Merryn said, her voice muffled against Bran's coat. "I felt it, too."

"I think a gifted person in the yard sensed that I would be trouble and impulsively did something to cause the mast to drop," Bran said.

"That's . . . very disquieting," Davey said. "Why would someone want to kill you when you're a stranger here?"

"He may not have known why, but he was sure he wanted

me dead." Bran frowned, wondering how to explain. "There are different kinds of gifts. Sometimes one knows something must be done, but not why until later. Maybe never."

"Being gifted sounds rather erratic," Davey said. "Unpredictable."

"It is, but sometimes gifts are life saving." Bran's brows furrowed. "Have we reached any conclusions about the safety of Plymouth Dock? It's vital for the Royal Navy to protect Britain. But from what I saw today, the dock isn't likely to be vulnerable to a direct attack."

"Not with all the defenses and artillery installations," Davey agreed. "Perhaps the French might commit acts of sabotage, but those would be small scale compared to a full-fledged assault."

"Even if they managed to blow up a ship like the *Amphion*, that wouldn't do serious damage to the overall yard," Bran said, though he felt uneasy about the possibilities. "Do you know if there are guards for individual ships? If not, there should be."

"Commissioner Fanshaw should be back next week," Davey said. "I'll call on him and explain that one of the Home Office special agents visited the yard and had some suggestions."

"Matthew, do you know *everyone* in Devon and Cornwall?" Bran asked.

Davey laughed. "Hardly, but lawyers deal with a wide variety of people. I'm known in Plymouth as someone who is good at resolving conflicts peaceably, so I'm consulted on a variety of matters."

"Very useful. Have you considered working for the Home Office?" Bran said half seriously.

"I'm quite busy enough now, thank you!"

A thought occurred to Bran. "Are there some people from the Penhaligon area who work at Plymouth Dock?"

"I believe so," Davey replied. "Because of the distance they usually stay in a boardinghouse during the week and go home to spend Sundays with their families. A Plymouth Dock carter has a regular wagon service to pick up workers in Penhaligon to take them to work Monday mornings and then drive them home Saturday evenings."

"Sensible. It seems like the sort of thing I should know." Because the more Bran knew about the shipyard, the better.

As the carriage neared the inn, Merryn straightened in her seat and set to work reshaping her smudged bonnet, which had been flattened by the mast. It would never be the same, but by the time the carriage stopped in front of the inn, it resembled a proper bonnet again. She placed it on her head and gave Bran a slanting glance from under the rim.

He smiled. "You're looking very well for someone who became a heroine today. Do you want me to carry you inside and up to our rooms?"

She shook her head. "Walk."

Bran climbed from the carriage first and helped Merryn to the ground. "Matthew, would you like to join us for luncheon? I'll have food sent up."

"I'd like that," Davey said. "Though I must then return to my office."

"We've been taking up far too much of your time," Bran said as he offered Merryn his arm.

"But you've made my life more interesting," Davey said with a smile.

The three of them entered the inn. The landlady, Mrs. Morrison, was sitting at the registry desk. She looked up, then frowned. "You're not allowed to bring girls who look like street ware to your rooms, Mr. Tremayne! This is a respectable establishment."

Street ware? Startled, Bran took a moment to reply. He gave her his most trustworthy smile. "This is my young cousin, whom I brought as my companion. I listed her on the register as Martin Tremayne, as it seemed simplest. It's her sixteenth birthday, and at her mother's request, I escorted her here. She's a tomboy and loves riding astride, so she wore her brother's clothing. Now that we're in town, she's been dressing as a young lady."

"A likely story!" Mrs. Morrison scoffed. "You're a dab hand at lying, Mr. Tremayne, but I'll have none of it! I want you and your bit of muslin out of here now!"

"You quite mistake the matter!" Bran said sharply. "Mary is a well-brought-up young lady who wanted a bit of an adventure, and to say otherwise is ridiculous!"

Mrs. Morrison's glare shifted to Davey. "I'm shocked that you're lending your countenance to such disgraceful behavior, Mr. Davey, and you a lawyer!"

"I assure you that nothing untoward is going on, Mrs. Morrison," he said stiffly. "Miss Tremayne is indeed a young lady."

"I *am*," Merryn said in a very young voice as she looked innocently out from under the brim of her bonnet.

"From the looks of your clothing, you've been entertaining men on your back in alleys! I want you *out*! *Now!*"

"As you wish, madam," Bran said, fighting a rare impulse to lose his temper. "I shall certainly tell the woman who recommended we stay here how unfortunate our experience has been." He glanced at Davey. "Matthew, would you please go to the stables and ask the ostler to prepare our horses for our departure?"

Looking bemused, Davey said, "Of course."

Deciding he should be conciliatory, Bran said, "While you have interpreted this situation wrongly, Mrs. Morrison, I understand why you find the appearance of impropriety upsetting. My cousin and I will leave as soon as we have changed and packed."

He gestured for Merryn to go up the stairs and followed her

before Mrs. Morrison could object. The light muslin of her cream-colored gown did indeed show smudges from being knocked to the ground when the mast had nearly hit her, but only a person obsessed with the possibilities of sin would have jumped to the conclusion that she was a streetwalker.

When they reached their rooms, Bran said, "I'm sorry you had to endure that nonsense."

Merryn looked more annoyed than upset. "Fool woman."

"She is." Bran smiled. "I imagine you'll be happy to put on your boy's clothing again for the journey home."

She nodded firmly, then moved into the other room and closed the door. She had the right idea. The sooner they left this place, the better.

Chapter 19

Ten minutes later, Bran and Merryn had packed their belongings and were leaving the inn. She looked entirely at home in her boy's garments. She descended the stairs ahead of him, head held high. She gave the landlady a cool gaze as Bran settled their account, paying the amount originally agreed on and refusing to pay the "outrage fee" Mrs. Morrison had tried to add.

Davey was in the stables and their horses were saddled and ready to go. Bran offered his hand. "Thank you for all your assistance, Matthew. I hope we didn't disrupt your real work too badly."

His friend grinned. "Life will be dull now. Miss Merryn, it has been a pleasure to meet you. I hope you are nearby if any masts are about to crush me."

She smiled a little and inclined her heard, then swung onto Shadow with Bran's aid. Once she was in her saddle, she looked at Bran and said, "See the sea?"

"You'd like to stop at a place where you can get close to the water?" When she nodded, Bran said, "Matthew, is there a cove or beach where it's possible to enjoy being right by the water? I will buy some food at the cook shop down the street so we can picnic there. Would you like that, Merryn?"

She gave him her rare full smile, her face lighting up.

Davey laughed. "I'll take that as a yes. There's a lovely little quiet cove about halfway between here and Penhaligon." He explained how to find the cove, then said farewell as Bran and Merryn rode out.

Bran had noticed that Merryn was fascinated by the water when they took the ferry across the wide harbor on their way to Plymouth Dock. The same was true when they and their horses took the ferry the other way. She hung over the railing, smiling at the water. He kept a close eye on her in case she fell overboard, but she didn't. He wondered if she'd grown up by the sea and yearned to be beside it again.

The weather was mild, which made for a pleasant ride south. The sun was at its zenith when they reached the narrow track that led down to the cove Davey had told them about. The track was gentle enough that they could ride the horses all the way down to the narrow sandy curve of beach.

The cove was lovely and very private, the water calm because the encircling cliffs protected the area from the open sea. A log that had washed ashore would make a good seat and a small stream ran into the cove, so there was fresh drinking water for the horses.

Merryn gave a happy sigh as she slid from Shadow and tethered the mare near a patch of grass by the stream. The cove was a perfect picnic place.

Bran also dismounted and secured Merlin beside Shadow. Merryn had already tugged off her boots and socks and was walking along the edge of the water, her feet splashing in the low waves. He hadn't seen her so happy since Shadow had returned to her. She bent and picked a shell out of a patch of seaweed that had washed up on the sand. She studied the shell, then brushed the sand off and brought it to Bran.

"For you," she said as she placed it on his outstretched hand. It was a small whorled shell, dark and gently textured, spiked on the outside and delicately pink inside.

"It's lovely," he said. "Thank you. May I keep it?"

She nodded emphatically. He fingered the shell, knowing whatever happened in the future, he'd keep this shell forever. He tucked it into an inside coat pocket, where it would be safe.

"I don't know about you, but I'm hungry." He moved to his saddlebags and retrieved the food he'd bought before leaving Plymouth Dock. More of the ubiquitous pasties and small fruit tarts, since they traveled well and tasted delicious. Plus a stone jug of ale to wash down the food.

He scanned the small beach to decide where best to set up their picnic—and froze when he saw that Merryn was stripping off her clothing. Her coat and shirt were already gone and she was tugging off her breeches and drawers. Then she freed her blond hair so it fell over her back and shoulders.

He managed to croak, "Merryn! Stop!"

She turned to look at him. "Why?"

She looked like the famous painting by Botticelli called *The Birth of Venus*. The picture depicted a young nude woman emerging from the sea, her body slim and exquisitely female, and her long pale hair waving gently around her. Merryn could have posed for that painting—except that the Venus of the painting modestly covered her private parts.

Merryn had no such self-consciousness. She was a child of nature and lovely beyond imagining. He was nearly paralyzed by the flood of desire that burned through him. More than anything in his life, he wanted her, wanted to take her in his arms and make intoxicating love to her.

Impossible, of course. His brain was so scrambled that all he could manage to say was "Can you swim?"

She thought briefly. "Yes?" Turning, she waded forward until she was shoulder deep, then plunged forward and disappeared.

Chapter 20

Bran thought his heart would stop when Merryn vanished from sight. Giving thanks that he could swim, he ripped off his own clothing and crashed into the water after her, praying that Merryn also knew how to swim. The water was cold, but not as cold as he expected, and he vaguely remembered reading that the south coast of Cornwall was bathed by warm currents from the southern seas.

Where was she? Dear God, was she already gone? He wondered if there were snags below the surface that might have dragged her down. How long had she been under the water? Too long.

Heart hammering, he swam full speed toward the spot where he'd last seen her. Suddenly she erupted from the water in front of him, her blond hair streaming over her shoulders. She laughed with delight. "Bran!"

She waved to him, then dived under the surface again. As his heart returned to its normal rate, he realized that not only could she swim, but she must have mermaid blood. She frolicked about like an otter, showing enticing bits of herself as she dived up and down. Her elegant back as she slid below the surface, then a glimpse of her lovely slim legs. Her perfect little breasts, the nipples tight from the cold water, when she propelled her body upward.

When her initial exuberance had worn off, she swam toward him, still smiling happily. "Thank you for the sea!"

"You swim like a sea goddess," he told her as he treaded water and struggled to find sanity.

Sanity vanished when she swam right up to him and wrapped her arms around his shoulders so they were pressed together, bare skin to bare skin. Her warm, soft femininity paralyzed his judgment. He instinctively embraced her, and they sank together below the surface.

He was struggling for breath as his feet touched bottom. He kicked upward, propelling their heads above the surface again. He coughed several times before he could breathe properly. Then Merryn drew back a few inches so she could skim her hand down the front of his body. Her hand paused at his genitals and cupped him curiously.

Heat shot through him, and he wished the damned water was much, much colder. "No!" he gasped.

He pushed away from her and looped an arm around her waist, then paddled them back to the shore. When his feet were solidly under him, he tried to speak.

Words vanished when she lifted her head and kissed him. Warm lips and shivering fire. She really was going to drive him mad. Her mouth was welcoming, and every exquisitely bare inch of her was pressed against him. As his arms went around her again, he felt as if they were Adam and Eve discovering desire in the Garden of Eden.

That hadn't ended well! He wrenched himself away from her. "Merryn, we must not do this!"

"Why not?" Her great aquamarine eyes were confused, and her lovely nude body shimmered with drops of water.

"We both need to get clothes on *right now!*" He pulled away from her and dragged his garments over his wet body.

Merryn frowned, but did the same, looking like an adorable damp sea nymph. Once her lovely body was covered, he was able to speak with some sanity. "You asked why not," he said. "It would be utterly wrong of me to take advantage of you when there is still so much we don't know about you or your past. What if you have a husband?"

Frowning, she sank onto the trunk of the tree and absently combed her fingers through her wet hair to remove snarls. "You asked me if I had a husband before." After consideration, she shook her head. "No, I do not."

"But you can't know for sure." How much did she know about marriage? "When two people marry, they vow to lie only with each other. If you have a husband, he would be angry if he knew that you have lain with another man. Many would consider it a crime if you and I came together like that. Since your past is still unknown, I refuse to cause that kind of trouble for you or for me."

She pondered his words, clearly not understanding, then gave a frustrated sigh. "Time to eat."

"Yes," he said, relieved to return to the mundane. And past time for him to keep his distance from her.

Bran set the food and drink on the log, then sat on the other side. As Merryn ate pasties, sipped ale, and stared at the sea, she tried to make sense of what had just happened. She felt herself becoming clearer in her mind and remembering bits and pieces about the world around her, but still didn't really understand who she was or how she should behave.

But she knew that Bran was the center of her world. His kindness and protection had been necessary to her survival, and she gave thanks for it, but today she'd realized how much more she wanted of him.

When she had embraced him in the water, it had seemed simple. Touch him everywhere. Lie with him unclothed. Let him touch *her* everywhere, because he wanted to—that had become clear. And the more they touched, the more she had wanted something she couldn't name or understand, but knew would change her forever.

But he wouldn't let that happen, and despite his attempts to explain, she didn't really understand. If she understood, would this craving go away?

She didn't think so. She glanced sideways at him. She always loved looking at Bran's beautiful, strong body and appealing, kind face. His gentle hands. The way he helped her understand, and his patience with her. He was everything to her, but to him, she was . . . like his horse. A creature who needed help and protection.

She'd saved his life. Surely, that mattered. But they were still not equals. She didn't know if they ever could be. She reminded herself of her thoughts at the inn in Plymouth Dock, how she must be strong. Such a long way to go!

He met her gaze and gave a half smile. "Don't look at me like that, my little mermaid. You make it very difficult to do the right thing."

As their gazes held, she recognized how very important it was to him to do the right thing. Much as she desired him, it would be wrong to lure him into actions he'd regret. Being strong enough to be worthy of him meant she must control her desires. She gave a nod, then turned her gaze away.

By setting the food on the log between them, he had put himself out of touching distance. He was wise.

But she couldn't help wishing that he wasn't.

Chapter 21

To Bran's relief, Merryn kept a polite distance between them as they ate and resumed their journey. His willpower had already been stretched to the breaking point today. She didn't seem angry about his rejection, but instead was thoughtful. He guessed that she'd understood his attempts to explain why they shouldn't do what seemed so utterly natural.

He really wished he knew what was going on in her pretty blond head. Every day she seemed more aware and independent, but she was still a mystery. He couldn't wait until Tamsyn arrived at the dower house. His sister had a gift for healing troubled spirits, and he prayed that she could fix whatever had been done to Merryn by her captors.

In midafternoon a cold steady rain began to fall, an unpleasant reminder that spring weather was variable. Bran glanced at the clouds, which didn't look as if they were going anywhere soon. Not long after, the road ran through a hamlet, right on the water, that had a small tavern advertising rooms for travelers. Luckily, two rooms were available, tiny but clean, and suitable for a gentleman and his young cousin. The tavern also served a very tasty fish pie for supper.

As Bran and Merryn finished eating and were about to head upstairs to their beds, she glanced out the front window. The rain had stopped and the sun was setting in a scarlet blaze.

Merryn turned and went outside to the narrow shingle beach. Bran followed. The tide was in, so the sea was only about fifty yards or so away. Merryn began walking parallel to the water, watching the setting sun.

"A pleasant way to end the day," Bran observed. "But no swimming tonight."

Merryn glanced at him with a faint smile. "No swimming."

They ambled along the shingle, which ended in a pile of boulders. When they turned back, the sun slid beneath the horizon. It would be full dark soon.

As they approached the tavern, Merryn said haltingly, "Want to read."

"Do you think you can read now?" Bran asked, surprised.

"Maybe." She nodded. "I hope."

"Then we'll find you a book as soon as we return to the dower house tomorrow." As he followed her into the tavern, he gave a silent prayer that she was right and that reading was now possible. Every day she was growing closer to normal.

Because the next day dawned sunny and warmer, Bran asked, "Would you like to do some exploring before we reach the dower house? It's a pretty day and I'd also like to delay our return until almost dinnertime. Then I can go to the castle and be very polite and gentlemanly, but leave fairly early with the excuse that I'm tired. That will mean delaying your reading for a few hours, but it is a very fine day."

She considered before saying, "Ride now."

They had a good time seeing scattered villages, an ancient abbey, and more spectacular scenery. Not to mention that Bran simply liked being with Merryn. There was something about her that felt warm and natural. She seemed to enjoy being with him as well.

They returned to the dower house not long before he needed to go to the castle. After they'd tended to the horses, he said, "I need to shave and change before going to dinner. You'll be all right here alone?"

She gave him a level stare. "Book *now*?"

Bran chuckled, pleased by her determination. "As you wish." He led the way to the small library and scanned the titles. Sermons and books on history and agriculture. Not very interesting to a new reader.

Ah, there! He pulled out a likely volume. "*Robinson Crusoe!* It's an adventure story about a sailor who is lost on a desert island and how he survives. He has many adventures." He placed the book in Merryn's hands.

Her brow furrowed as she carefully opened it to the title page. "May have read it before."

"That's very good news. I hope it makes the book easier for you to read." Bran traced a finger above the author's name. "This is the man who wrote it. Can you read his name?"

"Dan-i-el. De-foe," she sounded out slowly.

"Wonderful! Can you read the title?"

She frowned, then began. "*The Life and Strange Surprizing Adventures of Robinson Crusoe, of York, Mariner: Who lived Eight and Twenty Years, all alone in an un-inhabited Island on the Coast of America, near the Mouth of the Great River of Oroonoque.*"

The title was even longer than that, but her reading speed improved as she went along, and after finishing with only a couple of small stumbles, she looked up with a shining smile. "Reading!"

"Very well done indeed!" He wanted to hug her, but realized that would be a bad idea, so he refrained. "The book should keep you busy until I return from the castle. If you get hungry, one of the Penhaligon servants told me that they would stock the pantry with simple foods like ham and cheeses. I'll try not to be at the castle long."

She nodded, not even looking at him as she moved to a comfortable chair that had good light from a window. She was so involved with her book that she hardly noticed when he left after rendering himself presentable.

His mother and sister were glad to see him; though, as expected, Lord Penhaligon gave only a narrow-eyed scowl. After they dined, Bran quietly passed a letter from Davey to Glynis, then made his excuses. The moon was close to full, so the road back was well lit.

Glancing up at the moon, he wondered how long it would be until Cade and Tamsyn arrived. If they made really good time, perhaps tomorrow?

After settling Merlin in the dower house stables, he went inside and found that Merryn was still reading, though she'd moved herself and the book to the kitchen. By the evidence she'd foraged bread and cheese and toasted it for supper.

"Good evening," he said. "The reading is going well?"

She looked up from the book. "Yes! Faster." Then her gaze dropped back to the book.

Bran grinned. She'd clearly been a reader before, and now she was again.

He was about to toast some cheese for himself when the front door swung open with a bang and a familiar baritone called, "The lights are on, so someone must be home!"

Cade had the same talent for doorknobs that Bran did, so a locked door was no barrier to him. Knowing who had arrived, he exclaimed, "Cade and Tamsyn are here!"

Swiftly he made his way to the front, where a petite blonde leaped into his arms. "Bran, tell us of your adventures!"

"Tamsyn!" Laughing, Bran gave his sister a hug that lifted her from her feet. She looked exquisitely and misleadingly ladylike, but she was as much a tomboy as Merryn.

Setting Tamsyn down, he said, "You made good time," then offered his hand to Cade, who was carrying a sizable hamper, probably containing food and drink from their mother.

"I had the feeling you needed help," Cade said as he shook Bran's hand energetically. "So we didn't tarry."

Tamsyn set down a large reticule and dropped her flower-decorated bonnet on top of it. "Now . . . where is this fascinating female you wanted us to meet?"

Bran turned and saw that Merryn had followed him and was warily examining the new arrivals. She carried her book in one hand and looked ready to bolt. She still wore her boy's clothing, but her blond hair was loose and she looked like a delightful imp.

He put a hand on her shoulder and guided her forward. "Merryn, as you've surely guessed, this is my sister Tamsyn and my brother Cade."

While Cade studied Merryn, using all his fine-tuned talent for observation, Tamsyn moved forward and clasped Merryn's free hand. "I'm so happy to meet you, Merryn," she said warmly. "From what Bran said, you've had a difficult time of it, but you're safe now."

Merryn began to relax under the warmth in Tamsyn's voice. Bran had known very few people who could resist his sister's charm and genuine interest.

Cade said, "You'll have guessed that Gwyn sent supplies to ensure we wouldn't starve, and there are a couple of good bottles of wine here, as well as more in the carriage. Bran, help me settle the horses and bring in the rest of the bags."

Bran glanced at Merryn. "Will you be all right with Tamsyn?" The two had just met, and Merryn might be wary of a stranger.

But Merryn nodded. "Kitchen now." She returned to the kitchen with Tamsyn, while Bran lit a lantern and followed Cade outside.

The carriage waited at the front door, so they moved bags and hampers inside, and then Cade drove to the stable yard. The team of horses were tired and deserved some pampering.

Bran entered the stables and hung the lantern on a hook. "You decided not to bring a coachman?"

"I had the feeling that this was a delicate situation and the fewer people we involved at this point, the better," Cade said as he led the horses inside.

"As usual, your instincts were correct. I'll save my explanations until I can tell you and Tamsyn at the same time," Bran said as he started forking hay.

When they finished and headed back to the house in a light flurry of rain, Cade asked, "Merryn is very special to you?"

"Is it that obvious?" Bran asked ruefully.

"For someone who knows you well, yes. She's in good hands with Tamsyn."

"Don't repeat this to anyone, but Tamsyn is my favorite sister," Bran said.

Cade chuckled. "Mine too. But definitely do not tell her that!"

As always, Bran loved working side by side with this truest brother. Strange to think they'd started their journey together from near this place when they'd both been despised, discarded children. They'd come a very long way since then.

Now that they were working together, heaven help anyone who got in their way.

Chapter 22

Merryn eyed Bran's sister warily. She wasn't sure quite how she felt about this invasion of her sanctuary with Bran, but she liked Tamsyn and clearly Bran and the dark and rather fearsome Cade were very fond of each other.

As Bran had said, his sister was similar in size and coloring to Merryn, but she was so beautiful and elegant that Merryn felt plain and awkward beside her. But the warmth in Tamsyn's voice was impossible to resist when she said, "I've brought a nice selection of clothing that should suit you well, but we can look at it later. Now it's time to go to the kitchen and make strong, hot tea. It's cold out there!"

Stronger than she looked, Tamsyn picked up the heavy hamper of food and followed Merryn into the kitchen. While Tamsyn set the kettle on, Merryn collected the box of tea and the largest teapot from the pantry. Setting *Robinson Crusoe* aside, she perched behind the table to watch Tamsyn pulling food from the hamper.

Bran's sister had a subtle glow to her, and Merryn realized that Bran and Cade did as well. The glow was slightly different for each and Merryn guessed that she was sensing what Bran called gifts. Perceptions and talents beyond what most people possessed. The Tremaynes had them, and Bran said Merryn did, too.

There was a thumping from the front door and the two men entered the kitchen, droplets of water on their hair from a light rain. Tamsyn glanced up with a smile. "I'm scrambling up eggs, cheese, and fried potatoes, since Cade and I are hungry and there is nothing like sharing a meal with family and friends after a long journey. Not to mention that I've never known you to turn down food, Bran."

"Very true, Tam. I barely ate up at the castle this evening and Merryn only had a bit of toast and cheese," Bran admitted as his gaze shifted. "Merryn, do you mind these strangers moving in? Has my sister Tamsyn been alarming you?"

Merryn blinked, then shook her head. She was glad that Bran hadn't forgotten about her in the excitement of greeting his family.

As Bran set the kitchen table, Tamsyn finished cooking and Cade poured steaming hot tea into four large cups. When they sat down to enjoy their meal, Bran took the chair next to Merryn. She was intrigued by how the three Tremaynes worked with smooth coordination, though there was very little family resemblance among them.

Merryn wondered wistfully if she'd ever had a warm family like this one. If so, she had no memory of it.

When they finished their supper, Tamsyn arranged sweet biscuits from the hamper on a plate and encouraged everyone to refresh their tea and move to the drawing room. Bran gestured Merryn to the sofa, then sat down on her left.

When everyone was settled and had taken a couple of sweet biscuits, Bran said, "It's time for the serious discussion to begin. Tamsyn and Cade, I told you only the bare bones when

I wrote to ask you to come down here. I'm worried about Merryn, and I'm worried about Cornwall and a possible plot against Britain as we stand on the brink of renewed war with France."

He turned his head and took Merryn's hand. "Most of all, I've been worried about Merryn. Is it all right if I tell them about your situation and how we met?"

She gave a small nod, glad that he'd consulted her. After a moment's thought he said succinctly, "I felt compelled to come to Cornwall after learning I was likely the Penhaligon heir. Once I moved into this house, I kept looking into the woods behind it, till one day I was compelled to charge out into the night. I found Merryn being pursued by several men and a pack of baying foxhounds."

"Dear heaven, Merryn!" Tamsyn gasped.

Merryn cringed at the memory, though it seemed very distant now. The time hadn't been long, but she'd changed so much in those days.

Bran squeezed her hand and continued. "Between us we were able to calm the hounds, and I carried her back here. She didn't even know her name at first. Her pursuers followed her to the house, and I claimed that I knew nothing about her, but they came again when I was away. She escaped the house that time because she sensed them coming and fled before they arrived. That's when we realized that she has significant foretelling ability, which is apparently why her captors were desperate to get her back."

"A strong foretelling gift?" Cade said thoughtfully. "That's rare and valuable. If they kidnapped her for her talent, they surely have wicked intentions."

Bran nodded. "They were certainly desperate to get her back. Merryn has other gifts as well. Among other things she was able to call her horse to come to her here." He continued, describing their visit to Plymouth Dock and how she'd saved him from the falling mast. That invoked a hard frown from Cade and another exclamation from Tamsyn.

Bran ended with, "I think the woman Merryn calls the Starling put a powerful mental block on her. Since her escape Merryn has been improving daily, but she is not yet free of what was done. Tam, do you think you can help?"

His sister turned her perceptive gaze on Merryn. "I've been sensing the damage that was done," she said slowly. "Merryn has broken many of the bindings, but a number still remain." She moved to the sofa on Merryn's right side. "May I take your hand?"

Merryn was nervous, but warily she extended her right hand. Tamsyn clasped it in both of hers and closed her eyes. Her glowing energy increased, and Merryn felt a shiver of reaction.

After several long minutes Tamsyn opened her eyes again. "Merryn, the lock put on your mind and spirit is very strong. It's a tribute to your own strength that you've recovered as much as you have. Left on your own, you will continue to recover, but I don't know how long that would take. There might be areas where you would remain blocked indefinitely."

"Can you remove the blockage?" Bran asked quietly.

"I think so," Tamsyn said. "If Merryn will allow me to try."

Merryn was again grateful that she was being asked what she was willing to do, instead of being treated as a *thing*. Drawing a deep breath, she asked, "Hurt?"

Tamsyn hesitated. "There shouldn't be physical pain, but your mind will feel scrambled, like the eggs we had for supper, before it starts to sort out. Though it will be upsetting, I think that confusion should pass quickly."

"But you're not sure," Bran said.

His sister shook her head. "I've never encountered such a powerful block. I can't be sure of anything."

"Are you willing, Merryn?" Bran asked. "Tamsyn would never deliberately hurt you, but at the least this will be uncomfortable and probably frightening."

Merryn desperately wanted to become a real person and wasn't surprised that a price must be paid. She raised her chin and looked in Tamsyn's eyes. "Do it!"

"Very well." Tamsyn's left hand was clasping Merryn's right. Now she leaned forward and raised her right hand toward Merryn's forehead.

Merryn cried out and recoiled in shock. Tamsyn dropped her hand immediately. "Is this what that Starling woman did?" she asked softly.

Merryn caught her breath, then exhaled slowly. She realized that Bran was holding her left hand tightly, anchoring her to safety. She nodded. "Whenever bad, she did it again."

Tamsyn bit her lip. "To restore you to your normal self, I have to touch you, and your forehead is the most effective place to do that. I promise I won't take anything away from you. May I try again, slowly?"

To be herself again. Merryn wasn't even sure what that meant. She drew another deep breath, trying to calm her frantic heart. "Y-yes."

This time she closed her eyes so she didn't have to see that approaching hand, but she was shaking all over. Bran whispered, "You are the bravest mermaid in the world, and you *will* be all right."

She wished she really was brave rather than panicked and terrified, but she forced herself to hold still. Tamsyn's small, warm hand pressed across her forehead, and she gasped, but didn't pull away.

For a moment there was nothing. Then she was engulfed by

a horrifying sense that she was dissolving, falling to pieces, disintegrating. *Dying inside!*

She cried out and jerked off the sofa, yanking away from the hands of Bran and Tamsyn. Certainty shattered; incomprehensible images blazed across her mind. She crumpled to the floor on her knees, sobbing as if caught in a cataclysm.

Bran's arms came around her, a warm refuge from the chaos of her mind. Her emotions latched onto his essence, his unshakable strength and caring, which became her sanctuary from the shattering mental storm.

"*Breathe,*" Bran whispered. "Breathe with me. Inhale . . . exhale . . . inhale . . ."

She felt the rise and fall of his chest against her and worked to match her breathing to his. In, out, in, out . . .

Gradually her thoughts took firmer shapes, new yet hauntingly familiar. She realized that Bran was on the floor beside her and cradling her on his lap. She burrowed against his shoulder and tried to control her ragged breathing. A warm hand came to rest on the upper part of her back, and she sensed that it was Tamsyn, whose touch was calming.

As Merryn's shivering slowed, Bran asked quietly, "Has the tumult ended?"

She lifted her head and sorted out her thoughts and feelings. "I believe . . . that I've regained not only my thoughts and memories, but my pronouns. *I am! I am Merryn!*" Her brow furrowed. "Odd to be able to speak properly again."

"Odd but good, I hope." Bran shifted her from his lap, then stood and offered a hand to help her to her feet.

Cade said, "After all the tension I think brandy is called for. Merryn, would you like some, or do you want to avoid scrambling your newly regained wits?"

She considered. "Brandy, lightly watered, please." She turned to Tamsyn, who was back on the sofa, looking rather pale. "You have my most profound thanks, Tamsyn. Was healing me difficult for you? It looks as if it was."

The other woman smiled wanly and accepted a brandy from Cade. "It took a great deal of energy. I've never experienced anything quite like that."

"I hope you never have to do it again!" Merryn said fervently.

Tamsyn made a face. "My gift takes me into other people's nightmares, but I don't mind, because I can usually help them."

"You certainly helped me!" Merryn sat on the sofa beside Tamsyn and accepted a brandy from Cade. He was large and dark, and her first impression of him had been alarming, but now she saw that behind his intimidating appearance was a deep kindness similar to that of his brother and sister.

Bran reclaimed his seat next to her. "Do you remember your full name now?"

It took a moment to recall her identity. "My name is Merryn Penrose, and I grew up on the coast a little east of St. Austell." She drew a sharp breath. "My father! His name is Thomas Penrose! Oh, my! I've been gone over two months. He must think I'm dead!"

"We'll make sure he learns otherwise soon," Bran said. "Do you have other family at home? Mother, sisters, brothers?"

She had to think again. "No brothers or sisters. My mother died when I was young, so it was only my father and me." They'd been close and the thought of his grief was painful.

"A husband?" Bran asked in a carefully casual voice.

Her gaze met his. "No husband." Though there had been someone . . .

She was trying to remember more, but then a different thought snapped into clarity. "Crowley, the beast who kidnapped me!" Her voice became a hiss. "He's my uncle, my father's half brother! They're estranged, so I barely knew him."

"Did your uncle know about your foretelling ability?" Cade asked.

Merryn thought back. Though her mind felt normal, it took time to locate memories. "He did. In fact, he and my father fought about that. Crowley thought he could use my talent to make money on sporting events and investments. My father refused to allow me to be used for such selfish reasons. When Crowley kept trying to persuade him to give permission, my father lost his temper, which he almost never does. He told his brother to leave and never come near me or our house again."

"How old were you then?" Tamsyn asked.

"Thirteen, I think. A dozen years ago. I didn't see Crowley after that, until he kidnapped me." She frowned, trying to remember what she'd learned while his captive. "He has some plan he wanted to use me for, and he knew I'd never help him if I had a choice." Merryn shuddered. "I despised him as much as my father did!"

"How were you abducted?" Bran asked. "You didn't feel danger coming?"

Merryn thought back, reluctant to remember, but knowing she must. "I'd gone riding on Bodmin Moor. I always went up there when my mind needed clearing. On that day I was thinking about a decision I must make. I was worried, but thought it was because a storm was coming and I had a long ride home. I was still on the moor when Crowley rode up to me with the Starling. She's his mistress.

"I didn't want to talk to him, but he's family and didn't look dangerous. I didn't want to be rude." She grimaced. "I should have galloped Shadow away! Good manners can be dangerous. Crowley asked civilly about my father, then introduced the Starling.

"She stretched out her hand in a friendly way. I was reaching for it, when suddenly she leaned forward and slapped her hand to my forehead and . . . I don't remember any more. Just living in a cottage with the Starling, who fed me and took me for walks. After a while I started to recover more of myself and wanted to escape. One day I did. You know the rest."

Bran swore under his breath and looked ready to ask more questions, but Tamsyn said, "Let her rest, Bran! Merryn has had an exhausting day. We can continue this discussion in the morning after we've all had a good night's sleep."

"You're right," Bran said ruefully. "Tomorrow will be soon enough."

"I'm tired, too," Tamsyn said as she covered a yawn. "We had a long and very fast journey down from London. Bran, will you show me the bedrooms Cade and I will be using? I'll check what's missing in your preparations so I can remedy the errors."

Bran laughed as he lifted a lamp to light the way up the stairs. "It's not that bad, Tam! Lady Penhaligon sent two housemaids here to prepare the rooms."

"Excellent woman!" Tamsyn said approvingly. "I assume you'll take us over to meet her tomorrow?"

Bran nodded. "Yes, you will meet her and my sister Glynis. I'll go over first thing in the morning to say that you two have arrived. She will certainly invite you to dinner. Hard to tell if Lord Penhaligon will be there. He often isn't, and when he is, he does nothing but scowl at me."

"He's come to know you well in such a short time?" Cade asked innocently as he lifted several pieces of luggage to carry up to the bedrooms.

Merryn smiled as she lifted a smaller case. She enjoyed the easy banter among the Tremaynes. As an only child, she'd missed out on this. These people had not only given Merryn her life back—they were giving her their friendship.

With a start she realized that the moment when she'd desperately reached to Bran's essence had created a connection that she could still feel dimly pulsing inside her. She would have to think about that.

But for now she yawned and followed Tamsyn up the stairs, wondering what dreams would come.

Chapter 23

❧

Tamsyn was firmly in charge as she organized accommodations for herself and Cade. They had the two rooms on the south side of the house, separated from Bran and Merryn by the stairs and a passage. The Penhaligon housemaids had done a good job of preparing the bedchambers. A cold night wind was blowing from the sea, but fires had been laid and were waiting for the guests. Cade lit them to warm the rooms, while Bran took care of the fires in Merryn's room and his own.

His eyes warm and caring, Bran briefly laid his hand on Merryn's shoulder and wished her a good night. Then he and Cade descended to the drawing room to share a good-night drink and a brotherly discussion.

Tamsyn said, "Merryn, if you're not too tired, come into my room so I can give you the clothes I brought. If you're to pretend to be my maid, you need to dress the part."

Merryn glanced down at her rumpled boy's clothing as she followed Tamsyn into the guest room. "I suppose that means skirts again."

"Sadly, yes. I quite like wearing trousers myself when I have a good excuse." Tamsyn bent and lifted one of the cases onto the bed. Opening it, she said, "Nothing very exciting because maids aren't supposed to be noticed, but all the dresses fasten in the front for convenience. We're close enough to the same size, so they should fit fairly well. I also brought shoes, but size is more of a problem with shoes than clothing."

"Bran found me used riding boots and shoes in Plymouth that are a good fit." She glanced at Tamsyn's shoes. "That is fortunate, because my feet are larger than yours."

Tamsyn pulled two folded garments from the bottom of the case. "Here's a nightgown and a robe for you. Since your day clothing is boring, I thought you should have nightwear that's pretty."

The nightgown was a soft cream-colored material trimmed with blue embroidery that matched the warm blue robe. Merryn stroked the fabric with pleasure. So unlike the rags the Starling had given her. "Lovely! I'll sleep well in this."

Tamsyn closed the case again so Merryn could carry it to her room. "Have you minded living here with just a man?"

"I hadn't thought about that," Merryn said, only now realizing that she'd violated one of the cardinal rules of behavior for an unmarried female: A single woman should never be alone with a man. And she'd been living with one and enjoying it!

"There has been no problem. Bran has been everything that is kind. I don't know what I would have done without him. I'd still be a captive of the Crow and the Starling, I'm sure, and my mind would not have been my own." She shuddered at the thought.

"I'm so glad you escaped those horrid people!" Tamsyn covered another yawn. "Sleep now and know you'll be safe."

Merryn obediently went to her room and prepared for bed. She fell asleep quickly in her soft, pretty nightgown, but her newly awakened mind spun vivid, restless dreams.

The most intense came at dawn when she awoke sweaty and frustrated by heated memories of Bran. She remembered how she'd embraced him on the beach and the wondrous feeling of their naked bodies pressed together. His breath, his warmth, his taste, as she fell into his kiss. She was yearning to learn what came next when his damned conscience made him break away.

Honor was admirable, but sometimes annoying. Would his restraint toward her change now that her mind and spirit made her less vulnerable and in need of his protection? She smiled wryly and hoped for better outcomes in the future.

Knowing she wouldn't go back to sleep, she rose and washed up. Though it was early, tempting scents were wafting up from the kitchen, so someone was up and busy.

Feeling hungry, she donned a plain gray gown that Tamsyn had brought. When she pinned her hair back in a simple knot, she was interested to realize that her fingers seemed to remember what to do without conscious thought on her part. When she was done, her image in the small mirror was that of a modest and easily overlooked maid. All she needed now was a mobcap.

She headed down to the kitchen, expecting to find Tamsyn at work, but was surprised to see Cade expertly chopping onions and potatoes to fry together in a heavy cast-iron skillet. He was working in his shirtsleeves, with his coat tossed over the back of a chair, and looked intimidatingly broad shouldered and powerful.

But he smiled when he glanced up at her entrance. "Good morning, Merryn. Bran is off to the castle to announce that Tamsyn and I have arrived and to borrow a couple of riding horses that we can use while we're visiting. He shouldn't be long. There's tea in that pot if you'd like some."

"Thank you." She poured a steaming cup and added milk, then sat at the table out of the way of Cade and his flying knife. "Does everyone in your family cook?"

"Yes, our parents insisted on it. They feel that all their children should be capable of life's basic tasks. Bran and I are competent, but unexceptional. Our Lady Tamsyn is actually quite a skilled cook."

"Lady Tamsyn?" Merryn frowned. "Wouldn't that mean she's the daughter of a lord? Or is it a family nickname because she has such a commanding air about her?"

Cade laughed. "She does indeed! She gives orders to all of us, but her father is also a lord."

"Your family sounds large! How many children are there? You and Bran both have dark hair, but other than that, there's no particular resemblance."

Cade tossed the onions in with the frying potatoes and sprinkled a couple of pinches of salt over the contents of the skillet. "Bran never explained the Tremayne family to you?"

Merryn frowned and searched her memory. "I don't think so. If he did, perhaps I've forgotten, or he might have thought my muddled brain couldn't handle information that was complicated and not necessary for me to know then."

"That seems likely." Cade topped up his own tea and sipped it while keeping an eye on his skillet. "Our branch of the Tremayne family is headed by Rhys and Gwyn, Lord and Lady Tremayne. They are both strongly gifted. You know about gifted people, don't you?"

"Yes, though I have much more to learn."

Cade grimaced. "There's always more to learn. The sad reality is that gifted children are despised by some people. They are sometimes beaten, abandoned, even killed by those who hate them."

Merryn sucked in her breath. "Why?"

He shrugged. "Why do some people hate anyone who is different? It's one of the darker mysteries of human nature.

"At any rate, Rhys and Gwyn have three legitimate children

of their own, the oldest of whom is Tamsyn. They've also rescued gifted children who have been abandoned. They've found
good homes for some of those children, and others they've kept
and raised as if we were their own. Bran and I are in that cate-
gory. I think there are . . . ten of us fosters? Plus their three actual offspring. So thirteen altogether."

"How did you come to be fostered by them?" Merryn
asked, fascinated.

Cade stirred the potatoes and onions with a wooden spoon.
"Bran and I escaped a Cornish baby farm near here, before the
owners managed to kill us with neglect. Even though we were
very small, we managed to make our way to London in mid-
winter."

He paused for a long moment, his expression distant with
memory before shaking off the past. "Rhys and Gwyn found
us in an alley full of rubbish near Covent Garden. Bran and I
aren't actually blood kin, but we had decided we were brothers
and the Tremaynes accepted our kinship. They took us home
that night and ever since we've been members of their family, a
generosity for which I thank God daily."

Merryn stared at him, stunned. "That is an amazing story!"

"Yes, and entirely true. Feel free to ask Bran or Tamsyn if
you want confirmation."

She shook her head. "No confirmation needed. Your parents
sound like the next thing to saints."

"I wouldn't disagree with that." He topped up their tea
mugs.

"You and Bran and Tamsyn seem very close. Is that true of
all the children in the family?" Merryn asked.

"I would die for any member of my family," Cade said in a
matter-of-fact voice. "I think every one of us children, whether
legitimate or fostered, feel the same way. But since the family is
large, we tend to form smaller groups based on age and inter-

ests." He grinned. "Gwyn once called Tamsyn, Bran, and me her 'Three *B*'s.' Tamsyn for beauty, Bran for brains, and me for brawn."

Merryn laughed. "I hope none of you were offended! Certainly, Tamsyn is beautiful, but you and Bran are both entirely presentable, and while you're a little larger than Bran, you both look remarkably strong and healthy."

"We both fight very well, and so does Tamsyn, even though she looks like a spun-glass angel," he said. "But there is truth to Gwyn's description. Bran is the one who is best at figuring things out. I'm better at cracking heads."

"Do you have to do that very often?" she asked with interest.

"No, but it does happen." He hesitated, then continued. "You know that Bran and I both work for the Home Office? Which means it's our job to protect Britain from her enemies. Bran is a brilliant investigator, excellent at finding larger patterns in seemingly random events. I'm more likely to dress like a stevedore or a farm laborer and buy beer for local people at their taverns, which is a good way to learn what's going on."

"Both valuable skills." She studied the hard planes of Cade's face. "Why are you being so forthcoming? I wouldn't have thought that you usually are."

"I'm not, but Bran doesn't talk much about himself." Cade gave Merryn his full attention while the frying potatoes sizzled gently. "I think this is information you need and have a right to know."

And Cade wanted to look after his brother's interests. "Thank you," she said quietly. "I'm glad to know more about Bran and about you also."

In fact, she wanted to know everything about Bran.

The silence that followed was broken when Tamsyn drifted into the kitchen, elegant in pale green and covering a yawn with one hand. "Good morning, Merryn, Cade. One thing my brothers will be happy to tell you is that I am not fond of early mornings."

"Neither am I," Merryn admitted. "But I was drawn downstairs by the combination of restless dreams and the smell of good cooking."

Tamsyn poured herself a mug of tea and sat down beside Merryn. "I imagine your mind is churning, now that you are yourself again."

"Exactly." She frowned. "I think I dreamed some things I heard while a prisoner. I hope they may be helpful."

"Wait until Bran gets back from the castle," Cade suggested. "We've always found that tossing ideas among us brings up new possibilities." He pointed his wooden spoon at Tamsyn. "You, my lady, can mix up the eggs so they can be cooked quickly when Bran returns."

"I would refuse, except that my eggs are better than yours," Tamsyn said as she rose.

"Excessive modesty is not one of her failings," Cade said as he sliced a loaf of bread. "Are you any good at toasting bread, Merryn?"

"I managed to do it last night for my supper," she said as she also got to her feet. "I've never done much cooking, but I am most intrigued by Cade's descriptions of how everyone in your family knows their way around a kitchen."

"If you keep company with the Tremaynes, you'll soon know the basics of cooking also," Tamsyn said cheerfully. She'd found an apron in the pantry and put it on to protect her clothing before she started cracking eggs into a large bowl.

As Cade handed Merryn a pair of toasting forks, she realized how much she loved this friendly domesticity. It was unlike anything she'd ever known, warming her heart in wonderful new ways. She and her father had always gotten on well, but he was usually busy with his studies or the estate, and Merryn had often been alone. Rather lonely, in fact, which was why she'd been considering marriage to a man who was merely pleasant, and no more. She'd been thinking about him the day she was abducted.

Bran entered the kitchen with a breath of chilly spring air. "Ah, breakfast is imminent! I'm glad for that, since I refused breakfast at the castle, and I've worked up a good appetite. I've borrowed two very decent-looking riding hacks, so we can all explore the countryside together. Now that we have several horses in the stable, a full-time stable hand has been assigned to us."

He took off his coat and tossed it over Cade's. His warm gaze met Merryn's. "How are you this morning? Is your mind burning with activity?"

"Exactly so." She dropped her gaze when she remembered her vivid and indecent dream of him. "I really like the way you Tremaynes behave together. Can I be fostered into the family?"

Bran looked a little startled. "We would have to take a vote."

"I say we keep her," Tamsyn said promptly.

"I agree," Cade said. "What's your vote, Bran?"

"I want very much to keep her," Bran said, his intense gaze on Merryn. "She fits in so extremely well."

A weighted silence followed until Tamsyn said, "I'll scramble up these eggs now. Merryn, how are you coming with the toast?"

Merryn jerked, startled. The bread fell off one toasting fork and the piece on the other one was burned. "I'm sorry! This is harder than it looks."

"Even things that look simple take practice." Bran took the forks away and stuck pieces of fresh bread on both. "I'll do the toasting and you can set the table."

That, she was capable of doing. By the time she finished lay-ing out the plates and tableware, breakfast was ready and they all sat down to eat. Merryn wondered how long it would take her to learn how to cook simple breakfast foods.

The teasing and laughter continued while they ate. After the table was cleared, Bran clinked his teaspoon against his mug to collect everyone's attention. When everyone else fell silent, his gaze moved around the table. "With hunger satisfied, it's time for us to discuss the storm clouds that are gathering over Cornwall and Britain."

Chapter 24

∽

The silence was broken when Tamsyn whispered rather loudly to Merryn, "It's always like this. When Bran decides that we've done enough larking about, he calls us to attention and gives us a schoolteacher scowl if we keep chattering."

Bran smiled. "She's not wrong. But we've all felt danger approaching, haven't we?" After Caden and Tamsyn nodded, his sober gaze went to Merryn. "Have you had a chance to think about comments that Crowley might have made? Anything that might suggest what he's planning?"

She bit her lip. "Only small fragments. I don't know if they make any sense."

"There's a method gifted people use that might be useful here," Bran said, his gaze continuing to hold hers. "We simply all join hands in a circle and see if that helps clarify your memories. Are you game to try?"

"If you think it might help," she said doubtfully.

"Unlike removing the block from your mind, I promise this technique won't hurt," Tamsyn said encouragingly. "It's rather nice, actually."

Merryn drew a deep breath, then reached to her left for Bran's hand and Cade's on her right. Tamsyn, sitting opposite, completed the circle.

"Just relax and see if you feel us," Bran said.

She closed her eyes and obeyed, startled to realize that she could feel their energy. Subtle essences of her companions formed like musical chords, each a separate note, but harmonizing together: Tamsyn, bright and clear. Cade, a deep, utterly reliable foundation. Bran . . . the touch of his essence shook her to her core. His wisdom, his kindness, his protectiveness . . . and the intense desire she felt for him.

She swallowed hard, not wanting to know what he felt from her. "Yes, you're all there, distinct and different. I can feel you calming and strengthening my mind."

"What do you remember about your time as Crowley's captive?" Bran asked.

She sent her thoughts back into those murky missing months. "It's like a night landscape, with tiny points of light becoming clearer as I focus on them. Now what?"

"I'll ask a few questions and you can see what surfaces," Bran explained. "To start, did the Crow ever mention his plans to the Starling?"

"He didn't talk to her much," Merryn said, and was surprised when new memories took shape. "But several times other men visited. The cottage was small, and I could hear them talking. They paid no more attention to me than if I'd been a piece of furniture."

"Did you get a sense of their overall goals?" Bran asked quietly.

She let his question sink in, then whispered, "Wealth, through violence if necessary."

Bran asked, "Do you feel that Crowley is a French agent or sympathizer who is helping to organize an attack by the French Navy?"

Merryn kept her eyes closed so she wouldn't lose her focus on her internal landscape. "Noooo," she said as she tried to clarify her understanding of the Crow. "He owns several fishing boats and is a smuggler. Money interests him, not politics. He referred to some scheme that would soon make him rich."

"Is he working alone or with someone else?" Bran asked.

"He works with . . . a Guernsey man. A smuggler?"

"Guernsey is under English rule, but it has many ties to France. A large number of goods smuggled from France come through there," Bran said thoughtfully. "In fact, I met a Guernsey captain called Dubois who might be a smuggler with French leanings. He seemed rather unsavory."

"So the island could be a conduit for French agents establishing themselves in Cornwall?" Tamsyn asked. "Crowley might be working with the same people, but just for his personal good, with no direct involvement with French agents."

"That feels very possible," Bran said slowly. "We need more information."

"Don't we always?" Cade said. "There may be several things going on that are unrelated. Crowley's scheme for wealth is one. Greed is fairly simple and common. But there may also be French plots to damage Britain as war resumes."

Bran gave a soft whistle. "I think you're right that they are separate—yet, at the same time, they could become related."

"Not making a lot of sense, Bran," Tamsyn said.

"Figuring out connections takes time," Bran replied mildly. "Merryn, why did Crowley want you and your talents so badly that he abducted you and blocked your mind and personality?"

"He thought I could help him achieve . . . whatever it was he wanted to do. The Starling assured him that she could pull me out of my trance when it was time to use my talents."

She frowned as another thought clarified. "He also wanted me because he despised my father and wanted to hurt him and me." More memories. "Crowley is illegitimate and resented the fact that my father was the heir to a substantial property. I think their father set Crowley up with his fishing boats, but it was nothing like what my father inherited."

Bran swore under his breath. "A very unpleasant man. But we knew that."

Feeling tense, Merryn opened her eyes and rolled her shoulders. "That's all I know right now."

"Well done, Merryn. It's a start. Perhaps later, something more will occur to you." Bran released her hand and the others did the same. "But for now I think more tea is called for. Then we can resume our planning council."

There was a shuffling around as tea was made and Tamsyn produced a seed cake from the supplies they'd brought. Thinly sliced, it went well with fresh tea.

Once they were settled around the table again, Bran asked, "What else needs to be done in Cornwall?"

"I need to visit my family," Cade said in a hard voice.

"Can you find their cottage?" Tamsyn asked.

"Yes."

"Then what?" Bran asked. "Murder is probably not a good idea."

"I don't intend to kill anyone. I'm just . . . curious."

Merryn barely knew Cade, but suspected that his feelings were more complicated than that. Perhaps he wanted his family to see what the child his parents had thrown away had become.

Frowning, Cade continued, "I feel this is something I need to do."

Merryn was beginning to realize that among the gifted, this was a way of saying that intuition was urging them to do something. She needed to listen to her own intuition more.

Bran said, "I'll go with you."

"That's not necessary," Cade said. "I don't plan on killing my father."

"I know, but I have the sense that I should go with you."

Intuition at work again, Merryn thought. "I also need to go to my father."

"Of course he must know that you're all right, but it might be better to write him a letter," Bran said. "Going in person could be dangerous if Crowley is keeping a watch so he can capture you again."

Merryn gagged at the thought. "You're right. My father is a quiet, scholarly man, a naturalist. I don't want Crowley to have any reason to go near him." She frowned. "Can you write and assure him that I'm safe, Bran? I have a strong feeling that it's best that he not get a letter directly from me."

"You're probably right. You can return home when we better understand what's going on," Bran said. "For now it's safest to be with us."

Her intuition said he was right. And her heart said that she wanted to stay with these welcoming people who were becoming friends, and more.

When the others were at the castle, Merryn spent the hours organizing her augmented wardrobe, and also doing some mending for Tamsyn, as if she really was a lady's maid. Then she returned to *Robinson Crusoe*.

She was glad to hear when the others returned. Tamsyn came in alone, saying, "The lads are taking care of the horses."

She removed her cloak and Merryn took charge of it. "I'm trying to be a proper lady's maid," she explained as she brushed the fabric. "How was the evening?"

"Bran's sister Glynis is very nice. She asked if my maid had come with me and offered to lend me one if needed. I explained that my maid stays with me because she is similar in size and coloring, and enjoys receiving my castoffs."

Merryn smiled. "All true, except for the implication that I'm a competent lady's maid. What is the rest of the Penhaligon family like?"

"Her ladyship is pleasant and hospitable, but his father!" Tamsyn's nose wrinkled. "I am very glad not to be related to him! I think Bran wishes he wasn't."

Merryn led the way to the kitchen, which had become their communal gathering spot. As she put the kettle on for tea, she asked, "How do the two of them get on?"

"Bran becomes very polite and detached and impossible to read," Tamsyn said. "Though Lord Penhaligon seems to hate everyone, he reluctantly accepts that he needs an heir. It's not a happy situation." She frowned. "Perhaps Penhaligon is so awful because his health is failing, and he knows he won't last much longer and resents Bran for being young and healthy."

"You can see that the end is near for him?" Merryn asked, surprised.

Tamsyn nodded. "My gifts are for health, both mental and physical. I can usually help people who are hurting in some way."

"You certainly helped me! But it must be a demanding gift."

Tamsyn poured boiling water on the tea leaves. "It is. Everyone in the family is protective of me, which isn't really necessary."

"I think it sounds rather nice to have a large, protective family," Merryn said wistfully.

Tamsyn grinned. "Be careful what you wish for, because I think you're on the verge of being absorbed into the Tribe of Tremayne."

Merryn liked that idea. She liked it a lot.

Chapter 25

After tea and casual conversation, they all went to their bedrooms. Merryn should have fallen asleep immediately after such an eventful day, but her mind was too restless. Her mind and body both.

She had felt desire for Bran from the beginning, and her feelings only intensified when she started regaining her wits. She had burned for him when they went swimming and embraced naked on the beach. If not for his restraint, they would have become lovers that day.

Now that she was fully herself, she understood that restraint. For a gentleman to take advantage of a female who was eager, but mentally impaired, would have been disgraceful, and Bran was nothing if not honorable.

But now she was herself, and no longer a bold innocent—merely bold. On the day she'd been abducted from Bodmin Moor, she had been pondering the proposal of a young man who lived nearby. They liked each other and he certainly liked the fact that she was the only heir to her father's considerable property.

But his family was also comfortably off, and having reached the ripe old age of twenty-five, she'd realized that she wanted to be married. To enter the adult world, to be the lady of her house, to have children. She liked her neighbor better than any of the other young men she knew. They should be able to rub along together quite comfortably. But were those feelings enough for marriage? She wasn't sure.

Then she'd been kidnapped and rescued by Bran and discovered how intensely one could care about a man. Care about and desire. He desired her also—she was sure of it—and he no longer needed to be concerned about taking advantage of her vulnerability.

That didn't necessarily mean she could seduce him. Becoming lovers would be momentous for both of them. But she wanted that, wanted him, and she could think of no good reason to wait.

She smiled a little. Her father had once said that her motto was "It doesn't hurt to ask." Which wasn't always the case, but it was certainly her philosophy!

She slid from her bed and donned the pretty blue robe, which Tamsyn had given her, over her shift. Then she located her new hairbrush and brushed out her hair so it fell straight and shining.

Hoping she had the courage to follow through with her intentions, she set out to do battle with a gentleman's conscience.

Bran prepared for bed, but knew he couldn't sleep yet. He put on his robe and added more coal to the fire, then settled by the lamp on his desk and began jotting down thoughts of what dangers might be hovering around them. Though it appeared that Merryn's kidnapping had not been carried out by French spies, his intuition said that there was some connection to the threat of espionage.

Unfortunately, whenever he thought about Merryn, logic

vanished. Tamsyn's healing ability had produced a miracle. Merryn had intrigued him from the beginning and aroused his protective instincts. Now that she was fully restored, she entranced him. She was so emphatically *herself*.

There had also been the stunning moment when they had first joined hands and felt each other's essence. They resonated together in a way different from anything he'd ever experienced, and it was even more intense than that passionate embrace on the beach. Just thinking of those shattering moments aroused him. He was amazed that he'd been strong enough to step away before it was too late.

He had been blessed with a foster family whom he loved beyond measure. But his connection to Merryn was different, and even more powerful than his connections with Cade and Tamsyn, the brother and sister with whom he was closest.

He and Merryn were deeply connected on many levels. The question was, what to do about it? She had only just come back to herself again.

He finished the glass of brandy he'd been sipping, thinking it was past time he turned off the lamp and went to bed. Then he heard a soft tapping at his door. Cade?

He rose and opened the door, then stopped breathing for long moments when he found Merryn. Dressed in an elegantly simple blue robe, she was softly and deliciously female, with her blond hair spilling over her shoulders and glinting in the lamplight. She was petite, but at the same time emphatically occupied the space in front of him.

He must have looked bemused, because she smiled a little as she said, "May I come in?"

"This is not a good idea," he said, but even so, he stepped aside so she could walk into the room.

She smiled mischievously. "One can't always tell if an idea is good or bad until one tries it."

He had to laugh. "That sounds like an elegant rationalization for getting into trouble."

"Very likely it is." She turned and lightly rested her palm on the middle of his chest. "But I do think that ignoring the attraction between us is most emphatically *not* a good idea."

He caught his breath as his heart rate increased under her touch. "Perhaps you're right, but passion is as dangerous as it is powerful, and the pull between us is . . . very powerful."

She raised her hand to cup his cheek with a touch of fire. "I'm no longer the dazed girl you rescued," she said softly. "I'm a woman grown, and one who has been justly accused on occasion of being entirely too headstrong. Because of a certain recklessness with a charming stable boy when I was sixteen, I am also not a virgin, if that matters to you."

He covered her hand with his and said a little unsteadily, "It matters, but only a little. I'm less concerned with the past than the present, and the present is full of uncertainty."

"Then we should seize what we know is certain." She stood on her toes and slipped her arms around his neck as she rose into a kiss.

He had always prided himself on his self-control and balanced judgment, but both fractured when she kissed him.

In a calmer time and place, he would have courted her in a traditional way, with conversation and flowers and rides in the country.

But danger hovered over them, and he'd be a fool not to embrace passion and life while he could. He kissed her back, wanting to devour her. He wanted Merryn for now and always, and if his courtship led through a bed, he'd take it.

They set each other aflame with their mouths and hands. "Merryn," he breathed as he smoothed his hands down the enticing curves of her back. "Dear God, Merryn!"

"We're both wearing too many clothes!" She said as she slid her hands under the fabric of his robe so she could caress bare skin.

He sucked in his breath. "So we are." He tugged at her sash and peeled the garment from her shoulders. It slid to the carpet in a drift of blue wool, leaving her clad only in a lightweight shift that revealed every shadowed curve of her body.

It took only moments more to strip each other to bare skin. She was deliciously alluring, equally delicate and strong, and her passion shattered every last remnant of his control.

He tossed back the covers, then swept her up in his arms and laid her onto the bed, coming down beside her as he worshipped her throat, her breasts, the smooth arc of her belly, with his mouth and hands. Every texture, from silky skin to the soft roughness of hair, increased the fierceness of his arousal.

"You are beautiful beyond belief," he whispered raggedly. And she blazed with silver light.

"As are you, my dearest lord," she breathed as she separated her legs for him.

Tenderly he stroked the delicate folds of heated intimate flesh. She gasped and dug her nails into his arms, pulling him down onto her. "Now!"

Though the fierceness of her desire drove him to the brink of madness, he had sufficient control to enter slowly, careful not to hurt her. When they were fully joined, rapture seared through every fiber of his being. He wanted this to last forever, and at the same time he desperately craved the ultimate release.

"Ah, Bran!" she moaned as her hips rocked to bring them ever closer. He caught her cry in his mouth when she convulsed around him and had just enough sanity to withdraw before it was too late.

Gasping for breath, he rolled onto his side and enfolded her in his arms, amazed and awed by the intensity of sensation and emotions beyond anything he'd ever known. She was more than he had ever dreamed of, more than he deserved.

He whispered, "I feel as if I've loved you forever, but only now discovered you."

"I feel the same," she murmured as she rested her head on his shoulder and slid her arm around his waist. "My beautiful Bran."

As his breathing slowed and sanity slowly returned, he tugged the covers over their bare bodies and thought about what must come next.

What could be lovelier than lying in her lover's arms? Merryn thought dreamily that in some ways it was even better than the annihilating fulfillment of making love.

As Bran toyed with a tangled strand of her hair, he asked softly, "What is the story of you and your charming stable boy?"

She smiled reminiscently. "Henry and I were both young and hot-blooded and desperately curious about passion. We loved . . . playing with each other when we had the chance to be alone. One day we went too far. Neither of us regretted it, but we both realized that we had been very unwise. So we kissed goodbye and I returned to being a well-bred young lady, while he went off and joined the army."

"Were you in love with him?" Bran asked.

Her brow furrowed. "No, but we were very fond of each other. I thought of him when I was older, and men had begun to court me seriously. Some of them were very pleasant, but there wasn't one I wanted to pull down in a haystack." She rolled a little and kissed the side of his throat. "Until I met you."

"For which I am grateful beyond measure." He cupped her head and turned it so that their gazes met. "You may not have recognized it yet, but we're now basically married."

"What!" She jerked up to a sitting position and stared down at him. "We have become lovers, and I hope that we continue to be for a long time. But that's not the same as marriage!"

His gaze was calm. "That's true for most people, but those of us who are gifted often come together with a bond far deeper than marriage vows," he said. "My foster parents, Rhys and Gwyn Tremayne, have that kind of bond. I've envied the power of their union, without really understanding it or thinking I'd ever be so lucky." He raised her right hand and kissed it. "Then I met you."

"Are you proposing to me?" she asked rather hopelessly.

"I can't imagine *not* marrying you," he said thoughtfully. "It's interesting, because while I was attracted to you from the beginning, what I feel now is so far beyond mere attraction." He fell silent for the space of a dozen heartbeats. "I can't imagine feeling this for anyone else. I think we are meant to be together."

"It's also possible that you're mad!"

He chuckled. "You may be right. What do you feel?"

She drew a deep breath as she moved from simply feeling to thinking about *what* she was feeling. "I can't imagine being with another man, or caring so much for anyone else," she said hesitantly. "But *marriage*?"

"We won't be calling the banns tomorrow," he said reassuringly. "You weren't raised among gifted people, so you need time to adjust to the idea. You certainly have the right to think that I'm madder than a March hare! But I believe we're each other's fate."

She collapsed back on her pillow and stared at the ceiling, shadowed in the dim light. "Tamsyn and Cade. Will they know what we just did?"

"If they don't know already, they will as soon as they see us." He clasped her hand and raised both their arms so she could see them clearly.

"We're glowing!" It was almost a squeak.

"As I said, there's a powerful bond between us that's visible to those who have the eyes to see." He brought their joined hands back to the mattress. "I will never coerce you into anything you don't want to do, Merryn. But I do hope that as you get used to the idea, you will come to be as happy about our bond as I am."

She released her breath in a sigh. "I need lessons in what it means to be gifted. I don't want any more surprises like this!"

He laughed and drew her close to his side. "This is the largest surprise you're likely to experience, but Tamsyn and Cade and I will happily expand your knowledge of what it means to be gifted."

She closed her eyes, realizing how exhausted she was. She had trouble accepting the idea that she and Bran were more or less married. But she liked the idea of sharing a bed with him very much . . .

Chapter 26

Merryn had planned to rise early and return to her own room, but by the time she woke with Bran's arm around her, the sun was almost up. She slipped out of bed and retrieved her robe, pulling it on while she collected her nightgown.

Bran still slept, his dark hair tangled and his face relaxed and young. She patted his shoulder, then returned to her room, glad that neither Tamsyn nor Cade saw her. She heard sounds from the kitchen, though. One or both of them were early risers.

After she washed up, she brushed out her very tangled hair and secured it into a modest knot at the back of her head. Then she put on her dullest gray lady's maid gown.

As she headed down the stairs, she heard Bran's door open. Not wanting them to arrive in the kitchen together, she increased her pace.

The ground floor smelled of breakfast and she heard the easy murmur of Tamsyn and Cade talking. When she entered the kitchen, Tamsyn looked up from chopping spring onions and blinked.

Bran's voice came from behind Merryn. "Good morning to you two larks."

"It looks like a very good morning for you," Cade said, amusement in his voice.

Tamsyn wiped her hands on her apron, then headed around the kitchen table. "Congratulations!"

Merryn's face was burning like the sun. "Is it that obvious?"

"It is for us, because Bran is family." Tamsyn gave her a warm hug. "I'm so happy for you both!"

"It was my fault!" Merryn blurted out. "I went to Bran's room and seduced him!"

"More like ravished, actually." Bran stepped to her side and put his arm around her shoulders. "In an entirely mutual way."

Merryn was torn between wanting to crash a vase over his head and kissing him. She settled for leaning into his side. "I'm so new to this gifted business! I don't know what to expect."

"We can start lessons today," Tamsyn said. "Everything has happened so quickly! It was only yesterday that I cleared the mental block. I gather you've never known anyone who was gifted?"

"I was aware that some people had unusual talents, but I didn't really know what it meant."

"You probably did know gifted people, but most prefer not to talk about their abilities," Bran said. "Talents often run in families. There was no one in yours?"

"My father never mentioned the subject." Merryn frowned. "Perhaps my mother was."

"Then we'll just start at the beginning," Tamsyn said briskly. "While the lads are out adventuring, we can talk today."

Remembering what Cade had said the day before, Merryn asked, "Do you think that visiting your family will be an adventure, Cade?"

He shrugged, looking very opaque. "It shouldn't be."

She sensed that his visit would be unexpected and upsetting

to his family, but she didn't think he or Bran would be endangered. They were both very capable men.

Meanwhile, she had been revealed as a wanton woman, been congratulated for it, and now she was hungry! She began setting the table, glad she was useful in at least one small way.

After breakfast Bran and Cade left for the stables, and Merryn turned to Tamsyn. "Where shall we start my lessons in giftedness?"

"All good education about gifts begins with tea, pots and pots of it," Tamsyn said firmly. "It stimulates the mind."

Merryn chuckled as she put a kettle of water on to make a fresh pot of tea. "It's also good to have teacups to fiddle with while thinking. Will you start with defining what gifts are?"

"They aren't magic," Tamsyn said. "Gifted people can't conjure storms or turn lumps of coal into gemstones. Most gifts are a matter of increased perception and understanding, the sort of things that everyone does all the time, but more intensely. That's why it's so annoying when bigots hate the gifted. We don't do anything really different from everyone else, we just do some things better."

Merryn poured boiling water on tea leaves and left them to steep. "What gifts cause the hatred?"

Tamsyn pursed her lips. "Knowing things about people, sometimes things others don't want known. The ability to tell when someone is telling lies. Seeing future possibilities, as you do. Being a really good investigator, like Bran, who is very talented at ferreting out the truth."

"He did something to the back door knob so that I could open it even when the door was locked," Merryn said. "That seemed like magic."

Tamsyn frowned. "Not exactly. It's just a clever little trick he developed."

"Not magic? He affected something physical and solid. It wasn't a mental trick. It seemed . . . magical," Merryn said doubtfully.

"We never talk about anything we do as magic. It just upsets people," Tamsyn said firmly.

In other words, it was safer not to seem to work magic. Merryn recognized how such an action was much more dramatic than sensing emotions, and best not discussed. "What are Cade's gifts?"

Tamsyn considered her answer. "He has the skills of a first-class soldier, only more so. He's very quick and very strong. In a fight he can tell what his opponent will do, almost before it happens. He's a born hunter, very good at tracking criminals down."

"He and Bran seem exceptionally close."

Tamsyn nodded. "They considered themselves brothers even before they both became Tremaynes because of the way they worked together to survive."

A little shyly, Merryn said, "Bran told me that gifted romantic couples have very intense bonds."

"He's right." Tamsyn studied Merryn's face. "I sensed this was coming as soon as I met you. It was just a matter of time—and not very much time!"

"I didn't expect it!" Merryn felt her face color as she poured their tea. "Have you ever experienced this kind of bonding?"

Tamsyn smiled a little wistfully. "I've seen it with my parents, which is probably why I once thought I'd found my forever love, but I was very young, just a child. I outgrew that attraction with time when I realized it was impossible. Just a dream."

Despite Tamsyn's calm words, Merryn sensed there was still a lingering sadness for lost love. That sadness brought another question to mind. She asked hesitantly, "Is Cade going to feel that I'm coming between him and Bran?"

Tamsyn shook her head. "Cade is too generous for that. He wants Bran to be happy." She paused. "Cade is more self-contained. I don't think he feels the need to find a mate, but because he loves Bran, he doesn't begrudge him the kind of happiness you two have found together."

Before the conversation could go any further, a knock sounded on the outside door that led directly into the kitchen. Tamsyn stood. "I wonder who that might be?"

Tamsyn opened the door and said with surprise, "Glynis! I hadn't expected you. Is something wrong?"

"No, I just came to see what servants you need, now that there are more of you staying here," Glynis said apologetically. "Bran insisted on making do for himself, but we want you and your brothers to be comfortable."

Glynis stepped into the kitchen and glanced around, then gasped, "Merryn Penrose! Is that really you? You were reported dead!"

Merryn caught her breath, stunned at being recognized. Getting to her feet, she said, "That's me, but I had . . . an accident." Wondering if her memory was damaged, after all, she asked, "Were we friends?"

Glynis shook her head. "No, but once we both attended a festival in Polperro and were introduced very casually. I remembered because you were so very pretty. You gave me a friendly smile, but we didn't have a chance to speak."

Tamsyn gave Merryn a glance that said they'd better tell Glynis at least some of the truth. "Come in and have some tea. There is much to discuss."

Merryn poured tea for their visitor. "You heard that I was dead. What was supposed to have happened to me?"

Glynis accepted a cup of tea and took a seat at the kitchen table. She and Bran had a distinct family resemblance in their dark hair and gray eyes. "It was said that you went riding on

Bodmin Moor without a groom and never came back, though your horse returned to the stables with an empty saddle. It was assumed that you had a riding accident, and because so much of the moor is rough and remote, your body was never found."

Merryn remembered now that the Crow and his men had tried to capture Shadow, but her furious horse had bolted, so her captors concentrated on her. "I did *not* have an accident! I was kidnapped and held captive. It seems I'm gifted, and my captor thought I could be of use to him. I don't really remember much of the last two months because a mind block was laid on me so I was barely conscious."

Glynis gasped in horror. "How did you escape?"

"I knew I wanted to get away from those people, so one day I just ran into the woods. They set hounds on me, but luckily Bran rescued me and brought me here. Since we didn't know who might be after me, he's kept my presence a secret."

"So that's why he insisted he didn't need any help here in the dower house," Glynis said thoughtfully. "Now you've regained your wits, it appears."

"I was slowly improving, and then Tamsyn arrived and was able to clear the rest of my confusion." Merryn made a face. "I still have some mental cobwebs, but I think I am mostly myself again. Now Tamsyn is explaining to me what it's like to be gifted, since I know so little."

Glynis looked at Tamsyn and said shyly, "Could you include me in the lesson? Bran thought I might be gifted also, since it often runs in families. There are times when I've wondered if I sense more than others do, but I don't know."

"This calls for more tea! And shortbread." Tamsyn settled down and repeated some of the same information she'd given Merryn.

Glynis listened intently. "How does one even know if one is gifted?"

"It helps to be raised in a family where gifts are taken for granted, like mine. For those who aren't so lucky, like you and Bran and Merryn, there's usually some incident or incidents in which you know something you shouldn't know, and people around you find it very strange," Tamsyn said wryly. "Has that happened to you?"

Glynis frowned. "Sometimes I'll respond to something I thought a person said, but then I find they didn't say it aloud. People find that *very* annoying!"

"Indeed they would!" Tamsyn said. "Have you learned to tell the difference between when people are speaking out loud and when they're just thinking loudly?"

Glynis sighed. "Not really. I've found it best not to say much."

No wonder Glynis was so reserved. "But you have a sweetheart, don't you?" Merryn asked. "Do you have to stay silent around him?"

Glynis tipped her head to one side. "No, but how did you know I have a sweetheart? Did Bran tell you?"

"He didn't. Tamsyn, is this an example of knowing something I shouldn't know?"

Tamsyn laughed. "It is indeed."

"How did you discover your healing talent?" Merryn asked.

"I was about five years old when I found a kitten who had been hurt in the street. She was bleeding and had broken bones and was almost dead. I think some horrible person had kicked her. I picked her up and held her in my hands and cried over her and whispered that she was going to be all right and that I'd always take care of her."

"And she survived?" Glynis asked, fascinated.

"Survived and flourished." Tamsyn laughed. "My Angel cat lived to a ripe old age and was the queen of all the pets in my parents' house."

"That is a truly miraculous gift," Glynis said.

"It doesn't always work that well," Tamsyn said. "I can usually help a person feel better, but I can't always heal them." She sighed, her usual brightness dimmed.

Merryn reached across the table and laid her hand on Tamsyn's. "You healed me."

"You were well on your way to healing yourself." Tamsyn smiled. "I was so glad I could help." She leaned back in her chair. "Time for more tea? I can talk about being gifted all day."

Merryn and Glynis said together, "Please do!"

Chapter 27

As Bran and Cade rode south to St. Brioc, a hamlet a little beyond the village of Penhaligon, Cade was silent even by his standards. The day was cool with patches of sun and cloud. Pleasant for riding.

After they had ridden about an hour or so, Bran commented, "Even when we met as small children, you never spoke about your family."

"Neither did you," Cade said dryly.

"A fair point, but I talk more in general. Getting you talking is more difficult," Bran said with a chuckle. "You were a little older and might remember more. What's your family name? Assuming you remember it."

"Evans. My father is named Jago."

Jago was the Cornish version of James. "Do you remember what you did that made him throw you away?" Bran asked.

Cade glanced at him with a wry smile. "I'll tell you my story, if you tell me yours. You first."

"Just ahead there's a nice spot to take a break. Easier to talk there as well."

When Cade nodded, Bran guided them to a sheltered area on the left side of the road. The horses could graze on fresh grass, and a tree trunk made a good place for them to sit and admire the stunning view of cliffs and sea in front of them.

Bran gazed into the distance, remembering. "I'd forgotten what happened back then until I returned to Penhaligon Castle. I was very small, three years old or so, but always curious and looking into things."

"A born investigator, in fact," Cade commented.

"Apparently. That life ended the day when I felt that something was wrong, not acceptable. So I went exploring and found my father rogering one of the maids on the floor of the drawing room. I was too young to understand what was going on, but it looked painful and unpleasant, so I ran to my mother's morning room and told her what I'd seen.

"She turned white, then stormed out the door. I heard shouting. Looking back, I think that her expectations of Lord Penhaligon were never high, but she drew the line at him seducing the maids under her own roof. In broad daylight, no less."

Cade winced. "Of course he blamed you for the fact that he was caught."

"Exactly. The maid was discharged, my father beat me, and then took me to that baby farm and orphanage. You know what happened then. You found me and we became friends and helped each other survive until we escaped."

Cade grimaced. "I remember. Now that I'm here, I'm also remembering why I never wanted to return to Cornwall."

"Bad memories," Bran agreed as he gazed at the breaking waves below. "But the countryside is magnificent."

"True, and there's a sense of coming home, probably because I was born and raised here," Cade said, sighing. "Like with you, my sin was realizing something a normal child wouldn't have. My father had a fishing boat and did some smuggling as well. I told him one day that he shouldn't go out on that night's run. He'd been drinking, so he kicked me across the room and told me to mind my own damned business."

Bran grimaced. "This obviously did not end well."

"A revenue cutter caught him and his boat was confiscated. Jago managed to get out with almost no jail time, after which he came home and beat me for not giving him a better warning. Then he dragged me off to the baby farm."

"As with my father, he couldn't accept responsibility for his own bad behavior, so he blamed it all on a child." Most of the rescued Tremayne children had similar stories, Bran imagined. "We were very lucky."

"Meeting you was the luckiest day of my life, since you're the one who came up with an escape plan and guided us to Gwyn and Rhys."

Bran tried to imagine what his life would have been like if he hadn't met Cade. He would have died—terrified, dirty, and hungry. "It was teamwork, brother Cade. You're the one who figured out how to steal rides on the back of coaches and get us to London." Shading his eyes, he squinted out at the water. "There are the usual small boats, but there are a couple of very large ships farther out. Do you know what they are?"

Cade studied them, then gave a low whistle. "Royal Navy ships of the line. A first rate and a second rate, I think. Two of Britain's greatest fighting vessels. With war imminent, they may be going to Plymouth Dock for maintenance and refurbishing to ready them for battle. The Royal Navy has come a long way since war broke out with France ten years ago. I suspect it's now the greatest navy in the world."

"I hope so, because the navy is all that stands between us and Napoleon's ambitions." Bran stood and brushed off his coat. "How long do you think until the fighting starts again?"

Cade's expression became abstracted as he considered. "Two months at most. Quite possibly less. I can feel danger in the air."

When Cade made that kind of prediction, he was always

right. As Bran swung back onto his horse, he glanced at the distant sails of the warships. With a snap of certainty, he knew they were part of the puzzle he was trying to solve. A few more pieces and the puzzle would become clear.

It had better be soon.

As they resumed their journey, Bran asked, "Do you even know if your father is still alive?"

"He is," Cade said tersely.

Cade led them unerringly to the cottage at the end of a scraggly lane on the far side of the scattered buildings that formed the hamlet of St. Brioc. Built of whitewashed stone, it was solid and a little larger than Bran had expected, with a small barn behind; chickens and a pair of goats were scrabbling around the yard.

Bran and Cade tethered their horses and headed toward the front door. They both stopped dead at the sounds of gruff male voices coming from inside the cottage. A man with a strong Cornish accent growled, "How will we know when the ship with the confiscated goods arrives at Plymouth Dock?"

"I've got a fellow in the yard who will let me know," the other man said in a more educated voice. "The ship will be stuffed to the gunwales with confiscated silks and tobacco and brandy. Several fortunes' worth, and you and I will get most of it."

"As long as nothing goes wrong," the other man muttered.

Cade stiffened as he recognized the first voice, while Bran thought that the second man sounded familiar. They exchanged a glance, then walked up to the front door. Cade threw it open so forcefully that it banged hard against the inside wall.

"What the hell?" the first man snarled. "What are you doing comin' into my house like this?"

"It's my childhood home," Cade said with icy menace. "Surely, the prodigal son has the right to return home, Jago?"

As his eyes adjusted to the dim light, Bran saw that Cade was talking to a shorter, older, dirtier version of himself. Jago stared, then swore a filthy oath. "You must be the gifted brat I got rid of! They told me you'd died, and good riddance!"

"They lied," Cade said. "Baby farmers aren't paid enough to be honest."

Jago looked wary, and one hand went to a sheathed knife at his waist. "Why the devil are you here?"

Cade smiled, a dangerous smile with teeth. "Why, to thank you. After you beat me and delivered me to that hellhole, I made my way to London with my friend here. We were fostered by a wealthy couple who appreciated our abilities and raised us as gentlemen. I'm a wealthy man now, so it all turned out quite well."

Jago roared, "You bloody bastard!" He yanked his knife from his sheath and lunged at Cade. "You shoulda stayed dead!"

Cade caught his father's arm and spun around, slinging the older man through the open door to crash in the yard. "Not very welcoming, is he, Bran?"

The other man in the room had been silent, but now he said icily, "Why should he be welcoming when thugs invade his house? If you're really Jago's son"—the man squinted—"and with that face, I suppose you are, it's damned bad form to treat your father like that in his own home."

Bran inhaled sharply, as he realized why the voice sounded familiar. "Mr. Crowley! Did you ever find your poor, simple niece?"

Crowley focused on Bran, then stiffened. "Penhaligon! No, we never found her, alas."

Bran suppressed a violent urge to toss Crowley out the door to join Cade's repellent father, but he suppressed it. "I know you broke into the dower house and searched when I was out, but you didn't find her, because she wasn't there."

After a swift instant of calculation, Crowley said, "I shouldn't have done that, but I was so worried that I hoped she might have got in somehow without your knowing." He shook his head with seemingly genuine regret. "The poor girl was always drawn to the sea. I fear she went all the way to the channel, then fell off a cliff and drowned. Tragic. She wasn't capable of looking after herself, but she was a sweet thing."

A sweet thing, Merryn? She was wit and will and fire, not *sweet*. Bran said flatly, "Then you should have damned well taken better care of her."

Crowley gave Bran a look of acute dislike as he headed for the door. "I'm going to take my friend Jago into the village for a drink and to sympathize about his unnatural beast of a son. I trust you'll both be gone by the time we return." He exited, slamming the door so hard the windows rattled.

Cade's face looked carved from granite. Bran wondered what he'd hoped or expected from this meeting. He was about to suggest it was time to leave, when the door leading to the back of the house opened and a woman stepped through. She was middle-aged, with red hair, a bruised left cheek, and an uncertain but friendly smile.

"Sorry you didn't have a better return home, lad," she said to Cade. "Would you like a cup of tea before you leave?"

She was so incongruously pleasant that all Bran could do was stare. But he realized immediately that there was something — or someone — here that he and Cade needed to learn about.

Chapter 28

It took a moment for Cade to collect himself before he could say politely, "Are you Mrs. Evans? I suppose you must be my stepmother."

The woman shook her head as she gestured them into the kitchen in the back of the house. "I'm Annie Fletcher and I'm what passes for the lady of the house. Your father and I aren't married, though. He doesn't believe in marriage and has always avoided it, but he likes a woman around to cook and clean, and for . . . other reasons." She gave Cade a wary glance.

"If you're wondering whether I know that I'm a bastard, the answer is yes," Cade said in a cool voice. "I don't remember much about my life in this house other than trying to avoid beatings, but I do remember Jago railing against marriage."

Annie Fletcher relaxed. "He's not an easy man, but he pays for food and don't hit me too often." She touched her bruised cheek unconsciously. Bran thought that some women had very low standards for the men they lived with, but a woman alone didn't have many choices if she wanted to eat.

Tea had been steeping in a large pot, and now Annie Fletcher poured three cups. "Mint tea, can't afford the real kind, but it has a nice taste and there's honey in this pot if you'd like it sweeter."

"Thank you for the tea," Bran said as he added a spoonful of honey and stirred it. He handed the honey to Cade, then sat down on a battered wooden chair. "I'm Bran. Cade and I became brothers at the baby farm, where we were both sent. We went to London together and were fostered into the Tremayne family."

Cade had pulled himself together and accepted the mint tea, adding twice as much honey as Bran had used. His hands were not quite steady.

The mint tea was pleasant and soothing. As Bran took a second sip, a door to the backyard opened and a redheaded child peeped in. Annie said, "It's safe to come in, Danny. He's gone to the village."

The little boy entered, his gaze flicking around the kitchen warily. Behind him were another redheaded boy and a dark-haired girl. All were under ten, Bran guessed. They looked nervous, which any child in this house should be, but they appeared to have enough to eat, and their old garments were carefully mended.

Annie smiled at the children. "The redheads are Daniel and Henry, and the little dark one is Eselde. Here's your tea." She poured tea and honey into three smaller cups, then gave each child a piece of biscuit. "Now out in the yard with you!"

"They're nice healthy children," Bran said, for lack of anything better to say.

Annie gazed toward the back door, her expression troubled. "They are. The little redheads are mine, of course." She turned to Cade with a sober expression. "But I think that Eselde is your half sister, and she's in danger."

* * *

There was a moment of dead silence after Annie Fletcher spoke. Then Cade drew a harsh breath. "Eselde is Jago's child?"

"He says so. One reason he brought me in was to take care of her," Annie said. "Her mother was his last woman. When she died, Eselde was too young to go into service, so he told me that if I kept her and my brats out of his way and ran the household, I could buy food on his account. I've been here three years now."

She seemed to want to talk, so Bran asked, "You're a widow?"

She nodded. "My husband had died several months earlier and I was getting that desperate, so it was Jago or the poorhouse. I thought Jago would be better—though there've been times I've wondered," she added bitterly. "It helps that he's out fishing or smuggling a good bit of the time."

"A sister," Cade said softly. "Why do you say she's in danger?"

"Because she's gifted and she's seeing things about Jago that would make him kill her if he found out," Annie said bluntly. "You, most of all, know how Jago feels about gifted children."

"Her eyes are like yours," Bran said quietly. "Even if she isn't your sister, we need to take her to a safe place."

"You're right, of course," Cade said, his voice firm. "But what about you, Mrs. Fletcher? Are you safe here?"

She shrugged. "Safe enough. At least my lads and I have enough to eat."

Moved by impulse, Bran asked, "If you left here, is there somewhere else you could go?"

Annie sighed. "My sister Alice is a widow, too. She wrote that I could come live with her, but I've no way to get there, and she doesn't have much more than I do, so she can't help me move myself and my boys."

"Where does she live?" Bran asked.

"Plymouth Dock," Annie said. "Her husband died in the

navy, and she rents out rooms in her house to get by, but she'd
rather have me. She says I can easily get work there to help her
with the costs." She sighed. "But how can I get us all that distance when I haven't a penny to bless myself with?"

Plymouth Dock again. Another puzzle piece, or did it just
reflect the fact that the shipyard was, far and away, the largest
employer in this part of the world?

Cade said immediately, "We can take you there. How much
do you have to carry? Any furniture that would require a
wagon? Or will a carriage be enough for you and the children?"

"You'd do that for a stranger?" Annie said with amazement.

"You've been caring for my sister," Cade said. "Besides,
Bran and I don't like to see women and children mistreated."

Annie locked her hands in front of her, her eyes blazing. "If
you would do that, I'd pray for you both every day for the rest
of my life!"

"When would be a good time to collect you?" Bran asked.
"And will Jago cause trouble if you leave?"

Annie shrugged. "He wouldn't miss me, as long as I take my
annoying brats with me. He only puts up with me because he
likes meals on the table and a woman in his bed. It won't be
hard for him to find another desperate woman to take my
place." She gave a faint shiver. "It would be best if you came
when he's away, though. He's going off in his boat day after tomorrow and will be away for several days."

"So three days from now," Cade said. "If you give me your
sister's full name and address, I'll tell her to expect you and the
children."

Bran's brows drew together. "Mrs. Fletcher has been taking
care of Eselde, and this is the only family your sister has
known."

Understanding what Bran meant, Cade asked, "It was very
kind of you to take such good care of a child not your own,

Mrs. Fletcher. While I could place her with my adoptive parents, would you prefer to keep her with you if I pay for her upkeep?"

Annie looked stunned. "I'd love to keep her! I always wanted a daughter, and she's like one of my own."

"That's settled then. The third day from today and a carriage large enough for you all, along with some possessions."

"Not many of those, but dear God, please don't say you'll do this unless you mean it!" There were tears in Annie's eyes.

"I always keep my promises." Cade stood. "Can I see Eselde again?"

"Of course." Annie stood and opened the back door. "You can come in now!"

The three children skipped through the door, Eselde behind the boys. Once in the kitchen, she looked up at Cade with grave dark eyes and said solemnly, "I knew you'd come."

The girl was definitely gifted! After a startled moment Cade bent and offered his hand. "It's a pleasure to meet you, Eselde. I'm your half brother, Cade. I didn't know of your existence before today, so this is a lovely surprise."

Gravely she shook his hand. "You're going to take us away from Jago?"

"Yes, to a better, happier place."

"Good." Eselde released Cade's hand and glanced at Annie Fletcher. "I told you this would happen, Mama."

Annie smiled as she produced a pencil and a ragged scrap of paper. "So you did, love!" After writing down her sister's name and address, she handed the paper to Cade.

"I'll see you three days from now, mid morning, Mrs. Fletcher," Cade said. "Thank you for what you've done."

Bran also took his leave and followed Cade out to the horses. As they mounted and rode down the lane, he said, "Your little sister is most certainly gifted."

Cade gave a rare smile. "She is! I don't want to uproot her

from the only family she's known, but I'll make sure she gets proper training for her gifts."

Bran loved seeing Cade falling into a fatherly role. Good for Cade, and good for little Eselde. "What did you hope for, or expect, when you decided to visit your father?"

"Having a good excuse to break his neck would have been satisfying," Cade said thoughtfully. "But I think it was more a matter of showing him how very well I've done without him. He's still a drunken swine, while I'm a gentleman of sorts. There didn't turn out to be much satisfaction in that, but finding Eselde feels very satisfying. We were rescued, and now it's our turn to rescue others."

"Amen to that!" Bran replied with a smile. And Merryn was the best rescue of his life.

"The day is yet young," Cade said as they rode carefully through St. Brioc's very small market square. "Is there anything in particular you'd like to do?"

When he thought about it, Bran realized there was indeed something that they should do. "I think we need to stop for a meal in Penhaligon at the Admiral Drake Arms, which is presided over by the amiable Mr. Fellowes, who probably has a cellar full of smuggled alcohol. We may also meet Captain Jacques Dubois, the Guernsey sailor and likely smuggler, there." Bran thought a bit longer. "And perhaps much more."

"You think he might be connected to the looming danger?"

"I'm almost sure of it. I'd like your opinion on him and Fellowes, if possible."

Cade gave him a sidelong glance. "Does the Drake Arms have good food?"

"It does."

"Then lead on, brother Bran." Cade gave the smile that had teeth. "Good food and a villain. A splendid way to spend a day."

Chapter 29

The distance from St. Brioc to Penhaligon wasn't great. Bran felt like a hound on the hunt, following an invisible trail. Cade looked around with interest as they entered the village, memorizing the streets and the piers. Captain Dubois's ship, the *Sea Maid,* was moored in the harbor. Good, Dubois would be somewhere near.

After securing their horses in the Drake Arms stable, they entered the inn. It was much busier than on Bran's first visit, but Fellowes waved from behind the bar, where he was filling tankards of ale.

As the buxom barmaid began to distribute the tankards, Fellowes came around the bar to greet the newcomers. "Good to see you again, Mr. Penhaligon! How are you liking Cornwall, now that you've had more time to look around?"

"I'm liking it very well and remembering some of my early years here." He gestured to Cade. "My brother Cade Tremayne is visiting from London, but he was also born here and is finding some old memories." Not all of them good.

After Cade and Fellowes shook hands, the innkeeper glanced

around the nearly full taproom. "It's a busy time of day, but it will slow down soon. Order some food and I'll join you for a drink later. The shepherd's pie is particularly good today."

"That sounds appealing." Bran scanned the taproom. "Isn't that Captain Dubois in the booth in the corner? I met him when I was here before. I'll say hello now."

Bran led Cade across the room, narrowly avoiding being sloshed by an energetically swung tankard of ale. When he approached Dubois's table, the captain was frowning over a notebook. Even more noticeably than when they'd met before, he roiled with dark energy. He looked up when Bran called his name.

"Captain Dubois? I don't know if you recall, but we met briefly down at the harbor a while back."

Dubois's gaze sharpened as he saw who was approaching. "Mr. Penhaligon! Good to see you again."

Bran saw the captain's energy flare with dark menace; not just the sign of a powerfully gifted man, but a recognition by Dubois that Bran and Cade were also gifted and potential adversaries.

But they were all very civilized. Introductions were made, hands were shaken, and Dubois invited them to join him at his table so they could eat while waiting for Fellowes to join them.

The barmaid came over promptly with tankards of ale, then took their orders for shepherd's pie. Bran sipped from his tankard and his brows arched appreciatively. "Excellent ale."

Dubois nodded. "It's made by Fellowes's mother. He claims that she's the best ale wife in Cornwall, and he might be right." The captain sipped at his own ale. "The food here is . . . very English, but the drink is always worth a visit."

"I'm told you're a Guernsey man," Cade said after sampling his own drink. "Guernsey is even closer to France than Cornwall. Have you seen warships around the island readying themselves for a renewal of hostilities?"

Dubois frowned. "Aye, occasional French naval vessels. More from the Royal Navy. They've always patrolled the Channel regularly, but there seems to be more of them. I'm glad that my *Sea Maid* is too small to be a target for either side."

"The sailor's life has always been hazardous," Bran commented. "And surely more so now."

Cade added, "While we were on the coast road earlier today, we saw two ships of the line sailing north. Fearsome, even at a distance, even though they're on our side."

A spark of sharp amusement showed in Dubois's eyes. "There is actually some pleasure attached to those vessels. They are heading to Plymouth Dock for a last round of maintenance, and I'm told that another ship of the line will be joining them from the north. In a few days a public festival will be held at the yard to celebrate the grand power of the navy. This way people can appreciate how well Britain is protected."

"Really?" Bran said, startled. "I'm surprised the commissioner allows it. I visited the yard recently and they seemed very careful about who was admitted."

"Usually so," the captain agreed. "But there is a history of such public days. It's a kind of gift to the local residents, many of whom work at the yard or have family members who do."

"What sort of festivities?" Cade asked.

Dubois shrugged. "I'm not sure. Music, a parade, booths selling different goods, a roast ox or two. I believe that a few lucky visitors get tours of the ships. I'm told that the harbor fills with local boats that wish to enjoy the festival."

"Will you be taking your boat there?" Cade asked.

"No, it will be too crowded for my tastes, and I need to return to Guernsey with my cargo."

Bran and Cade exchanged a glance. Such a festival would certainly present opportunities for mayhem. "It sounds interesting," Bran said. "Perhaps we'll make up a party from Penhaligon Castle to attend."

The taproom had been emptying and now Fellowes joined them, tankard in hand. "Has Captain Dubois been telling you about the Royal Navy Festival at Plymouth Dock? It's just been announced." He took a deep swallow of ale. "I hope I can get up there to attend. It will be a grand event. They usually even have fireworks!"

Exactly what Bran was afraid of.

Tamsyn opened the back door of the dower house as the three young women returned from a walk in the woods. "Aren't you two tired of hearing me talk?" she asked.

Merryn laughed. "No, but you're beginning to sound a little hoarse, so you're entitled to a respite."

"This has been the most marvelous day," Glynis said, her face bright. "You're showing me whole new worlds. I no longer feel like I'm strange beyond belief."

"You aren't, Glynis," Tamsyn said warmly. "You're one of us."

"After that splendid hike, surely it's time for more tea," Merryn said as she led the way into the kitchen. Directed by Tamsyn, the three of them had talked for hours about what it meant to be gifted. After putting together a light lunch, they'd gone for a walk in the midday sun to enjoy the mild spring day. "Do you have more lessons for us this afternoon, Tamsyn?"

Tamsyn nodded. "Before tea I'd like for the three of us to hold hands and see what our energies feel like, individually and together."

The three of them settled around one end of the kitchen table, close enough to join hands. Having done this once before in a circle that included Bran and Cade, Merryn found the connection similar . . . but different. The combined energies of the three women were startlingly intense. Tamsyn, bright and clear and powerful. Glynis, with depths she was just beginning to explore. Merryn wasn't sure what she contributed, but she loved being part of this circle of three. She gave a soft sigh of delight. "Wonderful!"

"Indeed," Glynis breathed.

"Our energies blend together really well," Tamsyn said thoughtfully. "I think together we are formidable. I wonder what we might accomplish if we try?"

The front door opened just then and male feet tramped to the kitchen. Bran and Cade had returned. Bran gave Merryn a smile, which warmed her in unexpected places.

"Tea?" she asked.

"Yes, tea," Cade said. "And news. We have a new sister."

"We do?" Tamsyn straightened up. "Tell us about her!"

As Merryn put the kettle on, the men joined them at the table, with Bran between Merryn and Glynis, and Cade between Glynis and Tamsyn. Cade said, "I found my father and he's as dreadful as I remembered, but he has a small gifted daughter, my half sister. About eight, I think?"

"That would be my guess," Bran said. "She already has a strong talent."

Tamsyn said worriedly, "You didn't leave a child with that man, did you?"

"Don't worry, Cade is going to abduct Eselde and her foster mother and two brothers and take them away to Plymouth Dock where her sister lives," Bran said. "Cade, it's your story, so you fill in the details."

As Cade spoke, Merryn steeped the tea and handed around cups. When he ran out of words, she said, "All roads seem to lead to Plymouth Dock, don't they?"

Bran nodded agreement. "When you take Annie Fletcher and the children to her sister's, perhaps you can use your talent for investigation in some of the local taverns."

Tamsyn frowned. "A good idea. Also, I want to meet this new sister and her family. I wonder when we might visit?"

"Soon. A public naval festival is to be held at the yard, which is a good excuse for all of us to travel up there."

As soon as Bran mentioned a festival, Merryn choked on her tea and began coughing. Bran spread his hand on her back. "What's wrong?" he asked quietly.

She drew a deep breath, then took a cautious sip of tea to steady her nerves. "There's a great potential for danger there," she said in an unsteady voice.

"Can you see what kind of danger?"

She closed her eyes and tried to sort out what she was seeing. Opening her eyes, she said, "No, there's too much going on, too many possibilities. But one possibility is surely the potential danger you're sensing."

He nodded gravely. "Cade and I have come to the same conclusion. We met the Guernsey smuggler Dubois at the Drake Arms in Penhaligon, and he told us what would be involved in the festival. Glynis, have you ever attended one of these naval celebrations? I gather they've taken place before."

She nodded. "They're only held every few years, but we used to go regularly. It's the most excitement we ever get down here! We haven't attended recently, not since my father's health has declined. They're great fun. Very lively and may attract a few cutpurses, but they're well run, and I've not seen any danger in the past."

Cade said, "I think it would be wise if we attended, just to keep an eye on things."

He was right. But Merryn couldn't shake the feeling that this year the danger would be much greater.

Glynis rose reluctantly from the kitchen table. "This day has been marvelous, but it's time to go home before someone thinks I've been abducted." Seeing Merryn wince, she said apologetically, "I'm sorry. That's not a joking matter."

Merryn smiled and patted Bran's leg under cover of the tabletop. "No need to apologize. The abduction was dreadful, but the rescue has turned out wonderfully well."

He gave her a pleased sideways smile.

"Thank you for taking my thoughtless remark in good

humor, Merryn." Glynis glanced around the table. "I assume I'll see everyone but Merryn at dinner? My mother has extended a general invitation to Cade and Tamsyn for all meals, for as long as you're here. She enjoys having young people around and says it's good for me as well."

"As we are welcome at the castle, you are always welcome here, Glynis," Bran said as he got to his feet. "I don't think you're likely to be abducted, but I'll walk you home. We haven't had many opportunities to talk, and I'm interested in what you think of your explorations into giftedness."

"I'd like that," Glynis said with a shy smile.

"In that case, I won't offer to accompany you," Tamsyn said. "I'm so glad you called on us, Glynis, and look forward to getting to know you better and better."

As Bran and Glynis left the dower house to follow the footpath to the castle, he offered her his arm. She took it with a smile of pleasure. "You're much nicer than my other brothers."

"Even if I'm not actually your brother? Your father has his suspicions."

"Suspicions are his hobby," Glynis said dryly. "Mother and I have no doubts, and the estate needs an heir, preferably one who will be kind to my mother and me."

"If your father refuses to accept me as his son, who would inherit?" Bran asked curiously. "Matthew Davey said the next man in line is a second cousin, whom your father loathed. Have you ever met the cousin?"

"I've heard my father rant about Cousin George and his failings, but I've never met the man. I think he died several years ago. I believe there was a son, but I don't know anything about him or even if there is such a man. If you aren't acceptable, the next heir would be even more distant." She squeezed Bran's arm. "But that doesn't matter because we have you, and Matthew thinks you're the real Penhaligon heir."

He liked having acquired Glynis and Lady Penhaligon as relatives, but he still wasn't interested in becoming the next baron. It felt . . . wrong. "Do you miss your older brothers?"

She made a face. "Not really. They never listened to anyone else and were very selfish. They certainly weren't interested in a little sister."

"The more fools they," Bran said. "I'm quite sure that you were an adorable little sister. You still are, in fact."

Glynis laughed. "You say the nicest things, and you don't make them sound like false flattery."

"I don't lie without a very good reason," he said firmly. "And never to family."

"I love your Tremayne family. You and Cade *listen*, the way Matthew does," she said wistfully. "Can I be adopted into the Tremayne family the way you've adopted Merryn?"

Bran hoped that Merryn would soon be a Tremayne legally, but his family of the heart was nothing if not flexible. "Of course you can join. My mother Gwyn Tremayne says that the families we choose are the best, so you can choose us, as well as those members of your birth family whom you want to keep."

"If only it was that easy! I'd keep my mother, of course. My father . . ." She sighed. "He was never what I would call easy, but he wasn't always as difficult as he is now. We have a rather nice house in Plymouth, and we used to stay there regularly, as well as for the festivals. But for the last several years, my father has been in pain all the time, I think, and that makes him bad tempered. He hates not being able to do so many things that he used to do easily."

Bran considered how he would feel about his own ailing health when he was Lord Penhaligon's age. He didn't think he'd be as bad tempered, but he would not be happy about increasing limitations, particularly if he was always in pain. "I'll try to be more patient with him."

"My mother and I would like that." They were at the castle

walls, so Glynis released his arm. "Thank you for escorting me home. I'll see you at dinner tonight."

He watched until she entered the castle, then turned back toward the dower house. He had no problem imagining Glynis and Matthew Davey living long and happily together.

Now that he was in love with Merryn, he wanted everyone else to be just as happy.

Chapter 30

❧

Dinner at the castle was unusual because Lord Penhaligon joined them at the table. As soon as the food was served, he said brusquely, "Glynis tells me there is going to be a Royal Navy Festival at Plymouth Dock four days from now." He took a large swallow of wine. "I haven't been to one in years, but I'm going to this one."

Lady Penhaligon looked concerned. "Are you sure you're well enough for such an event, my lord?"

"I don't know if I'll ever have another chance, so I'm damned well going to this one!" he barked. "We will all stay in Tamar House, which is quite convenient to the yard. That means all of you."

He glanced around the table with narrowed eyes. "Lady Penhaligon. Glynis. Certainly, you, boy!" He glared at Bran. "You can show some filial feeling by pushing my wheelchair around the yard."

Next his gaze moved to Cade and Tamsyn. "You should come, too. It's a fine show. Tamar House has plenty of space."

"I would enjoy that," Tamsyn said lightly. "Glynis has told us something about the festival and it sounds very enjoyable."

Thinking of Merryn, Bran said, "I'd like to see the festival, but I'll stay in an inn. The one I used on my previous visit was good, and it's less work for Lady Penhaligon and the servants."

"*No!*" Lord Penhaligon slammed his hand down on the table so hard that the silverware rattled. "You were supposed to be spending time at the castle and estate to learn more about them, but you've barely been here at all! You certainly don't act like my son, and maybe you aren't. It's hard to believe a bloodless man like you can even be a Penhaligon!"

"Being thrown away by my own father was hardly designed to create family loyalty," Bran said dryly. "Perhaps if I grew up here, I'd have developed a sufficiently bad temper to suit you."

While Tamsyn and Glynis winced, Lord Penhaligon let loose with a string of curses that included words Bran had never heard before. Cornish, perhaps.

The tirade ended when Lord Penhaligon lurched to his feet. "The hotels will be full for the festival, so you'll stay under my roof and act like a member of the family, or be damned to you!" Then he snarled, "Serve my dinner in my study" to the butler and limped off, leaning heavily on his cane.

Bran broke the uneasy silence, saying, "I'm sorry, Lady Penhaligon. It was bad of me to provoke him like that."

She smiled wryly. "I can't say that I blame you. He probably thinks better of you now, though he much prefers shouting to elegant verbal knives."

Bran said with equal wryness, "Perhaps I should practice my shouting."

"I can help you with that," Cade said, straight-faced. "I'm better at being bad tempered."

That produced a ripple of laughter and the meal resumed. After dinner there was discussion and planning for the festival, but the evening broke up early. Bran carried a lantern as he and Cade and Tamsyn took the footpath back to the dower house.

"I can't remember the last time I saw you lose your temper,

Bran," Tamsyn said. "I assume that it's because you don't want to stay at Tamar House and leave Merryn alone."

"Exactly right as always, Tam. I can't leave her on her own when she might not be safe." Bran sighed. "I'm considering alternatives."

"We can take her to Plymouth Dock with Annie Fletcher and the children," Cade said thoughtfully. "Annie's sister Alice apparently has a reasonable-sized house, so they should be able to find a corner for a little bit of a thing like Merryn."

Bran's annoyed "Merryn is exactly the right size!" clashed with Tamsyn's indignant "Merryn and I are the same size, which is exactly right!"

Cade laughed.

"You are both perfect petite princesses. But I think this is a good plan. Merryn will be safe and anonymous there, and she can become acquainted with Eselde."

Bran thought, then nodded. "Given the enormous favor you're doing for Annie and her family, I'm sure they'll be happy to help us." It was a very good solution. He just wished he and Merryn would be under the same roof.

Merryn was curled up on the drawing room sofa reading by lamplight when the others returned. She set the book aside and bounced up to meet them. "How was your dinner?"

"We had a lovely time storming the castle," Tamsyn said as she removed her cloak. "Bran lost his temper and showed some sharp edges, and Lord Penhaligon is threatening to disown him."

"Oh, my," Merryn said, not sure how Bran would feel about that.

"Worse was to come." Bran stepped up to Merryn and gave her a warm embrace, which included a very thorough kiss. "We're all going to Plymouth Dock for the festival, but you can't stay with us in Tamar House, of course, which is the Penhaligon home in town."

That was enough to startle her out of what had been a thoroughly enjoyable kiss. She leaned back, frowning. "Am I to stay here?"

"No, we've decided it's best to leave you with Annie Fletcher and her family, including Eselde," Bran explained. "It's Cade's idea and a good one, I think. We'll be close and you'll be able to see the festival, and I think you can safely disappear into a household of women and children."

Merryn thought about the suggestion, then gave a brisk nod. "Yes, that's exactly the right place for me."

Which was true. But her sense of gathering menace grew more intense.

Chapter 31

Annie Fletcher and all three children were waiting on the stone steps in front of Jago Evans's cottage when Cade's wagon rumbled up the rutted lane and pulled to a stop. Cade gave Bran the reins and jumped to the ground. "I'm glad to see that you're all ready for your journey."

Annie and the children stood immediately. "Ready and praying that nothing has happened to stop us from leaving!" Her gaze went to the others who climbed from the wagon.

"Eselde, you've already met my brother Bran. Your uncle Bran." Cade gestured Tamsyn forward. "This is my sister Tamsyn Tremayne, so she's your aunt Tamsyn."

Eselde's gaze went to her with interest. "You have pretty hair."

"Thank you," Tamsyn said with a warm smile. "You can call me Aunt Tamsyn or Aunt Tam, but *not* Aunt Tammy!"

Eselde nodded, then turned to Merryn. "Your hair is like Aunt Tamsyn's. Are you another aunt?"

"I hope to make her one," Bran said as he rested his hand on Merryn's shoulder.

She frowned at him. "Don't rush your fences, Bran!"

He chuckled. "We're still negotiating that, Eselde." Sobering, he said, "Merryn is being hunted by a dangerous man and we need to keep her safe." With a glance he passed the conversation to his brother.

"Yesterday I visited your sister Alice to let her know you and your children are coming. She and her daughter are delighted by the news," Cade said. "Since the Penhaligon household will be staying near Plymouth Dock for the festival, I asked if Merryn could stay in her house for several days. We'll be nearby, but it's better if Merryn is difficult to find. Your sister is willing to have an extra visitor and I hope you are, too?"

"I know it's a great deal to ask, Mrs. Fletcher," Merryn said softly. "I won't be any trouble and I look forward to getting to know Eselde and Danny and Henry."

Annie stepped forward and took both of Merryn's hands. "Please call me Annie! We'll be happy to have you, Merryn. My sister and I know quite a bit about difficult men." She grimaced. "And we do not approve of them!"

"Luckily, there are also men who are very good," Tamsyn said with a wave at her brothers. "Let me help you with your belongings so we can be on our way."

Cade skillfully turned the wagon around in the yard; then the pitifully modest possessions were packed in the back. There were three rows of seats. As Cade helped Annie into the second row, he asked quietly, "Do you have any last thoughts about Jago's cottage?"

She sighed as she glanced at the whitewashed stone. "We usually had enough to eat, but not much more. I left a note saying goodbye and that we won't be coming back. It won't take him long to replace me."

Then she settled in the middle of the seat, with one of her boys on each side of her. Tamsyn had already taken Eselde under her wing, with the little girl sitting between Tamsyn and Cade in the front seat.

The rutted lane made slow going until they got to the coast road; then their pace increased. Bran sat next to Merryn on the back seat, discreetly holding her hand. With the three children chattering excitedly, his soft voice could be heard only by Merryn. "I hate that we'll be separated for the next several days."

She gave him a mischievous glance. "Even worse is being separated for the next few nights!"

The warmth in her gaze made his heart rate increase. "Very true," he said, his voice thickening a little. "I'll just have to remember these last nights until we're together again." A thought struck him. "Will a few nights of sleeping alone give you more appreciation for the advantages of marriage?"

She gave him a rueful smile. "It might do just that!"

They made several stops along the way to eat and take advantage of bushes when necessary. It was late afternoon when they reached Alice Williams's house in Plymouth Dock.

Alice and her small daughter had been waiting, and they swept out of the house and down the steps when the wagon pulled up in front. Alice's daughter appeared to be about Eselde's age; both mother and daughter had the family red hair.

"I'm so glad you're here!" Alice said as she and Annie embraced. "It's been so long since we've seen each other!"

"Too long," Annie said, tears in her eyes.

Tamsyn introduced Annie's children to their cousin Emily, while Bran and Cade transferred the small bags of belongings from wagon to house. When that was done, Alice invited everyone in for tea and shortbread.

As the water heated, Alice said, "Merryn, I'm so happy to have you as our guest. It's like a grand lordly house party! Come with me and I'll show you to your room. It's small, but I've tried to make it comfortable."

Everyone followed Alice to a back corner of the ground floor. The room was furnished with a narrow cot, a chair, several shelves for storage, and a wooden box on the floor with . . .

"Kittens!" Merryn dropped onto her knees beside the box.

The mother was a comfortable-looking tabby and her five kittens were a range of colors and patterns. They were large enough to be active and curious, and a gray tabby promptly lurched out of the box and into Merryn's lap.

She cooed at the kitten, then raised her head. "Alice, you could not possibly have furnished this room better. I may never leave!"

The other adults laughed, while Annie's children knelt to exclaim over the kittens. "Handle them very, very carefully," Merryn cautioned.

The children obeyed, their faces shining with pleasure. Merryn suspected that mutual kitten love was breaking down any uncertainties the children might have about this blending of two families.

"We need more kittens!" Tamsyn said with a laugh. "One for each of us here. Emily, since you've been living with these little darlings, may I borrow the one you're holding?"

Emily stood, smiling shyly. "I call her Sweetie."

Tamsyn gently accepted the kitten, which was mostly black with white socks and face. "What a delight a kitten is!"

Danny, the older of Annie's sons, said, "Puppies are very nice, too."

"Indeed they are." Tamsyn set Sweetie on Cade's shoulder.

Startled, he gave a rare smile as he stroked the kitten with one finger, while Sweetie explored his shoulder, shedding white hairs on the dark fabric of his coat. "We definitely need more kittens."

Kittens and humans had a wonderful time, and it was with regret that Tamsyn said, "We must be going if we are to return to Penhaligon before it's full dark."

"But we'll be coming to Tamar House tomorrow," Cade said. He brushed a hand over his small sister's tangled hair. "I intend to visit regularly."

"And I hope for advice about what to see and do here in Plymouth Dock," Tamsyn said as the adults left the kitten room and headed outside to the wagon, the children following behind and chattering happily.

Bran lingered behind to give Merryn a private goodbye. "I really wish we weren't being separated," he said, his gaze intense.

"So do I," Merryn murmured as they slid into each other's arms. They'd been together almost constantly since he'd rescued her. "I've grown accustomed to having you around all the time."

His arms tightened around her. "The Penhaligons will be arriving en masse tomorrow, but the naval celebration won't begin for another two days. Shall I bring our horses so we can go riding the day after tomorrow? Matthew Davey says there are several good beaches within riding distance."

She loved riding with Bran, and an outing might offer a chance for real, mischievous privacy. Nuzzling his neck, she said, "I'd like that. Should I wear a riding habit or trousers so I can ride astride?"

"Since we're in town, the riding habit would be best. Do you have yours with you? If not, I can bring it with my things."

"Please do. A nice, long ride will make up for the sad fact that we're sleeping under separate roofs."

"Not for long." He bent into a kiss that rapidly turned serious. She fell into his embrace, wondering why she was resisting the idea of marriage with Bran. It was true they hadn't known each other long, but surely there was no other man anywhere who could affect her like this!

"I want to sweep you up and run away with you," he said huskily. "But it's a very long distance to Gretna Green, so we must wait."

She laid her hand against his cheek. "Since you pointed out Tamar House when we drove here, I know where to find you if necessary, and you know where to find me."

He stepped away from her and pulled a well-filled purse from an inside coat pocket. "Here's some pin money, since you don't want to be penniless in town."

Her eyes widened at the weight of the purse. "You're very generous!"

"Money is useful, not least to buy treats for children who haven't had many. Buy them sweets or new clothes or whatever is needed."

She would enjoy that as much as the children. She could see herself escorting Eselde through a happy crowd enjoying the celebration. Then a shocking new image seared across her mind.

She gasped and swayed dizzily. Bran caught her arms to steady her. "Did you see something upsetting?" he asked in a low, calm voice.

"Terrifying!" She drew a deep breath as she tried to master herself. "I saw a pistol being pointed right at your heart!" She bit her lip, appalled at what she'd seen. "And . . . and I heard it fire."

Bran's expression became very still. "I am now forewarned, and I'm very good at ducking."

"I hope that's true," she whispered.

"We haven't talked much about your foretelling ability," he said. "How often do you see things? Are they usually very dramatic or sometimes mundane? How accurate are your visions? Can you consciously try to discover what will happen?"

She blinked at the barrage of questions. "I'll think about all this so we can discuss it when we go riding. A simple answer is that nothing is absolute." She hesitated, considering. "Sometimes I see possibilities, events that may or may not happen. For example, my warning to you of the man with a pistol may help you be prepared so you can avoid disaster."

"We will have much to discuss." He brushed a kiss on her forehead. "Thank you. I promise I will be very, very careful."

As he turned and headed toward the front door, she stood

frozen, realizing that he hadn't promised that he would survive, only that he would be careful. If he was killed, how would she live without him? The thought made her realize just how very, very much she cared for him.

Chilled, she walked back to her room and settled by the kitten box again. This time all five little fur balls crawled onto her lap, exploring with tiny purrs. Very soothing. She reminded herself that she hadn't seen Bran dead, so either the pistol misfired or his dodging skills were excellent. She hoped both were true.

Alice Williams came in. "I'm so glad you enjoy kittens! If there is anything else you need, please let me know."

"I will, but I'm sure everything will be fine. It's very good of you to let a stranger stay here."

"Annie and I are happy to oblige. Cade Tremayne has already done so much for us!" She gave a fond smile. "You have a lovely family."

"The Tremaynes aren't really my family, though they've been beyond kind to me," Merryn explained.

"That Bran seems to want to make you a member of the family!" Alice said with a knowing smile.

Blushing, Merryn replaced the kittens in their box and stood quickly before any of them could return to her lap. "We haven't known each other long."

"Time will remedy that."

"I'm glad you and your sister can live together now." Wanting to change the subject, Merryn said, "Have you been alone long?"

"Seven years." The animation left Alice's face. "Jack was in the navy, a bosun's mate on the *Amphion*. You might have heard of it?"

"Oh, no!" Merryn said involuntarily. "Such a horrible disaster!"

"It could have been even worse," Alice said tightly. "The

ship was set to sail the next morning, so there were dinners and celebrations for families on board. I would have taken Emily so her father could say goodbye to her, but she'd fallen ill with a streaming cold, and I didn't want to take her out.

"I was sitting with her and holding a cold compress on her forehead when I heard the explosion." Alice shuddered. "Somehow I *knew* it was the *Amphion*. I scooped her up and carried her to the yard and we . . . we watched the ship burn. And heard the screams." She swallowed hard. "Emily was too young to remember, but I've avoided the naval celebrations at the yard ever since."

Merryn laid her hand on the other woman's arm. "I'm so very sorry," she said softly. "Life is often unfair."

"Yes, but there are kittens and children, and now my sister and her children are living under my roof, and Cade's contributions to the household will take so many worries away. I'm better off than most." She managed a smile. "Now to find out what those four little ruffians are doing!"

Merryn followed her hostess out, closing the door so the kittens couldn't escape, wishing she could eliminate the image of the burning ship from her mind.

Chapter 32

Moving the Penhaligon entourage was the equivalent of a small-scale military invasion, but by late afternoon the next day, they were settling into Tamar House a short distance from the naval yard. As his lordship had said, the house was sizable, so there was room for Cade and Tamsyn, and there would have been room for Merryn . . .

Bran forced himself to turn his thoughts away from her. His job was to be a useful member of the household. And to figure out what danger was hovering over them, and how to stop it.

The servants were still unpacking when Lord Penhaligon barked at Bran, "I want to visit the yard. Ask the butler to bring out my wheelchair and put it on the small carriage so we can drive over there. The roads in the yard are fairly smooth and good for the wheelchair. You can push me down to the docks so I can see the ships and watch how the festival preparations are going."

His lordship looked gray with fatigue, so Bran said, "Perhaps you should rest up a bit before going over there?"

"Don't nanny me! I want to go *now!*" he barked.

There was no arguing with that. Lady Penhaligon looked worried, but gave a nod to Bran indicating that he should obey.

"I'll locate the wheelchair and arrange for the carriage," Brian said peaceably.

"I'd like to go as well," Cade said. "I've heard so much about this famous Royal Navy Shipyard. It's time to see it for myself."

"It's quite a sight, Tremayne," the baron said, mollified by Cade's interest.

The butler produced the wheelchair, which was solidly built and rolled smoothly. The small carriage had a rack built on the back to carry it. Lord Penhaligon looked even more exhausted after they got him into the carriage, but he was adamant about proceeding.

As they left the house, Tamsyn and Glynis were giggling together, and Lady Penhaligon was busy getting the household in order, so it was a male party that set off for the yard.

The gate guards there looked harried, and they were less careful checking credentials than when Bran had visited before. But with a barking baron demanding entrance, their party was allowed entry with only a short delay.

The carriage took them a short distance beyond the gates, but had to halt because the road was blocked by preparations for the festival. Bran helped his lordship out and into the chair, and they went exploring. The yard was more crowded with people and wagons than on Bran's previous visit. He guessed the crowds would be dense during the actual festival. Anything might happen.

When they first reached a clear view of the ship basins, Cade gave a low whistle as he saw the enormous warships. Lord Penhaligon exhaled with pleasure, his bad temper fading. "What a sight! The nearest one is the *Royal William*. A first-rate ship of the line, with three gun decks. Carries a hundred twenty cannons and a crew of eight hundred fifty. That one just beyond is a second-rate ship, the *Formidable*. Ninety-eight guns and seven hundred fifty crew."

He shaded his eyes against the sun and squinted. "The smaller ship on the other side of the *Formidable* is a frigate. Can't make out which one. Frigates are fifth-rate ships, only about forty guns and maybe a crew of three hundred, but invaluable as scouts and for going after enemy merchant ships and privateers." He gave a gusty sigh. "No finer fighting ships in the world than the Royal Navy. Drive me closer."

Startled by the barrage of information, Bran obeyed the order to resume pushing. "You're very knowledgeable about navy ships, sir. You wished to join the navy yourself?"

Penhaligon scowled. "Aye, as a lad I was all fired up to become a midshipman. Used to watch the navy ships sail by, out in the channel. Wanted to become an admiral. My father got me a midshipman's place, but just before I left, my older brother died of fever, so I became the heir. My responsibilities had to be on the land." He glared over his shoulder at Bran. "An estate like Penhaligon is a vast responsibility and a vast amount of work. Would you be good enough for that, boy?"

"I won't know unless I try," Bran said calmly, thinking it was strange to think of this bad-tempered old man as a boy with hopes and dreams and disappointments. Bran needed to be more patient. "But I've never shirked my responsibilities."

Cade added. "That's true, Lord Penhaligon. I've never known Bran to avoid doing what needed to be done."

The baron snorted, unconvinced. "Take me home. I'm tired."

"I'd like to stay and look around more," Cade said as his gaze lingered on the warships.

"I'll see you later," Bran said as he turned the wheelchair around. It would be interesting to hear his brother's observations.

By the time they returned to Tamar House, Lord Penhaligon was so exhausted it took Bran and one of the footmen to get him out of the carriage and into the house. His wife clucked her tongue worriedly, but before he headed to his ground-floor bedroom, Penhaligon said to Bran, "Send a message to Davey to be here in the morning. We have business to take care of."

"Yes, sir."

Pleased to have a reason to leave the house and stretch his legs, Bran decided to walk to Davey's office. A solid brick town house, it was only a brisk ten minutes away. Davey leased the whole building and lived there, as well as maintaining his office and records. As he'd said when they first met, the arrangement saved him the time of having to walk to work.

Bran was admitted to the office by James Greene, a young man who was reading law with Davey and acting as clerk and general assistant. The front reception room was his office and it looked very lawyerly, with bookcases, wooden cabinets filled with files, and a sizable desk.

They'd met before, and Greene greeted him cheerfully. "Hello, Mr. Penhaligon! We're just wrapping up work for the day. I'm sure Mr. Davey will be happy to see you."

Bran gestured at Greene's desk, which held several neat stacks of paper, each topped with a rock to hold the pages in place. "It looks as if you're busy."

"We are, but Mr. Davey is going to give me the festival day off so I can enjoy it with my family." Greene glanced at the door that led to the inner office. "He should be almost finished with his last client."

As Greene spoke, Davey emerged from his office with an

older man. After an exchange of greetings and goodbyes, Bran was left alone with Davey.

Davey smiled at his visitor. "Bran! I assume this means that all manner of Penhaligons have descended on Tamar House?"

"Yes, and his lordship has summoned you to call on him in the morning to discuss business."

"Yes, there are several routine matters that we need to review. But that's for tomorrow. Care to join me for a glass of claret?" He opened the door to his private office.

"That's the best offer I've had all day," Bran said fervently as he followed his friend into the other room. "Moving a household is hard work."

Davey opened a cabinet and removed a decanter of claret. As he poured two glasses, he asked, "How is Merryn?"

"She's well and staying with friends nearby."

"And Glynis?"

Bran accepted his wine and settled in one of the comfortable leather upholstered chairs. "When last seen, she was wearing the happy smile of a young woman who is going to see her sweetheart soon."

"You probably made that up, but it sounds good."

On his previous visit Bran had seen only the outer office, so he studied his surroundings. The spacious room was furnished more like a gentleman's study than the businesslike reception area. There were several good watercolors of the rugged coastline, and a beautifully detailed ship model stood on a polished wood bookcase.

"That's a handsome model ship. A first-class warship?"

"Second class, but quite complicated enough. It's a model of the *Blenheim*. Lord Penhaligon gave it to me when he was particularly satisfied with some work I'd done for him." Davey smiled a little. "Have there been any major explosions between you and his lordship?"

Bran shrugged. "Nothing major, though he barks at me like I'm a rather unsatisfying footman."

The other man laughed. "I imagine you are very, very polite when ordered around."

"Of course. Frustrates him no end." The claret was excellent. After another sip Bran said, "When we arrived at Tamar House, he demanded I take him to the yard in a wheelchair. He's very knowledgeable about ships. I hadn't realized that he'd wanted a life in the Royal Navy."

"Yes, it's a pity his older brother died. Lord Penhaligon would have made a fine admiral."

"One who wouldn't have gone light on the floggings," Bran commented.

"Probably not, but he does love the navy. He once told me that he bought Tamar House so that he could visit the yard often. He used to spend more time here in Plymouth Dock, but not so much in recent years."

"He looked so gray that I was worried he'd collapse before I could get him back to the house," Bran said with a frown. "Is he seriously ill? No one talks about what's wrong with him."

"I have no official knowledge, but I think his heart is weak." Davey swirled the wine in his glass absently. "I suspect he knows he's running out of time, which is why he sent me heir hunting."

"To keep the estate out of the hands of his despised second cousin." A thought struck Bran. "Was the cousin in the Royal Navy? Did Lord Penhaligon hate him for being able to do what his lordship couldn't?"

Davey's brows arched. "Your intuition is working well. Yes, his cousin was an officer with a distinguished career who died heroically in battle."

"Did the cousin leave a son who could inherit?"

"That was a subject Lord Penhaligon never wished to discuss," Davey said with extreme dryness.

"A pity Lord Penhaligon can't leave his title and estate to Glynis. She'd be an excellent lady of the castle, particularly since his lordship doesn't like any of the other possibilities," Bran said.

Davey's brows arched. "I thought that finding you settled the question of inheritance."

"You're the only person who's seen the dragon tattoo on my back and you say it's blurred by the passage of time. Lord Penhaligon has never even asked to see it. I think he'd like to be able to deny that I'm his son." Bran shrugged wryly. "But if not me, who?"

Davey studied Bran's face. "Do you still dislike the idea of inheriting Penhaligon?"

Bran thought before he replied. "I realize that I may have no choice but to accept the responsibility of the inheritance, yet it feels . . . wrong."

"What feels right?"

"Merryn," he said instantly. "My goal is to find a way to safety through the hovering danger, and then persuade her to marry me."

"Are you making progress on that front?"

Bran remembered how well he and Merryn suited each other as lovers and hoped the thought didn't show in his face. "I think so. Speaking of Merryn, you'd mentioned that there were some pleasant beaches within an easy ride. I brought both our horses and we want to ride out together. Do you have suggestions?"

"I'll write out some directions for you." Davey rose and moved to sit at his desk, where he proceeded to draw simple maps showing the way to some of the nearby beaches.

Bran accepted the pages, and hoped that he and Merryn would find a day of relaxation and romance before the furies broke loose.

* * *

It was almost dinnertime when Bran made it back to Tamar House. The meal was leisurely and enjoyable, probably because his lordship was too tired to join his family. Lady Penhaligon was tired but happy because several of her local friends had called on her. Bran suspected that her life in the castle was rather lonely, with mostly her daughter for company. Glynis also looked happy after Bran said that Davey would call in the morning to go over business, and he'd surely find time to spend with her.

Bran didn't have a chance to talk privately with Cade until late in the evening, when they retreated to Cade's room with a bottle of brandy in hand. They both stripped off coats and boots and relaxed together as they'd done for most of their lives.

After pouring each of them drinks, Cade settled into one of the two chairs and stretched out his legs. "I'm going to miss times like this."

"Because we're not likely to be living under the same roof much longer?"

His brother nodded. "Our paths are going to be diverging, now that you've met Merryn."

Bran realized that his life was about to change irrevocably. Cade had been the most constant person in his life since they were small children working together to escape the baby farm before it killed them. They'd grown up together, studying, learning to fight, learning how to care for the younger members of their foster family.

When they both started to work for the Home Office, it had been time to leave Tremayne House, but it had been utterly natural to take a place together. They'd both traveled for their work, and sometimes weeks would go by without seeing each other, but sooner or later, they'd both return home, kicking back with a drink and just talking, or not talking.

Cade, Bran's big brother. He knew the bond between them was unbreakable, but he'd miss these casual times. On the positive side it would be pure joy if Merryn became part of his everyday life. "What about you? Have you had any thoughts of marriage? You're a couple of years older than I, so maybe it's time."

"It's not a matter of time, but of finding the right woman," Cade said dryly. "If I find one who affects me as Merryn affects you, I'll consider it, but I'm more likely to end up as the eccentric bachelor uncle to numerous Tremayne nieces and nephews."

No. Intuition kicked in and Bran knew with absolute certainly that Cade would find a woman who would own his soul, as he would own hers. But his brother would figure that out for himself when the time came.

Realizing that he could easily become an annoying matchmaker, Bran smiled to himself and changed the subject. "I presume that when you explored the yard, you were looking for weak points that could be exploited by saboteurs."

"I showed my Home Office credentials and talked to several officers of different ranks," Cade said. "I didn't see many obvious problems. Officials are aware that allowing the public in for the festival is potentially a problem, but nothing serious has happened during past festivals, so they aren't as worried as perhaps they should be."

"Is access to the ships guarded?"

"Reasonably well. All the vessels being built or repaired have guards on the gangways and there are regular patrols around the shops and offices. The yard is protected against casual troublemakers, but a determined agent could cause damage if he's capable and well prepared."

"Unfortunately, so many French agents fit that description." Bran covered a yawn and rose from his chair. "I'll let you do the worrying for now. Merryn and I are taking tomorrow just for ourselves."

Cade smiled. "You've earned that. And while you're enjoying yourself, your intuition will probably kick you with some answers."

Bran hoped so. Before he left the room, he rested his hand briefly on his brother's shoulder. Cade gave a small nod. They'd never really needed words.

Chapter 33

⌒

Merryn hadn't seen Bran the day before because he was help-ing to move his family to Tamar House, but he'd sent a servant over with a package containing her riding habit, boots, and a wide-brimmed hat with a veil so that anyone seeing her would have trouble recognizing her.

She waited impatiently for Bran to arrive the next morning. As soon as she saw him approaching, she went outside to greet him.

Why was he so compelling to watch? It wasn't just that he was handsome, though he was. Perhaps it was the quiet, con-trolled power he radiated. Or perhaps it was the way he under-stood her so well.

Or simplest of all, it might be the way he lit up when he saw her. He was riding Merlin and leading Shadow, who also lit up at the sight of Merryn. When the mare saw her, she yanked her lead from Bran's hand and whickered a greeting as she trotted up to Merryn.

Merryn stroked Shadow's sleek, dark neck, cooing, "I've not spent enough time with you lately, my darling, but soon this will all be behind us, and we can ride regularly again!"

The mare nudged her affectionately. If Shadow had been a cat, she'd be purring.

Smiling, Bran swung from Merlin and caught Merryn's hand for a brief, heartfelt squeeze. "I think all four of us, both humans and horses, are looking forward to this day together."

"I certainly am!"

"Should I go in and say hello to your hostesses?"

She shook her head. "Best not. It's lesson time and having a guest would be disruptive. Alice and Annie are both very serious about lessons. You can say hello when we return."

"Besides, you are vibrating with impatience to be off," he said with a laugh as he linked his hands together to provide a foothold so she could mount.

She settled herself in the sidesaddle, arranging her skirts to fall decorously over her legs. "I'm telling myself and Shadow that we must look very ladylike until we're outside of town. Then we can have a good gallop."

"Merlin is anxious for that also." Bran mounted his horse and they set off. "It will be a slow ride to open country. The streets are full of people who have come to town for the festival. I'm told that all of the inns and guesthouses are full to bursting."

"And the weather is lovely. A truly glorious spring day." A thought struck her. "Did you do something to make the weather so perfect for our ride?"

She assumed he'd deny it, but to her surprise, Bran said slowly, "I don't really know. Perhaps. When an outdoor event is approaching, I'll imagine the weather as being sunny and pleasant. I don't know if I have any effect on the skies, but if I imagine good weather regularly, it generally turns out like today."

"Generally?"

"Well, just about always. But I'm not really sure I'm doing anything," he said.

"It sounds like you do have a weather gift, which is not at all certain in England!"

He shrugged. "Perhaps I'm just lucky about picking good days to travel."

She suspected that it was more than just luck. Later today they could have a longer discussion on the nature of gifts; there was so much she didn't know.

They turned onto the main road that would lead them out of town. As Bran said, it was bustling with people and carts and carriages, with peddlers offering goods and entertainment. They slowed their mounts, wary of children or dogs who might dart under the horses' hooves.

Merryn had the disturbing sense that she was being observed by someone cold and calculating. She glanced around, unable to see any particular person staring at her, but with so many people around, it was hard to tell. As they moved beyond the crowds, she said under her breath, "I felt as if someone was watching me."

"Probably people were watching because you're beautiful. I really like watching you as well," he said promptly.

"I don't mind if you look at me," she said, glancing back again. "But this felt different. Intense and rather . . . unwholesome." She bit her lip. "Perhaps I'm just nervous because I've been hunted in the recent past."

Bran asked, "Do you think it might have been the Crow or the Starling watching you?"

She hadn't considered that they might have joined the crowds coming to Plymouth Dock. She shivered at the thought and tried to analyze what she'd felt. "It's possible, but I just don't know."

"When I said that you might be watched because you're beautiful, that wasn't just flattery. It's true," he said seriously. "It's an unfortunate fact that young women of exceptional beauty too often become the targets of the cruder sorts of men.

Tamsyn often feels that sort of interest and hates it. Are we far enough away from whoever was staring that you can't sense him anymore?"

She mentally tested what she was feeling. "Yes, I'm beyond that unhealthy interest. But I'm really looking forward to that lovely, private beach!"

"So am I," he agreed, his gaze skimming around them.

He was always watchful, she realized. Protective and looking out for trouble. She was grateful for that, because she also felt the gathering danger.

But she could put her concern aside for now as they moved into open country. She gave Bran a slanting glance. "Is your fell intent to take me to some private place so you can work your wicked wiles on me?"

"No," he said with a slow, devastating smile. "But if you choose to work your wicked wiles on *me*, I won't object!"

With a laugh she urged Shadow to a swifter pace as she put her fears aside. This day was for them.

The small beach was a lovely arc of white sand, with scattered tufts of tan grass, and mostly surrounded by a low sea cliff. They enjoyed shedding their jackets and boots and walking barefoot along the water's edge, holding hands and not talking much.

Beginning to feel hungry, Bran retreated to the cliff, where a shallow cave had been scoured by winds and waves. An overhang offered shade and protection from the wind, which made it a good picnic spot. He spread a blanket over the sandy floor, then sat down to explore the canvas bag of food and drink provided by the Tamar House cook.

Merryn was still standing ankle deep in the water, holding her skirts above the small waves, while gazing out to sea, the breeze blowing her loosened blond hair around her shoulders. He loved watching her. If such things as mermaids and sea nymphs existed, Merryn surely had a few in her ancestry.

He thought of the beach where they'd stopped to eat when returning from their first visit to Plymouth Dock. The sight of her stripping off her clothing and diving into the sea was burned into his brain.

Even more vividly he remembered how they'd emerged from the water, then embraced on the shore, naked as Adam and Eve. Mouth to mouth, skin to skin, eager hands and mutual heat . . .

The memory of those moments blazed through him like wildfire. How had he had the willpower to keep from making love to her? He damned well deserved a medal for his heroic restraint on that occasion.

He'd barely managed to walk away from her then, and it would be even more difficult, now that they had become lovers. Luckily, he didn't think that restraint would be called for today.

With a last look at the sun-touched sea, Merryn turned and walked lightly up the gentle incline, her bare feet leaving footprints in the sand. "Welcome to our private retreat, my lady."

She plumped down beside him in a flurry of skirts, and he handed her a small towel to brush the sand from her feet. "There's a beach rather like this on my father's property, though it's longer. I walked there almost every day." She sighed as she cleaned her feet. "I miss my father, but he's such a dreamy scholar, he's probably scarcely noticed that I've gone."

"Perhaps, but he'll certainly be happy to see you again. Remember, I sent him a letter explaining something of the situation and saying you were safe and would be home again soon."

She caught her breath. "You've received a reply?"

"Yes, I just received a letter from him yesterday." He pulled a folded paper from an inside pocket of the coat he'd taken off. "It's taken time because I gave him the address of a London postal receiving station I use. My father forwarded the letter back to me here. I didn't want to leave any visible connection between you and Penhaligon Castle and the Tremaynes."

She accepted the letter eagerly. "Do you think that was necessary?"

"I thought your Uncle Crowley might have an informant in your family home."

"You're right, that would be just like him. That's probably why I felt I shouldn't write him directly." She unfolded the letter and held it in the sunlight to read. It was very short, and tears showed in her eyes when she read it: *Tell Merryn I love her, and keep her safe. Thomas Penrose.*

"He said all that was necessary," Bran said softly. "You should be able to go home again soon."

She gazed at the note for long moments before folding it again and handing it back to Bran. "You keep it for now. Men's clothing has better pockets."

He lifted his coat and tucked the letter back into an interior pocket. "True in general, but if you hide that in your décolletage, I might be tempted to look for it."

"Sir, is that a wicked wile?" she asked with mock outrage.

"It could be," he said earnestly.

Smiling, she shook her head. "We can practice our wiles after we've eaten. What do you have there?"

He opened the bag of food. "Apple tarts, cheese, and Cornish pasties, which are permitted even though we're actually in Devonshire now." He offered her one. "And ale to wash it down."

She accepted the pasty, her fingertips brushing his with soft sensuality. Her gaze on his, she bit neatly into it, then licked fragments of crumbly pastry from her lips. As an exercise in provocation, it was very effective.

He poured ale into a mug and sipped from it, then turned the vessel as he handed it over so she would drink where his lips had been. It was a subtle kiss that she rewarded with an enchanting smile. "The wiles are increasing," she murmured.

She took a swallow of ale to wash down her first bite, then broke off the other end of the pasty and held it to his lips.

He accepted the tidbit with a kiss of her fingertips. "Mmmm, such delicious wiles."

Their meal continued as a mutual seduction, with lingering touches and teasing words. The rising sensual tension was so powerful that he would have had to drag himself away and dive into the cold sea if he thought she didn't feel the same way, but she did. It wouldn't be long until they caught fire together, but he thought it best to allow her to strike the spark.

After they finished the pasties, she emptied the mug of ale and set it aside. "The time has come to release the full measure of our wicked wiles!"

Not waiting for a response, she leaned across the blanket and pounced on him, catching Bran's shoulders and pushing him flat onto his back. Then she straddled him, her knees bracketing his hips as she bent into a kiss.

"I surrender to your glorious wiles," he breathed as he opened his mouth to her kiss. Her lips were luscious and her loosened blond hair spilled silkily around his face, scented by sea breezes and lavender.

"I've been sleeping with kittens," she said huskily, "and it was quite nice, but I would have *much* preferred lying with you." Her embrace was both sweet and searing as she settled on top of him, rolling her hips to fit the two of them together.

Though they were both fully clothed, the heat and pressure of her supple body was as erotic as when they'd first embraced, skin to skin, on that other beach. Now he knew the enticing reality of what lay beneath the layers of fabric: soft breasts, shapely hips, warm and welcoming thighs.

His hungry hands kneaded down her back and below, until he could catch handfuls of her full skirts. Raising the layers of fabric allowed his seeking hands to caress upward over her silky thighs until his palms cupped her round bottom. He pulled her against him more tightly so that their loins were pressed together, heat to heat, separated only by a few layers of inconvenient fabric.

"Merryn," he said intensely, "my magical mermaid!"

She pulsed her hips against him provocatively and said in a rough whisper, "My darling Bran, so calm and controlled, except when we make love!"

So true that his calm and control had vanished! Now all that mattered was his need to make love to her, to merge their bodies and spirits. He caught her waist and rolled them so that he was above, capturing her mouth again, while his right hand delved under the full skirts to find her hidden heat and moisture.

When he touched her intimately, she cried out, "Bran!"

After a paralyzed moment she tore at the fall of his breeches, yanking off one of the buttons as she released him into her eager clasp. "We must make up for our lost nights."

He shuddered, barely able to restrain himself as she guided him into her, joining them in all ways. Dear God, how was it possible to feel such passion and intimacy? His soul yearned as his body burned. They were made to be together, now and always.

Their union was swift and primal. When he was on the verge of culmination, he again stroked her most sensitive place. She cried out and convulsed. He barely managed to withdraw in time before he also fractured into passionate madness.

As they both gasped for breath, her arms encircled his waist, locking them together while she panted. "I look forward to the time when withdrawal isn't necessary!"

"As do I." He rolled to his side, holding her against him as her knee slid between his. "But even at my most delirious, I won't do anything that might hurt you." He pressed his lips to hers for a tender kiss. When he lifted his head, he whispered, "This is a good argument for marriage, don't you think?"

She laughed a little. "That's a discussion for another day. Now I want to learn more about the gifts that sometimes make others despise us."

"Very well, but in that case we need to sit far enough apart that you're not within distractingly easy touching distance," he warned.

"Sadly true," she said with a sigh as she sat up and moved farther away.

He smiled wryly as he also sat up and leaned back against the cliff wall, stretching his legs out on the blanket. Though she was out of easy touching distance, that didn't mean he'd stopped wanting to touch her!

Chapter 34

After they restored themselves to rumpled respectability, he dug again into the bag of provisions. He pulled out a pottery jug decorated differently from the one that had held the ale. He uncorked it, then poured the contents into two mugs, not just the single one they'd shared earlier.

He handed one to Merryn. "This is cold tea flavored with lemon and honey. The cook said it's pleasant and refreshing. Good for a serious discussion."

Merryn took a wary sip, then drank. "Very nice."

She leaned back against the cliff wall, stretching her legs out to mirror his position. "You asked about my gift for seeing the future. I've been thinking about your questions, and I've realized it's not something I have much control over. Sometimes I see images and they're often potential disasters, but it's never clear if they have already happened, certainly will happen, or just *might* happen. Not terribly useful, except perhaps as a warning."

"Did you attempt consciously to see what might happen? That could be really useful as we try to figure out the dangers ahead."

"I tried, but couldn't make myself see anything when I tried."
She made a face. "I don't see why my horrid uncle would find
my gift useful at all."

"Perhaps his obsession with you has less to do with your
usefulness than with the fact that he resented your father."

"From the fragments of conversation I remember, he had
some definite plans in mind, though I don't know what they
were." She shrugged. "Since he's a mystery, let's talk about
gifts in general. How many kinds of gifts are there? When do
they first appear? Can a person have more than one? Do gifts
ever just vanish?"

"You ask difficult questions," Bran replied. "It's hard to
generalize. Gifts usually start to appear when a child is very
small, though some are so subtle that they are just accepted as
part of the child's nature. They're most often noticed when the
gifts create trouble, as happened to me when I saw Lord Penhaligon rogering a maid in his drawing room, which led to my
being disowned and exiled."

She winced. "How could he do such a thing to a child? I
can't imagine it!"

"That's because you have a kind and loving heart, unlike
Lord Penhaligon," Bran said dryly. "Fortunately, Cade and I
found each other. Together we survived and ended up in a
much better place."

"Was Cade also banished from his home because of his gift?"

"Yes, he saw too much and was despised for it. I think that
many of the gifted children Gwyn and Rhys rescued have similar stories."

"How would you describe your particular gifts?"

He considered. "I have very good intuition about what actions I should take, though I often don't know why. For example, when Matthew Davey tracked me down in London, I had
little interest in discovering whether I was the Penhaligon heir,
but I had a powerful feeling that I should come down to Corn-

wall." He smiled at Merryn. "I had no idea that I would meet a lost mermaid fleeing through the woods, but my intuition was never more accurate!"

She laughed. "But you have other abilities, don't you?"

"I'm good at investigating and finding patterns in the information I collect." He thought more. "I usually have good judgment about people, though all these things might be aspects of my intuition."

Merryn sipped more tea. "Do people ever have multiple gifts?"

"Sometimes, but it's more common to have a main gift that shows up in different ways."

"Do gifts ever disappear?"

"I don't think so, but sometimes people will suppress a gift if it's too troublesome to use," he said slowly. "I think our abilities are an inherent part of who we are and it's difficult to repress them."

"From what you're saying," she said, "gifts are not as clear as a talent for music or for drawing. Is that the case?"

"Exactly. I've thought about this question often and haven't come up with any clear answers or rules."

Merryn drew up her knees and linked her arms around them. "Is it possible people aren't born with specific gifts, but rather a certain amount of potential? Then specific gifts appear as needed when a situation is of critical importance."

Bran's brows rose. "That's a very interesting thought. So perhaps a person with a large potential might find new gifts if a situation was desperate."

"Has that ever happened to you or Cade or Tamsyn or any of your other Tremayne family members?"

Bran remained silent as he thought of an instance that was still difficult to remember. "Tamsyn always had a gift for dealing with mental and emotional problems. Even when she was a small child, she could soothe gifted children who had been rescued by the Tremaynes. Such children were often frightened and angry.

"When Rhys and Gwyn brought Cade and me in, they put us in the same bedroom because we couldn't bear to be separated. Cade was particularly upset—the Tremayne house was so different from any other place he'd ever been. We were sipping mugs of warm spiced milk, which Gwyn had given us, when Tamsyn marched in. She was a tiny, beautiful little blond angel, even younger than we were. Just seeing her made me feel better. She walked up to me and smiled and patted me on the shoulder, as if saying not to worry, everything would be well.

"Then she turned to Cade, who was curled into a tight little ball on the bed. She took his mug from him and set it on the bedside table, then took both his hands in hers and just gazed into his eyes. I could see him unwinding as the fear fell away. When she gave a little nod, he smiled and kissed her right hand, a gesture he'd probably never even seen. When she left the room, she took our fears with her."

"What an extraordinary child she was," Merryn said in a hushed voice.

"Always. But you asked about developing a new gift when it was needed." He swallowed hard, having trouble talking about the incident even now. "Rhys and Gwyn have three natural children, and Tamsyn is the oldest. The youngest was born when Tamsyn was eleven, and Gwyn nearly died after the baby was born. The whole house was saturated with pain. Rhys was quietly frantic, and I was afraid that if Gwyn died, he might quickly follow."

"But she survived," Merryn said quietly.

"It was a miracle, I think. Tamsyn summoned everyone in the household, children, servants, everyone. We were all gifted, to a greater or lesser extent. She had us hold hands and gather in a circle around Gwyn's bed. Gwyn looked so pale, as if already halfway to heaven."

Hearing his pain, Merryn inched closer so she could take his hand. "What happened then?" she asked quietly.

"The bed was high, so Tamsyn had to climb up on the mattress. Then she laid her right hand over Gwyn's heart, while her left hand held Cade's. I was next to him; other members of the household circled around to Rhys, who was to the left of Gwyn. He rested his hand on Tamsyn's, over Gwyn's heart. No one said a word, but I felt an amazing energy rising and coursing around the circle as we all poured our prayers and love into Gwyn."

He drew a deep breath, shaken by the memory. "Tamsyn performed a miracle of physical healing. Gwyn's face gradually regained color and then she opened her eyes and smiled at Rhys and Tamsyn and whispered that they needn't worry, she wasn't going anywhere. It was . . . extraordinary."

"What a remarkable talent to appear when it was so desperately needed!" Merryn exclaimed. "Has Tamsyn ever done any other physical healing like that?"

"I don't believe so. After Gwyn was past the crisis, Tamsyn slept for twenty-four hours. Over the years she's worked to improve her talent for healing problems of the mind, but never again undertaken such a dramatic physical healing. Perhaps the ability to bring someone back from the brink of death could only appear in such a desperate situation as saving her mother's life."

Merryn squeezed Bran's hand, then released it and settled back against the cliff wall. "It sounds as if almost anything might be possible if the need is great enough."

"Perhaps, though usually gifts manifest in less dramatic ways." He glanced across at her, savoring her delicate, thoughtful profile. "Sometimes people have gifts that we don't recognize as anything special."

She smiled. "Like the possibility that you might be able to affect the weather?"

"The weather in Great Britain is so changeable, how can I tell?" he said with a laugh. "Do you have any abilities that you've taken for granted?"

"Nothing springs to mind." She frowned thoughtfully. "Well, the way I was able to call my darling Shadow after you rescued me."

"Definitely a gift," he agreed, "and one that you took for granted. Do you have any other such gifts?"

"If it's something I take for granted, how would I know?" she said reasonably.

"Very true." Bran sighed. "I hate to leave here, but our holiday is over. With the festival starting tomorrow, we need to figure out what danger is hovering over our heads and what can be done about it."

They retrieved their horses from grazing on fresh spring grass. "Maybe we can come back here another time," Merryn said wistfully.

"I hope so." Perhaps they might. But Bran felt that the danger right ahead of them was too vast and nebulous to look beyond to happier times. "We need a council of war as soon as possible."

"Whom would that include?" Merryn asked.

"Cade, certainly, and Tamsyn and Matthew Davey, if possible. We need a safe, private place to talk." He thought a moment. "Not Tamar House or at Alice Williams's house. Davey's would be best."

"How long will it take to collect everyone?" Merryn asked.

"That depends." Bran patted Merlin's neck, then bent his head and concentrated hard as he mentally searched for Cade.

After a long moment he lifted his head. "We can meet Cade and Tamsyn at Davey's house. With luck, Matthew will be there as well."

Startled, Merryn asked, "Can you and Cade talk mind to mind?"

"Not exactly." After helping Merryn onto her mount, he swung up on Merlin. "It's more a matter of sending feelings. I mentally searched for Cade, and when I felt him, I let him know we needed to get together as soon as possible. When he recognized that, in return he gave me a sense of Davey's house. He knew we were coming here today, so he can estimate how long it will take us to reach him."

"Is this a common gift?" Merryn asked curiously.

"I don't think so. It's probably because Cade and I have been close for so many years. We don't do this often, but the ability is there when a situation is serious."

She shook her head wonderingly as they started the ride back. "Will you and I be able to feel each other like that?"

"In time, perhaps." He smiled at her. "We'll just have to spend more time together until we find out."

Chapter 35

❦

When Bran and Merryn reached Davey's house, they found Cade, Tamsyn, and Davey sipping tea and looking worried. Once they entered and greetings were exchanged, Tamsyn poured two more cups of tea and said, "You called this meeting, Bran, so you tell us why."

"We've all sensed potential danger," Bran said. "Have you felt it also, Matthew?"

Davey nodded. "I have, even though I'm not gifted."

"Everyone has some degree of intuition," Tamsyn said. "Since Plymouth Dock is your home, you may be more aware when things are subtly out of balance."

"That's probably it," Davey agreed. "I hate not knowing what's bothering me!"

"Being gifted is often like that," Bran said. "Cade, you've been investigating among the taverns and sailors. What did you learn about the so-called treasure ship?"

"It's a real ship," his brother replied. "A revenue cutter that's supposed to dock at the yard tomorrow. It's said to carry a king's ransom of valuable goods that have been confiscated from smugglers. There's also a rumor that it carries a large amount of gold taken from one of the brokers who guarantees funds for buying and selling smuggled goods."

"If there's a great deal of gold, it's surprising that it's all being turned in to the government," Davey said dryly.

"Perhaps not all of it is," Cade said. "But the rumor is that even after various hands have dipped in, the amount is large enough to have been sent here so it can be stored securely."

Tamsyn asked, "Is there such a secure place at the yard, Matthew?"

"The office of the Clerk of the Cheque has a vault that would look at home in the Bank of England," Davey replied. "It probably also holds a substantial amount of cash for paying the ships' crews. Adding the value of the revenue cutter's cargo could amount to a huge sum of money. A tempting target for thieves."

"With two ships of the line and a frigate currently docked in the yard, that's a lot of sailors," Tamsyn said. "Do you think someone is planning a great theft?"

"Possibly." Cade frowned. "But it feels as if we should be looking for a larger danger."

"You have something in mind," Bran said. It was not a question.

His brother nodded. "There have been several Royal Navy mutinies in recent years, not just the ones at Spithead and Nore, but more violent ones in other places. Many sailors are restless and angry."

"Not without cause," Bran said. "The Spithead mutiny won sailors some improved working conditions, but the Admiralty seems to have gone as far as they're willing to go. The Nore mutineers did not fare as well."

"In another complication," Cade said, "a number of navy sailors are Irish, and some of them have sworn United Irish oaths because they despise England, even though they're willing to sail English ships. The French know this and delight in stirring up trouble at Britain's back door. That adds another piece of kindling to the fire. With war about to break out again, the Admiralty is understandably worried about more possible mutinies."

"Because Plymouth Dock is a major naval facility, it would be a good target for those who want to cause us trouble," Davey said, frowning.

"Could the ships themselves be targets?" Merryn asked hesitantly. "Not just the yard, but the actual ships?"

"Yes, but they're well guarded when they're in port. That's one of the first things I looked into." Cade smiled a little. "While you two spent the day larking about, Matthew and I decided we should talk to the authorities about possible dangers. Luckily, Matthew knows everyone, and he was able to get us in to see Commissioner Fanshaw, the man in charge of the whole yard."

"It helped that Cade has Home Office credentials and he looks alarmingly serious," Davey observed. "Fanshaw thought we might be overly concerned, but he doesn't want trouble, so he agreed to increase the guards on the ships, the revenue cutter, and the Clerk of the Cheque's office. There will also be pairs of Royal Marines patrolling the yard for the duration of the festival."

"Well done!" Bran said. "That may or may not be sufficient to head off trouble, but it's a good start."

"But is it enough if an enemy is orchestrating simultaneous attacks on the yard and the Royal Navy?" Merryn asked.

"Is your intuition telling you that will happen?" Bran asked.

She bit her lip. "I don't know. I'm not as adept at interpreting intuition as the rest of you."

"You may be a novice, but you're a novice with a great deal of power," Bran said quietly. "You may be sensing something the rest of us are missing. We need to remember that."

"The best strategy would be to cancel the whole festival and be very, very careful of anyone who wants to enter the yard," Tamsyn said tartly.

"You're right," Cade said, "but that's impossible. Too much planning and money have gone into this. Too many people are looking forward to the festival. It's a grand occasion in this part of England. There would be a riot if Commissioner Fanshaw attempted to cancel it."

"Fanshaw believes that the festival is essential for building goodwill between the Royal Navy and the community," Davey said. "He's not wrong, either. The Royal Navy is the backbone of Britain's military. The population needs to love, respect, and believe in it. There will be recruiting stations in the yard, where young men will be encouraged to enlist. The festival will go on, even if there's reason to expect trouble."

"I know all that, but like Merryn, I believe Commissioner Fanshaw is underestimating the potential for trouble," Tamsyn said with a frown.

"The marine patrols strolling about are well trained," Cade said. "They should be able to handle normal problems, like drunks."

"So they can concern themselves with general order, while we watch for unexpected disorder," Bran summarized. "Does anyone have any other thoughts?"

His companions shook their heads. Merryn rose, covering a yawn. "In that case I'm ready for an early bedtime. It's been a busy day." She gave Bran a swift, private smile.

Cade said, "I think trouble is more likely to happen later in the day, but I'll go to the festival in the morning when it's just opening. At midday I'll have lunch at Tamar House with Tamsyn and we'll return to the yard together."

"Merryn and I will go over at midday," Bran said. "Lord Penhaligon hasn't been feeling well, but he said this morning that he wants me to push him over in his wheelchair when the fireworks are scheduled to begin. If you're not too tired, Merryn, later in the day you can join Tamsyn and Cade. Matthew, will you be going with Glynis?"

"Yes, we'll go later in the afternoon." Davey smiled. "I don't know if we'll have to confront any dire plots, but we will enjoy spending the day together."

Bran stood and took Merryn's hand. "Let's hope our worries come to nothing."

Cade's ironic glance said that was wishful thinking.

Chapter 36

The next afternoon Merryn went to the festival with Bran, looking demure in a plain gray gown and a broad-brimmed bonnet. The day was bright and beautiful and the festival was crowded with happy visitors. "I know we're here looking for trouble," she said as she strolled along, holding Bran's arm, "but I'm thoroughly enjoying myself."

"I spent time imagining this as a perfect spring day, so you may thank me for the excellent weather," he said solemnly.

She laughed. "I wonder how many times you'll have to do this before it can be decided if you have a true weather gift or whether the skies will do what the skies will do without any help from you."

"It would take a lot of evidence to convince me," Bran said. "But I will start taking notes about the results whenever I do make an effort to alter the weather."

They were slowly working their way along the broad road that led from the entrance to the far end of the yard. Booths selling food and flowers, toys and trinkets, and everything else imaginable lined both sides of the road, and Merryn had brought a canvas bag to carry her purchases. As she told Bran, no normal woman would be visiting the festival without shopping. Her bag was beginning to fill with small toys for the children, a packet of cinnamon-flavored toffee sweets, and an old, used book of poetry, which she hadn't been able to resist.

Bran had laughed and agreed that shopping was required. When she fell in love with a silver chain necklace set with small sparkling garnets, he'd bought it for her with hardly any haggling over the price. She'd promptly put the necklace on, ridiculously pleased.

There were also entertainers: jugglers, musicians, a Punch and Judy show. Her eyes widened as a strangely dressed couple moved by on stilts, their steps slow and stately. "I've been to local fairs, but never anything like this!"

"It's a grand show," he agreed as he looked around them, his gaze missing nothing. "There's nothing wrong in taking pleasure where we can find it. It's a lovely sunny day and I'm here with my favorite lady. It's almost as enjoyable as yesterday was at our private beach."

"Mr. Tremayne, I believe you are trying to shock me!" she said, peering up from under the brim of her very demure bonnet.

"Am I succeeding?" he said teasingly.

She blushed. "You certainly are!"

"Then we will be very, very respectable for the rest of the day."

His words were light, but she felt the coiled tension in him. "You still sense danger, don't you?" she said quietly.

He nodded. "I can feel it from all directions. I think you were right that there will be multiple sources of trouble."

"But as Cade said, the security is good." She nodded toward the *Royal William*, the largest of the warships. Two intimidating Royal Marines were stationed at the bottom of the gangway, politely refusing entry to curious people who would have liked to board the massive ship. Four more guards were stationed behind them.

"It's fortunate that Davey and Cade were able talk with the commissioner," Bran observed.

Merryn smiled. "When Cade speaks, people listen."

"He's a born leader," Bran said. "If he'd gone into the army, he'd be a general by now."

"And where would you be?"

Bran chuckled. "In the back room with the maps and the intelligence officers." He stopped by a booth that was selling pasties and tarts and sausages. "Would you like something to eat? It's beginning to feel like a long time since lunch."

"A pasty," she said. "They're good walking food."

He bought a pair of pasties and they nibbled as they continued toward the far end of the fair; Bran suddenly stiffened at the sight of a modest sailing ship gliding up to dock beyond the warships. "That's the revenue cutter coming in."

They stopped and watched as the crew maneuvered the cutter to its mooring. A crowd was gathering to watch, and Merryn felt a rough energy in the group.

"I see a Guernsey sea captain called Dubois there, and he has someone with him. They're French agents and here to provoke trouble," Bran said quietly.

Merryn caught her breath. "Are you sure?"

"I'm sure. The energy of both of them is dark and angry and excited." He looked down at Merryn, worried. "I need to take a closer look, but I daren't take you over there."

She glanced around them. A booth that sold sweets and another that offered used clothing were behind them and there was a gap between the two. "I'll wait between these two booths," she said. "No one will notice me back there—though I might succumb to some of the sweets before I withdraw into the shadows."

"You're already as sweet as any woman could be," he murmured as he brushed a light kiss on her temple. "Be careful."

He set off, calm and confident and ready for anything. She

loved watching him. The group he approached was all male, many of them the sort she wouldn't want to meet on a dark street at night. Her feeling of danger intensified with every step Bran took away from her. If he was right that Dubois and his companions were French agents, what could he do about it if they started a riot? Bran would be as vulnerable as any other man.

She bit her lip to keep from calling for him to come back, because she knew that he wouldn't turn away from his duty. Was Cade nearby? She'd feel better if they were together.

A hand fell on her shoulder and she turned—to find herself staring straight into the face of the Starling.

As she gasped, the Starling said with vicious sweetness, "Aren't you glad to see your auntie?"

As she spoke, she slapped her hand across Merryn's forehead and the world disappeared.

When Bran neared the rough crowd gathering by the revenue cutter, he focused his powerful gift for evaluating the natures of men. Many of the men in front of him were smugglers. Some were merely curious; others had heard the rumors of a treasure ship where they might find some profit if there was trouble. Dubois was darkly focused on the best time and method for triggering chaos.

But the riot was triggered not by Dubois, but a regular smuggler. A voice with a thick Cornish accent boomed, "Now's the time, lads, before any guards arrive to interfere! There's plenty for all!"

The crowd surged toward the cutter, some of the men producing crowbars and other tools because they'd come prepared. Bran and the French agents were caught off guard as the group dissolved into shouts and fighting to get aboard the cutter.

Bran's instinct for danger warned him to duck, but before he could, a brawling sailor cannoned into him and knocked him off balance. Moments later, a rock crashed into the side of his head. Blood was already streaming as he collapsed. He had had a single instant to reach out for Merryn before he lost consciousness.

But pain and blackness won.

Merryn couldn't move, but she had some mental clarity, more than the first time her mind was blocked. As the Starling bent over her to assure her weakness, Merryn whispered, "You're not . . . aunt. You're . . . Starling. Uncle's whore."

The older woman cuffed the side of her head. "You know my name is Doris, you filthy brat! Your uncle Crowley has promised to marry me after this is over, when we're rich."

"Starling."

"Call me Doris!" The order was accompanied by another strike, this time a hard slap across Merryn's cheek.

"Doris," Merryn whispered obediently. Under the effects of the mind block, she had almost no will. She wouldn't waste energy arguing about what name to call this horrible woman.

"We need to get her out of here," a gruff voice barked. The Crow. A blanket was loosely wrapped around Merryn, and she was lifted and carried a short distance before being dumped into what seemed to be a cart. Dusty. She began to cough.

The cart didn't travel far before it stopped and Merryn was transferred into a building. She guessed it was in one of the many workshops and outbuildings that were spread all over the yard.

When she was laid out on a hard floor, her uncle said, "Test to see if she obeys orders as well as she did before."

Doris laid her hand on Merryn's forehead again. "Stand up."

Merryn obeyed without any will on her part. She felt like a puppet, but she did have some ability to think, so she was better off than during her first captivity.

"Disappear!" The barked order had come from Doris.

Merryn blinked, trying to understand.

"Vanish!" This time the order came from the Crow, and it was accompanied by a fist slamming into her shoulder. "I've seen you do it before. Do it again!"

"She'll remember," Doris said grimly. "She just needs reminding." Another slap across her face.

Patchy memories began to surface in Merryn's mind. The time when she was a small child escaping from her minder when she was in the family garden. She'd slipped out to the path that followed the cliffs in front of the house. She'd loved looking at the sea and felt very brave for escaping.

When she realized she was out of sight of the house, she turned back, just as a rough-looking man came along the path from the other direction. He'd been drinking and was filthy and smelled foul. When he saw her, he leered and said she was a pretty little thing and her parents should take better care of her.

He grabbed her and said she'd fetch a good price in town. Then he kissed her with his wet, slobbery mouth. She shuddered at the memory. Instinctively she'd fought, biting his tongue and kicking him in the stomach. He'd dropped her, swearing and screaming threats as he lunged at her again.

She remembered being terrified and wishing she could just disappear. And . . . she did, though she didn't realize she was invisible until he started looking for her. He lurched in a circle, kicking and snarling for her to stop hiding. But there was no place nearby where she could have hidden.

Frightened and furious, she kicked his ankle. It was not very hard, because she was so small, but he lost his balance and fell over the cliff.

She remembered his scream. It had ended very suddenly. She didn't know whether or not he'd died. The cliff wasn't very high, so he might have survived. She didn't care, didn't look, just ran back to the garden. Her frantic nursemaid caught her up in her arms and took her into the house.

Her mother had asked how her dress had become so dirty. Merryn couldn't bear to say what had happened, both because she was upset and because she'd be scolded for running away. Seeing how frightened she was, her mother blotted away her tears and gave her milk and a sweet biscuit before sending her upstairs to be bathed.

But after that, when Merryn was scolded or upset, she became invisible, until her mother ordered her to stop doing it. She'd obeyed, because vanishing was disturbing; but looking back, she realized it was the kind of gift Bran had described, one that had appeared under dire circumstances.

Her mental blankness was pierced by the memory of the last time she'd vanished. Her uncle Crowley had been visiting the house and he'd frightened her when he tried to pinch her cheek. She'd never liked him, so . . . she disappeared. After the Crow left, her mother ordered her not to do it again. If she didn't like a visitor, she should just excuse herself and leave the room.

But the Crow had remembered what she'd done. He hadn't kidnapped her for her uncertain ability to tell the future, but rather for her vanishing ability. He wanted to force her to help him do something illegal.

Though her body was not her own, her mind was filled with rage. How dare he! *How dare he!*

But would she be able to resist the Starling's mental control? She must try.

The Crow's hard hand caught her wrist, and he squeezed it with painful strength. "Vanish!"

Perhaps vanishing would help her escape. Merryn concentrated until something clicked in her mind. She could no longer see her own body, nor the Crow's, though she felt the painful pressure of his hand on her wrist and smelled the scent of his sweaty body.

"She did it!" the Starling said triumphantly.

"Good! Now, little girl, we're going to walk around this room. I won't let go of your wrist and both of us will remain invisible."

Resistance was futile, so she walked around, as her uncle had ordered, while he held on to her. But though her will did not belong to her, her thoughts and vision were becoming clearer. She could see furniture and boxes around the room. Could she jerk away from her uncle? She tried, but her body would not obey her thoughts.

Bran! He would be wondering what had happened to her, first worried, then increasingly frightened. She drew a shuddering breath, wanting nothing more on earth than to have his arms around her.

Mentally she tried to reach out to him—and with a stab of horror, she realized he'd been hurt. She wanted to scream and rush to him, but she couldn't. She slowed her mind and tried to sense him again. Hurt, unconscious, but not mortally wounded.

"Sit!" the Crow barked, and he released her wrist.

There was a chair near, so she sat, staring dully into space. She would break free of these monsters as soon as she could. She would find Bran. But for now she must endure and wait.

Another man had joined them, and he gave a low whistle of shock when she suddenly appeared. "Amazing!" he said with a French accent. "Can I get her to obey me like that?"

"Take her wrist and tell her to vanish, Dubois," the Crow said. "It has to be bare skin to bare skin."

The Frenchman hesitantly took her wrist. "Vanish."

Merryn vanished, and Dubois with her. "*Sacré bleu!*" he swore. "I didn't believe it was possible, despite what you said. I've never heard of a gift like hers."

"Neither have I, but it's perfect for your purposes." In a hard voice her uncle continued, "That's why you'll pay a small fortune to borrow her and her gift for a few hours."

"Worth every penny, and a bonus as well." Dubois released Merryn's wrist and moved to a window that looked into the yard. "It's almost time. You'll get your payment when I've used the girl and am safely back here."

"I want a deposit."

"You don't trust me," Dubois said. "Wise, though I assure you that in this case, you have my sworn oath." There was a jingle and he pulled a heavy bag from inside his coat. "Your deposit. What your little niece will help me do today is worth a great deal to France."

The Crow opened the bag, then smiled with satisfaction. "You don't even have to bring her back safely. I'll want my money, but I don't care about her."

Merryn heard her uncle's words, and knew they were her death sentence.

Chapter 37

❧

"Bran. *Bran!* Wake up, dammit!" The voice was Cade's. The sharp tone and the wet cloth washing over Bran's face pierced the engulfing darkness.

Bran blinked blearily. He seemed to be lying on a table in a tent, maybe one of the booths that lined the festival road. He looked up to see that his brother had been washing blood from his face. "What happened?" he croaked.

Cade straightened and gave a sigh of relief. "You lost your usual ability to dodge at the right time and something like a piece of brick gouged a hole in your head. You were bleeding like a stuck pig."

"You know how it is with head wounds." Bran raised a tentative hand to the wound and found that a neat bandage had been applied. "There was a riot forming by the revenue cutter. Did they manage to loot the ship?"

"No, I came in with a platoon of Royal Marines and we broke it up."

"Marines?"

"I convinced them that I was their commanding officer," Cade explained.

It was the sort of thing Cade *would* do. Bran pushed himself warily to a sitting position, then held still until the dizziness passed. "What happened after I got my head bashed in?"

"The riot around the cutter was broken up so quickly that most visitors didn't even realize there had been a problem. The goods and gold were safely transferred to the Clerk of the Cheque's vault, up the hill, and are now heavily guarded." Cade crossed the tent and gazed out the narrow opening. "But the danger hasn't ended. If anything, it's worse. There are too many other things that might go wrong." His voice hardened. "So you need to wake up and use your excellent abilities to find what disaster is imminent, in time for us to stop it."

Tamsyn entered the tent. "No barking at Bran when his wits are still scrambled!" she said as she crossed the room and laid gentle hands on Bran's head, avoiding the bandaged area while she sent peace and healing through him.

Feeling better, Bran swung his feet to the ground and stood. Then he froze. "Merryn. *I can't sense her!* She's not here. I have to find her!"

He started to move to the tent's entry, but Cade caught his arm and said with brutal honesty, "If you can't feel her, she might be dead, in which case you can't do anything for her. It's far more likely that she's alive, but perhaps in hiding. She may have pulled in on herself, so you can't feel her."

"*I have to find her!*" Bran jerked away from Cade's grip.

Cade's dark eyes bored into Bran. "Our first priority has to be stopping this trouble before it turns into a disaster that could kill a very large number of people! Perhaps even weaken Britain before the French bring war down on us again."

Bran had a powerful desire to smash a fist in his brother's jaw—so he could leave this tent and look for Merryn—but Tamsyn stopped him. "He's right, Bran. I don't know where Merryn is, but I don't think she's been badly hurt or is in immediate danger. We need you to help us stop other threats."

Bran closed his eyes, shuddering. His heart said he must find the woman he loved, but his sense of duty, cultivated by years as an agent of the Home Office, said that his first responsibility was to protect Britain. "Very well."

There was a wooden chair by the table, and he sank into it and cleared his mind as he tried to arrange possibilities into a pattern. Frowning, he said, "I think the attack on the treasure ship might have been a distraction to draw a rough element to the festival and create confusion."

Cade caught his breath. "That makes excellent sense. The whole festival could have dissolved into chaos if things had gone differently, but we stopped that from happening. So, what was the attack meant to distract us from?"

"Commissioner Fanshaw is scheduled to give a speech soon," Tamsyn said slowly. "A viewing stand was set up at the top end of the quadrangle, not far from the entrance to the yard. The commissioner is supposed to march down from his headquarters, escorted by an honor guard of sailors and marines. I assume he'll talk about how the town and the yard are mutually fortunate to be celebrating the greatness and power of the Royal Navy."

A violent image seared across Bran's mind. "Assassination! It's a perfect time for someone to shoot the commissioner while he speaks, which would certainly cause rioting and chaos."

"Dammit, yes!" Cade swore. "We need to make sure that doesn't happen. Come on, he'll be speaking very soon."

Bran stood, but he was swaying on his feet. Tamsyn pressed him back into the chair. "Bran is in no condition to go with you. Find some more Royal Marines to help you prevent assassination from being done."

Cade looked at Bran. "Tamsyn is right. Both of you stay here."

Bran tried to bring the nightmare image into clearer focus. "Look for a Frenchman. Dubois was at the cutter, and he was with a man dressed as a sailor. It might be one of them."

"I'll find them before they can murder Fanshaw," Cade said flatly before he disappeared.

"Drink this," Tamsyn said as she pressed a glass into Bran's hand. "It's that cold lemon tea the Tamar House cook makes."

He took a swallow, then another one. He still felt shaky, but worry for Merryn focused his mind. "I need to find Merryn," he said tensely. "I know she's in trouble, even though I can't really feel her. Cade may be right that she's pulled in on herself because she's in danger. I need to strengthen our connection so I can find her. Can you help me, Tam?"

His sister frowned thoughtfully. "Perhaps. Let's see." She crossed the tent and laid one hand on Bran's forehead and the other on his heart.

As he inhaled deeply, he felt the smooth warmth of her power flowing through his mind. The remaining pain faded as his perceptions sharpened.

"Think of Merryn, her essence and your love," Tamsyn said in a low, compelling voice. "Think of her as a bright star in the center of your mind and heart."

Bran did as his sister said, visualizing Merryn in all her strength and vulnerability and passion. He had been drawn to Cornwall to find her and there had been a powerful connection between them from the first.

He must find her spirit and rebuild that connection again. His intrepid mermaid lady. He thought of her ability to call her mare to her and tried to call her in the same way. *Merryn, beloved . . .*

Between one breath and another, their connection sprang to vivid life, stronger than it had ever been. In fact, he realized, stunned, the connection was close to being mind talk. He'd told Merryn that unexpected gifts could appear in dire circumstances, and that was happening now as they connected, mind to mind, spirit to spirit.

Merryn, are you all right? Can you hear me? He felt her shock, and also a kind of paralysis. *Are you safe, love?*

Her words were erratic: *Crow. Starling. Mind block.*

He swore. *They caught you again?*

An affirmative response from her. With effort her mind formed more words: *Amphion! Royal William. Use . . . me . . . to board ship.*

The pieces snapped into a pattern. He shoved himself to his feet and spoke aloud. "She was caught by her uncle and his mistress and her mind has been blocked again. She's being forced to take them to the *Royal William*. Apparently, there is some way they can use her to get them aboard. I think they want to blow up the ship the way the frigate *Amphion* blew up several years ago."

"Then we will stop it!" Tamsyn gasped with horror. "Come on!"

As they emerged into the late-afternoon sunshine, he saw that they were only a couple of hundred yards from the *Royal William*, the largest of the three warships docked in Plymouth.

Tamsyn took his hand. He wasn't sure if she was sending healing or just keeping him from keeling over, but he was grateful.

His sister asked, "Do you know if Merryn is being taken to the ship?"

He mentally asked the question and sucked in a breath as he found her bright silver energy. "They're boarding the ship right *now!*"

The flow of visitors was moving in their direction as people flocked to hear the commissioner's speech. He tried to look over the heads of the crowd but couldn't see anyone on the gangway. Maybe Merryn and her captor were already on board. He quickened his pace, Tamsyn matching his stride.

"Have your Home Office credentials ready," his sister said. "You'll need them to get aboard."

She was right. He reached for the credentials in an inside pocket and his fingers brushed the shell that Merryn had given him the first time they'd visited a beach together. He'd carried the small twisting shell ever since; touching it made her seem closer.

They slowed as they approached the guards at the foot of the gangway. The men were dressed in the impressive red tunic of the Royal Marines and they looked as if they took their work seriously.

Bran pulled out his identification and said under his breath, "Prepare to charm them, Tam."

"I will," she assured him.

When they reached the guards, Bran handed over his credentials, while he snapped in his most authoritative voice, "I'm from the Home Office and need to board immediately! We have a report that there's a saboteur aboard the ship."

The guard, a corporal, studied his papers. "You're Mr. Branok Tremayne?"

Hiding his impatience, Bran said, "I am, and this is Miss Tremayne, my sister. She's with me because she can identify the saboteur."

The corporal frowned. "Dangerous work for a lady."

"Protecting Britain is everyone's job," she said with charming earnestness. "Please, sir, the matter is urgent!"

Stronger men than the corporal had melted before her mesmerizing blue eyes. He handed the credentials back to Bran. "I'm Corporal Richards and I'll go with you to show the way. Jenkins, take over for me."

One of the guards standing behind him moved forward and took the corporal's position. Bran guessed that Richards wanted to keep an eye on the unexpected visitors, which was wise of him, as well as useful for them.

They ascended the gangway at a swift pace. "Is this too fast for you, Miss Tremayne?" Richards called back.

"The faster, the better!" Tamsyn said. "The saboteur is French and very dangerous!"

"Do you know where he is?" the corporal asked.

"One of the powder magazines," Bran replied with horrifying knowledge pulled right from Merryn. The *Amphion* had exploded because of an accidental fire in a magazine. It was impossible to exaggerate the danger. If the powder was ignited in the *Royal William*, the explosion would turn the ship into a blazing inferno, which would surely also damage or destroy the *Formidable*, docked right next to it.

"The powder magazine!" Richards gasped, understanding the danger. "That's deep in the hold. Run!"

He reached out to Merryn again. *We're on our way. Slow him down as much as you can!*

The three of them raced single file through narrow corridors and down steep steps, Richards in the lead. Bran and Tamsyn were close behind, and Tam matched them step for step. Her small size was an advantage in the narrow spaces.

It was taking so long, so long . . .

"We're almost at the magazines," Richards said grimly

There was no natural light this deep in the ship, so oil lamps were set into small glass boxes built through the passage wall to shine light into the magazines. They were tended from the passageway so no fire was brought into the powder storage chambers.

Bran's heart almost stopped when he caught a faint whiff of smoke. Ahead on the left was a doorway covered by a wet curtain to protect against flames, and he knew with absolute certainty that the smoke came from inside that magazine. Merryn's captor had struck a flame. Did the bastard hope to escape alive or was this a suicide mission in which he planned to die nobly for France and take untold people with him?

A sliver of light showed between the panels of the wet curtains. The corporal swept the curtains aside and Bran blasted past him. He *knew* Merryn was inside, but all he saw was stacked barrels of powder. On top of one was a mound of black powder, and a tall candle was set in the middle of the mound.

It was a slow fuse designed to delay the explosion so the saboteur could escape the ship alive. And a flicker of flame hovered in midair above the candle.

"Merryn!" he shouted, sure she was here though he couldn't see her.

"Bran!" she called back, and in that instant she became visible. A large man was gripping one wrist, not Crowley, but Dubois, and he held a lighted taper in his other hand above the candle wick.

As the Frenchman swore at the sight of the intruders. Merryn wrenched her left wrist from his grip and clamped her right hand over the burning taper, extinguishing the small open flame instantly.

Dear God, Bran realized, Merryn had the legendary gift of invisibility! That was how she'd been able to bring Dubois onto the ship without being seen. He hadn't really believed such a thing was possible.

"You *bitch!* You weren't supposed to be able to defy me!" Dubois yanked a long, glittering dagger from a sheath under his coat and lunged at Merryn.

Bran grabbed the other's man's arm and swung him around, hurling him into Richards. The marine disarmed Dubois with a vicious twist of the Frenchman's wrist, then dragged him from the magazine into the cramped passageway. There was a brief, violent three-way struggle that ended when Bran chopped Dubois's throat with the edge of his right hand.

The Frenchman choked and staggered back. Richards shoved him to the floor and knelt on his back. "You'll hang for this, you devil!" he snarled. "This is *my* ship and she's filled with my friends! I'm tempted to kill you out of hand!"

Dubois stopped struggling, though he swore French oaths so vile that Bran didn't understand half the words.

Bran turned back to Merryn and engulfed her in his embrace. "Dear God, love, are you all right?"

She burrowed into his arms as if she'd been drowning and he was the only safety imaginable. As she did, Tamsyn laid her palm on Merryn's forehead and frowned in concentration. "I'll remove the mind block."

After a long moment Merryn shuddered all over, not loosening her grip on Bran. "Y-you cleared it much more quickly this time," she said raggedly. "Thank you so much!"

"Nothing like practice!" Tamsyn said cheerfully.

"Was Dubois the only one with you?" Bran asked. "Crowley isn't here?"

"It was just Dubois. The Crow and the Starling are in a room in a building in the quadrangle waiting for the ship to explode!" Merryn hissed.

"You're a heroine!" Tamsyn said admiringly. "You just saved hundreds of lives, including ours, as well as one of his Royal Highness's first-class warships."

Dubois was swearing viciously in French as Richards used a belt to tie his captive's wrists behind him. The corporal was efficient, but pale with shock. "I didn't believe you, Mr. Tremayne, but thank God for you and your cousin! This was so close . . ." He hauled Dubois to his feet. "We have enough guards on the dock for a firing squad."

His arm firmly around Merryn's waist, Bran said, "Believe me, I'd like to see that as much as you, but this man should be questioned before he's tried and executed."

"You're right," Richards admitted. His gaze moved to Merryn. "Who is this young lady?"

"My betrothed, Miss Penrose. Dubois had kidnapped her."

"Putting out the candle was a brave and clever act, Miss Penrose," the corporal said admiringly. "You're a lucky man, Tremayne."

"Believe me, I know!" Bran said fervently. "We'll be down

after you shortly. As soon as we get off the ship, we'll need to arrest Dubois's accomplices."

"With pleasure," Richards said, a hard gleam in his eyes as he turned and marched his prisoner away.

Still in Bran's arms, Merryn looked bemused. "Your 'betrothed'?"

He grinned and touched his mind to hers. *Are you still trying to deny the inevitable?*

Her mind blazed into his with love. Aloud she said, "I think that by now we've known each other long enough to promise forever."

As Bran kissed her, Tamsyn said, "About time you two made it official! Merryn, may I stand up with you?"

Laughing, Merryn surfaced from the kiss and put an arm around Tamsyn, drawing her closer. "I will be pleased and honored to have you at my side."

Bran regretfully loosened his grip on his betrothed. "Till later, my mermaid lady. Now there is still some business to take care of."

"Later," she agreed in a caressing voice.

Not too much later, he hoped.

Chapter 38

It took only a few minutes to reach the office in the metalwork building where Merryn had been held captive. The Starling was there, and she began shrieking when Merryn returned with Bran, Tamsyn, and three marines. "What are you doing here? Where's that damned Frenchman with our money?"

"He's been captured, the *Royal William* isn't going to explode, and you'll probably be hanged," Merryn said crisply. "I guess you won't be marrying my uncle, after all. Where is he?"

"Not here! You'll never find him," the Starling said sullenly as she struggled futilely to avoid being tied up by the marines.

"I doubt he's intelligent enough to escape," Bran said.

As the marines led the Starling off, one of them said, "Our captain will want to talk to you, Mr. Tremayne."

"I'll come to your headquarters tomorrow morning, though I doubt I'll have much more to tell him."

It was almost dark now. Tamsyn said, "Bran, didn't you say that Lord Penhaligon wanted you to push his wheelchair out here to watch the fireworks?"

"I'd forgotten. Thanks for reminding me, Tam." Bran smiled

dryly. "Lord Penhaligon will not be happy with me, but then he seldom is."

They started walking back toward the entrance of the yard. The crowds had thinned and most of the remaining people were lining up along the waterfront to wait for the start of the fireworks display.

Tamsyn remarked, "Strange that so many people are looking forward to explosions in the sky, when one of Britain's grandest warships almost provided the same sight."

Merryn shuddered. "Too soon to joke, I think."

"You're right. I'm sorry." Tamsyn peered ahead along the wide road. "Is that Cade?"

"Yes, and he looks relaxed." As his brother approached, Bran called out, "No assassination?"

"No assassination, and no warships turned into fiery tombs," Cade confirmed. "It's been a good day all around."

"Was there an assassination attempt?" Tamsyn asked.

"Yes, but we stopped it before the French agent could get his pistol cocked."

Cade fell in beside Tamsyn, and the four of them continued along, side by side. "Merryn, tell me your story?"

She did, succinctly. Cade gave a low whistle when she described how she was captured and forced to use her vanishing ability, and how Bran and Tamsyn had thwarted Dubois's attempted sabotage.

Cade listened in amazement. "Bravely done, all three of you! Merryn, I want to see a demonstration of your unusual talent later."

"It will be my pleasure." Merryn smiled. "Also, Bran and I are getting married."

"It was just a matter of time." Cade bent to brush a light kiss on Merryn's cheek, then shook Bran's hand. "When will the wedding be?"

"Soon, I hope." Bran glanced down at Merryn, who looked

young and happy and adorable. He was a very lucky man. "We haven't had time to talk about it yet."

"It's been a very busy day!" Tamsyn said fervently.

Bran saw a wheelchair rolling toward them. "Here comes Lord Penhaligon, and Matthew Davey is doing the pushing." Glynis was at his side, smiling.

When he was within talking range, his lordship glared at Bran. "Where the devil have you been?"

"Working for the Home Office," Bran said mildly. "Matthew, I'll take over. Thank you for filling in for me."

Davey stepped away from the chair so Bran could take over the pushing. "Happy to oblige, but how did you get that bandage on your head?"

Bran had half forgotten. "There was a small riot earlier and I got hit by a flying brick."

Davey looked appalled as he took Glynis's arm, but Penhaligon just snapped, "A brick to your head shouldn't have caused any damage!"

"My head is indeed too hard to suffer a serious injury, but I did bleed rather messily," Bran said, refusing to be offended. "By the way, I'm now betrothed to this lovely lady, Miss Merryn Penrose."

Penhaligon stared in shock. "Thomas Penrose's girl, are you? Thought you'd got yourself lost on Bodmin Moor and never returned."

"Reports of my demise were premature, my lord," she said demurely.

"It's a decent match," Penhaligon said grudgingly, "but you should have discussed it with me first, Branok."

"I needed to convince the lady to agree," Bran said.

Ahead, the first fireworks exploded into blazing showers of white and scarlet over the river. There was a soft murmur of pleasure from the onlookers and a few squeals from children.

Lord Penhaligon raised his gaze to the sky. "Quite a sight," he said, no longer angry. "One I didn't expect to see again."

More rockets flared, reflecting brilliantly in the water below. It was as good a display as at one of the London pleasure gardens, Bran thought. A grand ending to a terrifying, wonderful, rewarding day.

As everyone in their group gazed upward, a dark figure bolted from the crowd and stopped directly in front of the wheelchair. Crowley, blazing with mad rage as he raised a pistol in both hands and cocked the hammer. "You ruined everything, you bastard!" he snarled at Bran. "You stole my niece, my fortune, and my future! But you won't be around to enjoy any of them!"

Bran tried to dodge, but he was caught between the wheelchair handles and Matthew and Glynis were right behind him, blocking his retreat. As Crowley pulled the trigger, Cade lunged for him.

Bran tried to twist away, but the barrel of Crowley's pistol tracked his movement. With icy certainty, he accepted that he was about to die.

In one furious motion, Lord Penhaligon clamped his hands on the wheelchair's arms and shoved himself upward, shielding Bran from Crowley's pistol. The bullet blazed straight into his lordship's heart with an ear-numbing blast and a puff of acrid black powder.

Simultaneously Glynis screamed, her father pitched to the pavement, and Cade's tackle threw Crowley to the ground. Bran heard a ghastly cracking sound that he recognized as a breaking neck. Cade was a very skilled and dangerous fighter.

Glynis and Davey knelt beside Lord Penhaligon while Cade lurched to his feet and wrapped a hard arm around Bran's shoulders. "Dammit, Bran, I can't leave you alone for a minute without your trying to get yourself killed!" he exclaimed in a shaking voice.

Bran swallowed hard and briefly leaned into his brother. "Sadly true." Then he pulled away and knelt by Lord Penhaligon, who was surrounded by a spreading pool of blood.

"Sir ... !" Bran exclaimed, agonized, not sure what he wanted to say. He hadn't much liked Lord Penhaligon, but his father deserved better than to die like this.

The old man's eyelids fluttered open. "You're a good man, Bran," he said in a labored whisper. "I wish ... you could have been my son."

His eyes closed and he breathed no more. Sitting back on his heels, Bran said tightly, "I don't even know what that means."

Merryn's hand came to rest on his shoulder. "Didn't you say that he never quite believed you were the lost heir?"

"Very true." Bran stood and peeled off his coat, then gently laid it over Penhaligon's body. "I didn't want to be the heir, and I don't think he wanted that, either, but he didn't have an acceptable alternative."

Men hurried over, having heard the sound of the gunshot. A well-dressed fellow knelt by Lord Penhaligon's body. "I'm Mr. Jones, a physician." He checked Penhaligon's pulse and breathing, then shook his head and got to his feet again.

"The gentleman is gone. I'm sorry. He was shot?"

"Yes, by a deranged man who was aiming to shoot the Penhaligon heir." Matthew Davey was the one who answered, and there was a brief quaver in his voice before he calmly took over the situation. "We'll have Lord Penhaligon removed to his home at Tamar House, which isn't far. Lady Penhaligon must be informed."

Matthew kept a firm arm around Glynis. Bran realized that there were no longer any barriers to prevent them from marrying. That was a bright spot in this final tragedy.

The next hour was a confusing blur of activity as men arrived with a stretcher to carry Lord Penhaligon's body away. Bran and the rest of the group walked to Tamar House, while a Penhaligon footman collected the wheelchair.

Davey delivered the news to Lady Penhaligon in the drawing room. She closed her eyes for a long time before saying, "My husband was dying. I rather think he must have been glad to die in a way that had meaning."

Her gaze swept the younger people. "I want everyone to gather in the drawing room in an hour. There are matters that must be discussed."

Bran and Merryn went up to his room, but not to make love. They just wanted to hold each other. "This has been the strangest day of my life," she whispered.

"Very strange indeed," Bran replied, intensely grateful to have Merryn in his arms. "Except the getting-married part. That is most excellent." He hesitated, almost afraid to ask. "You're not going to change your mind, are you?"

"Never," she said firmly. "As you said, this result was inevitable. I love you, Bran, now and forever, amen."

"As I love you." They were sitting in the armchair in his room, and she was in his lap. The closeness was healing the bruises they'd both suffered in mind and body.

"Will Cade resent me for taking you away from him?" Merryn asked softly.

It was a serious question, but the answer was simple. "No, he is too generous for that. But we will both miss being a daily part of each other's lives."

"We'll just have to find him a woman who will love him as much as I love you," she said seriously.

Bran gave a startled laugh. "Are all women dedicated matchmakers?"

"I rather think so," Merryn said, a smile in her voice. "But that's a project for another day. Tonight is just about us."

*   *   *

The dinner gong sounded to bring the Penhaligon family and their guests to the drawing room. Lady Penhaligon sat in her favorite chair looking very calm, as if a burden had been lifted from her shoulders.

When everyone had gathered and received drinks, she said, "Glynis tells me that her father's last words were that he wished Bran had been his son. Bran, do you think he was refusing to recognize you as his heir?"

How to answer? "I believe so. He never asked to see the dragon tattoo on my shoulder, and he seemed to resent me."

"Perhaps he was saying that he wished you had grown up in his household and you'd had a normal father-and-son relationship. He had only himself to blame for that," she said tartly. Her gaze held Bran's. "You don't really want the title or the estate, do you?"

It was time for honesty. "No, though I liked having you for a mother and Glynis for a sister. But the estate needs an heir. If not me, who? His lordship mentioned a second cousin, whom he loathed. Is the cousin alive? If not, did he leave a son?"

Her ladyship's piercing gaze went to Matthew. "Mr. Davey? You are our legal expert. Speak to us."

He gave her a wry smile. "You know, don't you?"

"I knew your mother, my dear boy," she said gently.

Davey's gaze swept around the room. "My father was the despised second cousin. I believe Lord Penhaligon hated him because he was able to join the Royal Navy and have the heroic career his lordship wanted for himself.

"Heroism comes at a steep price, though. My father died when I was very young. I scarcely remember him. Lord Penhaligon had already cut all ties with my family. My mother was a practical woman, so she reverted to her maiden name, Davey, and I did also. She moved in with her brother and ran his household, and he became a father to me. They're both gone now. If I have a family, it's the people in this room."

254 Mary Jo Putney

Lady Penhaligon said, "Do you wish to succeed to my husband's title and fortune?"

Davey's jaw dropped. "But I'm just a distant cousin! Bran is the true heir—I have no doubt of that!"

"If Bran doesn't wish to lay claim to Penhaligon, you're the next in line." Her ladyship's gaze moved to her daughter. "Glynis, would you like to be the next Lady Penhaligon?"

Glynis was staring at Matthew in astonishment. "You never told me about this!"

"There seemed to be no point," he said simply. "I was the estate lawyer, no more."

"A great deal more," she said softly as she took his hand.

Her ladyship's gaze moved to Merryn. She and Bran were sharing a small sofa. "What about you, my dear? If you're going to marry Bran, you're entitled to express your opinion. Do you want to be Lady Penhaligon?"

Merryn raised her chin. "I don't want a title. I only want Bran. The choice is his."

Lady Penhaligon's gaze was very serious. "If you truly wish to renounce all claims to the ancient and sometimes honorable family of Penhaligon, Bran, you must do it now and forever, and no one outside this room will ever know."

He looked down into Merryn's warm aquamarine eyes. "The only forever I want is with Merryn. Matthew, by rights you should be the heir. You know the estate, its finances, its people, and from what I saw, you and his lordship had a close and caring relationship, far more like father and son than he and I had. If you wish it, take Penhaligon with my blessings."

Matthew's gaze moved to Glynis. "What do you think?"

She laughed. "Now that I'm getting used to the idea, I quite like it! I get to marry the man I love and won't even have to move to a new house!" She leaned forward and kissed his cheek. "Now you just have to ask me to marry you!"

His laughter joined hers and he leaned forward to speak soft words in her ear. Bran put his arm around Merryn's waist and pulled her close enough that their sides were pressed together. "The strangest day of my life just got even stranger, but I like the way this has turned out. What do you think, my love?"

She tilted her head up and whispered mischievously into his ear, "Do you think anyone will notice if I spend the night here with you?"

Epilogue

❧

The next day, Bran took Merryn back to her home. Penrose Hall was a great sprawling house overlooking the sea, and from what Merryn said, the estate was almost as large as Penhaligon. When their carriage halted in front of the house, Merryn tumbled out heedlessly. As she reached the front steps, she was intercepted by a lean silver-haired man who came down them to greet her. "*Papa!*"

He caught her up in his arms. "I knew you were safe, my darling girl! And that you'd come home." One arm around his daughter, he turned and offered his hand. "And you're my Merryn's young man, Bran Tremayne."

"Yes, sir." They exchanged a firm handshake. Thomas Penrose was small boned like Merryn and had the same aquamarine eyes. As they shook hands, Bran had a clear sense of where Merryn's foretelling ability had come from.

"I'll tell the vicar of our parish church to start calling the banns this Sunday," Mr. Penrose said.

Bran exchanged a glance with Merryn. "The sooner the better, sir."

"And now it's time for tea!" Merryn said as she took Bran's arm with one hand and her father's arm with the other.

Merryn and Bran were married a month later at her family's parish church. The wedding breakfast was held at Penrose Hall and was attended by local friends and a sizable contingent of Tremaynes down from London, including Rhys and Gwyn and several younger siblings.

It was a perfect sunny day in early May. Bran had been visualizing such weather. He still wasn't sure if he had a gift for weather, but perhaps he did. If not, he was grateful that today the weather gods were smiling down on them.

Merryn was the most beautiful bride imaginable, shining with the bright silver light that had drawn him to Cornwall. Tamsyn stood up with her and Cade with Bran.

After the sumptuous wedding breakfast, the guests spilled out onto the wide green lawn that led down toward the sea, sipping champagne and becoming better acquainted. By mutual consent, Bran and Merryn walked down to her beach, kicked off their shoes and strolled along the sand, holding hands and laughing together as the small waves washed over their feet. He brushed a kiss on her forehead. "Welcome to the Tribe of Tremayne, my love!"

She smiled up at him. "Always and forever, amen!"

Author's Note

In 1588, English naval ships sailed out of Plymouth under the command of Admiral Drake to confront and defeat the Spanish Armada, a pivotal event in British history, so the roots of the Royal Navy run very deep in Plymouth. The naval base at Devenport which figures so importantly in this story was established in 1690 by King William III. It was intended for shipbuilding and repairs and was technically innovative from the beginning. Today it's the largest naval base in Western Europe.

At first called Plymouth Dock, the name was later changed to Devenport. The yard has had its share of disasters, including the horrific fire that destroyed the frigate *Amphion* in 1796 and a major fire in 1840 that destroyed two ships as well as buildings and equipment. Nonetheless, some of the original buildings are still in use even though the shipyard suffered severe damage in the Plymouth Blitz of World War II.

The festival at the end of the story came from my imagination. I have my doubts that so many civilians would be allowed entrance to the shipyard, but the Royal Navy has a long tradition of celebrating its people and their communities.

The Treaty of Amiens created a short-lived period of peace from March 25, 1802 until May 18, 1803, the only generally peaceful period in Europe between 1798 and 1814. Naturally Britain and France concentrated on reorganization and rearming themselves during that period, as one does.

Aristocratic Britons hastened to France during this interlude, since Paris was the sparkly fashion capital of Europe. Those who didn't return to Britain in a timely fashion ended up interned in France until 1814, but that's a story for another day!

—MJP